THE

COMPLEX

ARMS

THE

COMPLEX

ARMS

A NOVEL

DOLLY

DENNIS

DUNDURN
TORONTO

Publisher: Scott Fraser | Acquiring editor: Rachel Spence | Editor: Dominic Farrell
Cover designer: Courtney Horner
Cover image: istock.com/Floriana
Printer: Marquis Book Printing Inc.

Library and Archives Canada Cataloguing in Publication

Title: The Complex Arms : a novel / Dolly Dennis.
Names: Dennis, Dolly, author.
Identifiers: Canadiana (print) 20190204494 | Canadiana (ebook) 20190204508 | ISBN 9781459746244 (softcover) | ISBN 9781459746251 (PDF) | ISBN 9781459746268 (EPUB)
Classification: LCC PS8607.E671 C66 2020 | DDC C813/.6—dc23

We acknowledge the support of the Canada Council for the Arts and the Ontario Arts Council for our publishing program. We also acknowledge the financial support of the Government of Ontario, through the Ontario Book Publishing Tax Credit and Ontario Creates, and the Government of Canada.

Printed and bound in Canada.

VISIT US AT

   dundurn.com | @dundurnpress | dundurnpress | dundurnpress

Dundurn
3 Church Street, Suite 500
Toronto, Ontario, Canada
M5E 1M2

Remembering Black Friday

There is a luggage limit for every passenger on a flight. The same rules apply to your life. You must eliminate some baggage before you can fly.

— Rosalind Johnson

JUNE 21, 1987

AIRBORNE

There is a woman in the air. She seems almost as if she were afloat, suspended above the city. She clutches her three-year-old daughter in one hand, and with the other she clings to her spirit. For a moment she is suspended, moving in slow motion, her gauzy summer dress billowing like Mary Poppins's umbrella, the wind propelling her to stay aloft. She has lost the combs that had kept her waist-length black hair neatly in place. Long strands now tumble about her face. She cannot see anything. Then her body hits the ground. The little girl lands on her mother's belly, a pillow for safety. Dead eyes stare at storm clouds above; dead eyes guard the fourth-floor balcony.

"Where you going?" He was sitting at the kitchen table drinking coffee. He had just woken up. Night was the start of his day.

"I'm going to Vera's bridal shower," Jan reminded him.

"And where's that?"

"At her sister's. Not far from here."

"What's her name?"

"Shannon. You know her. She used to work with me at the hospital, remember?"

"I don't believe you. I know where you're going. You're going to some bar to meet some guy. You're staying put tonight."

"I've got to go! They're waiting for me."

"They?"

"My friends."

"What friends? You don't have any."

"But I promised. I have to go!"

He sighed. His head slumped to his chest as though he carried the weight of the world and could no longer hold it up.

"Come here."

She approached the table with frightened steps, felt her body fold inside out, her face drain of colour.

He gripped her wrists. "How are you going to get there?"

"The bus."

He released her hands then swung them back with such force that her shoulder blades almost snapped.

"What bus?"

He knew how to get there. This was just a game, an invention of his sadistic nature created to amuse himself, tease her. He loved to listen to her whimper; it heightened his carnal excitement.

"Go on, TELL ME." He was shouting now.

"I'll take the bus on the corner of our street, then four blocks later get off, cross the street, and there's Shannon's house. It's not far and I promise not to stay long."

He whacked her on the side of her head. She became disoriented, kept pointing to the living room window.

"See, come here. I'll show you where the bus stops."

"Don't you dare talk back to ME. Not a word. I said NO."

"Let me at least call Shannon, let her know I can't come. They're expecting me."

THE COMPLEX ARMS   3

And then.

The tears. She knew he hated tears. She rubbed her eyes, pretending they were itchy. Tears triggered some demon in him. *Oh God!* She shut her eyes. *Don't cry*, she willed herself, *don't cry*. She could see Nina hiding behind the sofa trying to make herself invisible, sobbing softly. *What will she remember of her childhood?*

And then.

The belt. She cowered, screeching like a pig sent to slaughter, spinning, twirling, running in circles, dodging his buckle, screaming, squealing.

He shoved her into the bedroom, onto the bed. She lunged toward the phone on the nightstand, her hands blindly searching for the receiver.

Too late.

"Do you think I'm stupid, huh? Do you think you can lie to me?"

And he wrapped the telephone cord around her neck until she pleaded, "No, it's me that's stupid. I'm sorry. I won't go. Please, please, I'm sorry. Plea—" Her words were cut off, fading into a chokehold of surrender.

He wanted sex, and she let him use her because she was afraid he would hurt her again. And when he had finished with her, he laid his head with tenderness on her lap and moaned, a baby in search of a mother's womb, a mother's love.

"I'm sorry, Jan, I'm sorry, sweetheart. I didn't mean to hurt you. I promise I won't do that no more."

"No, it's my fault," she said.

It was always like that.

After he had left for work she bathed herself, determined to erase every sense of him. She scoured her inner thighs and stomach with an SOS pad, brushing lightly over the welts and abrasions. He would punch her in places invisible — never her face.

No one knew the secrets her body carried, so no one could help, no one knew to care.

She let her head slide down the back of the tub — submerging, drowning, weeping, the water a melding of scented soap and salty tears. For a moment there was only a kaleidoscopic muffle of water on water, whirling, swirling; a tunnel of bubbles surging toward the surface. She held her breath and felt her life explode.

At thirteen, the school nuns had inspired her to consider a life in Christ; instead, she compromised and became a nurse. The idea appealed to her innocent vision of herself as a modern-day Florence Nightingale, a lady in white, a beacon to the sick and dying, the wounded, and the needy.

She had always considered herself an intelligent, well-educated professional — independent, proud, sophisticated — so how had it come to this? How had she allowed her life to sink into this nightmare?

They had met at the hospital. He was her patient, a lost puppy with a broken leg — injured, needy, hungry for affection, looking for a good home.

"There. You should feel more comfortable now. Doesn't that feel better?" She had just finished washing him.

"Ah, Jan, you're so good to me."

"It's my job."

"Just that?"

She smiled and covered his good leg. "Are you warm enough?"

"Not unless your body is pressed next to mine, sweetheart."

The day she arrived at her apartment and found a bouquet of flowers outside the door was the day her life changed forever. A steady stream of miniature white roses, her favourite, continued to greet her every evening until she finally relented and brought the puppy home. It took a week to yield to his charms.

The sudden upsurge of water flooding her nose made Jan gasp for air. She instinctively bobbed to the surface, a survivor still.

"Mommy, Mommy."

At the bridal shower Vera sat on her throne, coloured streamers adorning the only armchair in the apartment, ribbons cascading down her hair like spray from a water fountain. Queen for the day. Someone had planted an enormous bow on top of her head, she a bridal offering to be opened on her wedding night. Silver and gold wrapping paper carpeted the floor; boxes from Birks, the Bay, Stokes, and Totem Outfitters littered her domain. There were gift cards to shop for a lawnmower, a snow blower, furniture, electronic toys, appliances, and gadgets. Her parents had bought them a house in an exclusive neighbourhood, a wedding gift. A forever gift. If any time could be called perfect, this night was it. Her friends shrieked at the size of her diamond, embraced her, and envied her good fortune.

"You're so lucky. He's such a hunka, hunka, hunka," they said in a scatter of words. And Vera's face flushed as it always did when she drank too much wine.

"You should see what he does with his tongue," she burped. They all giggled and snickered like twelve-year-olds who had just seen their first male centrefold.

"Hey, Jan, come on over here and join the fun. You need a refill," Shannon called out.

Jan rarely drank but this was a special occasion. She had parked herself in an inconspicuous corner just outside the main bedroom in the rear of the living room. Her disobedient, defiant legs had found their way to Vera's shower, and now she kept an eye on the door for signs of him.

"I'm okay. I want to stay near Nina just in case she wakes up." A three-year-old could only survive on so much cake and ice cream before collapsing into sleep.

Shannon bobbed to the disco rhythms of the Bee Gees. Ten drunken women joined the chorus, a crescendo of voices soaring, flying, ricocheting off the ceiling, airborne, slightly askew, notes off key. Jan smiled at their giddiness. If only they knew. It wasn't that easy.

On Jan's wedding day everyone had thought she and the groom also made a beautiful couple. Theirs seemed to be the sort of relationship that could make you believe in fairy tales. Here was Prince Charming, who was not only incredibly handsome, but also a gentleman — a six-foot-two, dimple-cheeked Adonis, black curls caressing his forehead, cobalt-blue eyes: a Paul Newman look-alike who had no right to be more beautiful than the bride. He displayed all those attributes advertised in personal ads on the back pages of questionable magazines — polite, kind, considerate, sensitive, and generous to a fault. His charisma captivated all.

"He's got a job, money in the bank! What more does a woman need? He'll give you security, honey. Listen to your mother, I know," she had sighed and patted Jan's knee for reassurance.

Her friends had commented on the size of the ring. "My God, Jan, he really loves you."

And when he wasn't lining her living room with flowers, he was offering exquisite gifts, entertaining her at the most expensive restaurants, bribing the other nurses on her floor with chocolates and doughnuts. "Make her say yes, girls."

"He's so romantic," they would swoon.

And so obviously in love with Jan — arms always in motion — draping her shoulders, playing with her hair, kissing the palms of her hands, her fingers, her cheeks, her forehead — protective, supportive, dependable.

"You'd be a fool to let this one go," everyone cajoled her. No pressure.

Her mother may have thought that he was perfect husband material, but she still insisted he convert to Catholicism, a religion that didn't recognize divorce, a religion that had held her own spirit hostage in a thirty-year marriage to an alcoholic. Yes, to justify the expense of a large wedding, he would have to convert; insurance for a marriage that might go wrong, an obligation to honour their vows and stay the course until death did them part.

At her wedding reception Jan had danced with an old friend. Perhaps he had held her a little too close; perhaps for a moment she had leaned into him, permitting herself to become lost in a high-school memory.

Suddenly.

Someone dashed brusquely by her. There was the breezy scent of whisky and Old Spice, the rapid snapping away of bodies, splitting, separating, and stumbling backwards.

"Don't you dare look at my wife that way. EVER." He dragged Jan away, cornered her in the dark, and slapped her face. "And YOU. Don't you ever embarrass me like that no more." And he walked away.

Jan was stunned.

His mother discreetly brushed by her side and murmured, "He's been so stressed out lately with the wedding and all, dear ..."

It was one of life's transitional moments. Jan excused his behaviour, made the mistake of measuring the intensity of his love by the intensity of his jealousy. She forgave him.

The real nightmare began five months into the marriage. He was fixing a light switch and had forgotten to shut off the fuse box.

"You'll electrocute yourself," she had warned. There he was prodding at the switch with a screwdriver.

"You're going to hurt yourself," she kept insisting. "You'll see. Call Adeen."

"I know what I'm doing," he shouted back over his shoulder, but she persisted.

Perhaps if she had held her tongue; perhaps if she had called Adeen, the resident manager, herself, the outcome would have been different. He repeatedly stabbed at the switch, punching holes in the surrounding wall, unleashing a buried fury, a steady jab-jabbing, leaving a trail of dents on its surface, jab-jabbing, and her nag-nagging voice in his ears, finally resulting in the convulsion in his hand.

"See, I told you," she scolded, "I told you, but you wouldn't listen." And he charged at her, flinging her body across the room.

"Shut up!"

When Nina was born, he had denied his paternity and called Jan a slut. He was drunk. He demanded she quit her job. The thing that had initially attracted him to Jan was gone. She became dependent, and he resented the attention Jan lavished on the child. To him, Nina was an irritant, an obstacle for Jan's affection.

That was when he began to drink heavily. Then the fights really began.

"You should be able to live on what I give you. What do you do with it?" he would holler.

But he never gave her enough money. In the day, while he slept, she would salvage bottles from the apartment building's Dumpster, hoping to find enough empties so she could buy Nina milk. She would often battle with her neighbour, Payton, over a found empty beer can. "It's a fundraiser for the Boy Scouts," she would say. "Let me have it." A life just held together, glued by secrets and lies. Once she had whispered in the confessional, "He's been hurting me, Father," and her parish priest had sighed and told her to be a better wife and not argue. As penance, he made her recite fifty Hail Marys.

Jan shut her eyes and rolled the sides of the wine goblet along her forehead, cheeks, and chin, massaging the heat out of her pores.

"You okay?"

Shannon had flitted her way across the room in a gyration of various dance steps from the jive to the twist. Startled, Jan sprang from her chair, spilling wine across her skirt, the chair, the carpet.

"Oh, I'm sorry … I'm so clumsy. I better go. Sorry. Sorry."

But before Shannon could dissuade her, the doorbell rang. It was one of those frozen moments, seconds really, when the soul leaves the flesh, when brain cells collide, then die, when fears hurl themselves through the body like so many meteorites hitting earth, electrifying the entire nervous system.

Two gorgeous young studs were on the doorstep, handsomely dressed in full tuxedos. Shannon ushered them into the room and offered them up to her sister — a surprise present. And there they were. Vera could only giggle. "Oh, you shouldn't have."

Shannon had seen their amateur Chippendales-type act in one of those nondescript lounges on the outskirts of Red Deer and thought they would be a novelty, a last hurrah for Vera before settling into married life. The other women certainly seemed to appreciate the muscular bodies of the two men, who stripped down until they wore only black bow ties, white cuffs at their wrists, and thongs concealing bulging packages. It was an intoxicating evening. The room vibrated with the hot mix of old and new sounds — the Bee Gees, Rod Stewart, Santana.

The girls gyrated their hips, slid their butts against the two performers, ignited dormant passions. Then they lunged for the duo, teasing them with sweaty dollars peeking through revelations of Wonderbras and fancier Victoria's Secret lingerie. Jan, too, rode the crest of a fantasy — inebriated, loaded, stoned, smashed, drunk, bombed out of her mind on too much wine and maybe life. The doorbell had mercifully silenced her fears this one time, giving her permission to fly.

Jan was spinning in the air. If she stretched her arms upward, she could touch the ceiling. One of the young men had lifted her, securing her pelvis against his cheek, and now she was whirling in space, a frenetic dervish, her hair combs come undone.

"Put me down," she lashed out in a sudden panic of nerves. "Put me down."

Her kicking tipped their balance, and both collapsed on the floor.

"You're one sexy babe," he flirted, and he held her with a tight grip, pressing his lips against her throbbing heart.

Her husband had been the only man she'd ever slept with, so she didn't know how it was supposed to be. It was never gentle. He'd twist her arms behind her back, hurt her, and when he was done, he'd take a shower and leave for work. As far as he was concerned, Jan had fulfilled her duty as his wife. She, instead, craved tenderness, to be smothered in soft, loving kisses, and this young man was about to satisfy her wishes.

"Aren't you glad you stayed?" Vera wiggled by singing a duet with George Michael's "I Want Your Sex."

"I'm a married woman, and my husband is a very jealous man."

"That's what they all say," he laughed.

The distant relentless ringing. Insistent. Incessant. Unceasing. Unnerving.

"Will someone please get the phone!" a voice shouted above the din.

And then.

"Jan. It's for you."

Something pierced her heart, jolted her nervous system again, and then came the tiny voice outside the bedroom now, "Mommy, when we going home?"

Oh God. Oh God. Oh God. Suddenly sober, Jan fastened her hair combs back into place, gathered Nina in her arms, and ran for the door.

"Jan. Jan. You forgot your jacket." Even Vera couldn't catch her attention.

"Oh God. Oh God. What have I done? Oh, Nina, he's going to be so mad at us. Oh, Nina!" And she smothered the child against her chest, rushing out of the house and into a drizzle of rain, running the four long blocks back to the Complex Arms, Nina wailing, both stumbling, faltering on slippery pavements, plunging into puddles, scraping knees and elbows, Nina still wailing, Jan now crying, both uncertain where the tears ended and the rain began. A borderless pain.

He wouldn't let her in. She rang the doorbell with frenzied fingers, yelling into the intercom until her shouts became sobs. "Please, please. I'm sorry. Sorry." She pounded the double glass doors, pushing more buttons helter-skelter. "Please, please."

"All right. All right. I'm coming." Adeen poked her head out her apartment door, saw Jan, and buzzed her in.

"Forgot your keys?"

But Jan had gone deaf to any voice but her husband's. She poured into the lobby in a torment of tears, Nina still wailing in her arms.

"Jan, wait! What's the matter? Jan!"

No time for explanations. Nina hung on to Jan like a precarious dishtowel swinging on a clothesline in a wild wind, the two tripping over frantic footsteps.

Adeen stood on guard outside her apartment, listened until she heard the slam of a door. Then there was nothing except the music from Cody's oddly retro record collection drifting out of his apartment and into the corridors. "You Really Got Me," the Kinks staccato tribute to love. But then, a thunder of ugly swearing: *Slut. Whore.*

Later Adeen would berate herself for not doing anything. She, against her better judgment, had ignored her intuition, didn't go upstairs to check; instead, she had hesitantly locked the door behind her. For once she'd followed Frosty's advice: *None of your business.*

He was waiting for Jan, still dressed in his security guard's uniform. "A uniform makes a man," he had once told her. "People respect you." He wanted to join the air force but had failed the written exam. This was the next best thing.

Dawn was breaking. His shift was over. The day was the start of his night. Had she stayed at Vera's shower too long? She faced him.

"YOU." He stabbed his finger at her. "YOU —"

Nina scampered behind the couch.

"— ARE DEAD." He whipped out his billy club and lunged toward her. "I'll teach you to disobey me!"

What was this inner strength that now impelled her? Was it the image of Vera, sitting in that armchair surrounded by dreams that reminded Jan of an earlier time when she, too, believed in fairy tales? She wanted to reclaim that woman. After all, she was entitled to some joy in her life. Nina's childhood memories shouldn't begin and end with the fear of coming home and seeing her mother beaten by a madman. She and Nina deserved more than this. If for no other reason, she would do it for Nina.

Jan dashed into the bedroom and locked the door. She was leaving. She could hear his threats, feel his ugliness flowing under the door sill like red-hot, toxic lava. She gathered only what they both needed — a change of clothes, underwear, toothpaste, and toothbrushes — enough to fill a shopping bag, enough for a day's stay at the women's shelter. And then she lay on the bed.

Catatonic.

She stared at the peeling white paint on the ceiling, studied its cracked surface, dissociating herself from the ranting in the living room.

"Whore! Whore!"

It was Nina's scream that roused her, and a savage howl sprung from the very core of her body.

"Don't. You. Dare. Touch. Her."

Jan flung the door wide open and pounced on him, positioning herself between her daughter and the billy club. The sight of Nina lying on the floor kindled a fury in her, like that of a mother bear protecting her cubs. There was Jan growling, snarling, biting, kicking, scratching, thrashing. Her books and spilled photos from family albums were hurled from shelves. A life erased.

"You little whore. Who do you think you are?" And the billy club smashed down on Jan. She crumpled to the floor with a scream, tried to secure her footing, but the club came down again, again, again, on her ear, her jaw, her stomach. She lay there, blood framing her.

"You try leaving me and Nina goes over."

"Hey, what's going on up there? Hey." Adeen barged up the stairs; other tenants peeked through half-chained doors.

Jan was disoriented but managed to roll onto her side. She could make out the blurry images of greyness against the balcony railing — he, leaning over the edge holding a rag doll. She tried to lift up off the floor, but her legs failed her.

Adeen knocked on the door. "Open up or I'll call the cops." Bang, bang, bang.

"Give her to me. Give her to me, you bastard."

Jan managed to crawl on her hands and knees to the balcony, reaching it just as Adeen finally succeeded in ramming the door open.

The rain had stopped; only a scatter of drops, the crack of lightning and thunder a faint rumble.

"If you try to leave, I'll kill you both, you and Nina. You and Nina. I'm warning you, Jan, I swear. I swear."

What power again reinforced her, drew her up, pulled her to the railing? "Give me back my baby, give me back my baby, give me back —" Her last susurrus mantra. And then she reached out.

There is a woman in the air. She seems almost as if she were afloat, suspended above the city. She clutches her three-year-old daughter in one hand, and with the other she clings to her spirit. For a moment she is suspended, drifting in slow motion, her gauzy summer dress billowing open like Mary Poppins's umbrella, the wind propelling her to remain airborne. She has lost the combs that had kept her waist-length black hair neatly in place. Long strands now tumble about her face.

In the morning the bus passes in front of the building and we crane our necks to point and whisper, "There, there is the balcony. There is where she fell."

Neighbours light candles and plant wooden crosses on the spot where she came to rest; strangers decorate tree branches with black satin ribbons; the media pay attention; her friends and colleagues pray for a life cut short; a parish priest performs the last rites; a mother weeps for a son's misdeeds; another buries a daughter; a child misses her mother; and he, he covers her grave with miniature white roses.

Every day.

JULY 1987

ADEEN

So it happened first day of summer. That's how I'll always remember Jan. Summer solstice girl. Stopped raining after that night. It usually pours like a broken water main out here every June. Everyone else's April showers are Alberta's June showers. But not a drop after that.

In my years of managing the Complex Arms, and all the times I've lived in apartments — and I've been in a few — I'd never experienced something like that. I mean I got the drunks and pretty party animals, but to throw your wife and child over a balcony? When I burst into the room, he was just standing there with weird vacant eyes, like he was possessed. Possessed of a devil's temper for sure. "She fell," he kept babbling. "She fell." Just that. His voice had this tone of disbelief. I called emergency right away and they arrived in minutes, as though they were expecting my call from that number. She was dead, of course, but Nina survived. Thank God for small mercies.

Jan never mentioned any problems with her marriage ... although on occasion I could hear shouting matches between them, and that first week when they moved in they had a doozy of a fight. I suspected the usual arguments between a man and his wife and that was all, but nothing like … like what happened. We used to go for strolls in the fields nearby, me and Nina. She never said a thing. Kept it a secret from me. Sometimes I would bring my little girl, Irene, who always liked to push Nina in her stroller. Those times were really special. Sometimes we would stop and rest on the scratchy grass, have a picnic of sandwiches and lemonade, the usual stuff. I felt like Jan was the daughter I should have had.

I still can't believe it. Still have nightmares. If you saw them together, you would have sworn they were the most romantic couple since *Love Story*. It's always like that, isn't it? You just never know. It's the quiet ones you have to watch for. They hide their bruises well. Smile in the face of pain. That was Jan.

Anyhow, that's the story there.

ALBERTA

Adeen carried her curiosity with her when she arrived in 1982. She learned that Mill Woods was named after the Mill Creek Ravine, the little valley that cuts through the northeast portion and into the woods nearby, home to a First Nations reserve. It was no surprise to learn that once settlers decided they wanted the land for themselves, the Indigenous people on the reserve were evicted and split up, forced to move elsewhere. The province acquired possession and Edmonton created a blueprint for its use: cheap starter homes were to be built on the swampy, unstable soil where nothing grew except prairie weed.

As soon as the general public learned that the city was going to develop Mill Woods — and that the lots were to be sold for only one hundred dollars — crowds camped outside the sales office. It was a crazy time, reminiscent of the gold rush. Speculators bought up the neighbouring farmlands, hoping to cash in when the municipality decided those properties were needed also to accommodate the ever-increasing population. Over time, apartment buildings like the Complex Arms were added to the housing mix.

The city planners said Mill Woods was "an experiment in community living, an inclusive neighbourhood for a diversity of cultures, languages, and incomes to thrive, where everyone is welcome." Adeen didn't fall for all that marketing drivel, of course, but after she moved there she did eventually grow to love the neighbourhood — so unlike where she had grown up in the grimy streets of Montreal's East End, the slummy part of town.

Adeen knew that Mill Woods certainly wasn't the only place people flocked to. Easterners, Maritimers mostly, forced from their homes because the fish were dying from oil spills in the Atlantic, were settling in the satellite towns around Calgary and Edmonton, portaging to their jobs wherever they were assigned, joining the husky farm boys on the rigs up north in Fort McMurray, or Fort Mac as it was commonly known.

Hired on as welders, pipefitters, and ironworkers, the new residents tramped through the land to install and maintain the pumpjacks, build the refineries, flush out the soil's riches, construct new towns. Like Adeen, many settled in Edmonton, Alberta's capital, a blue-collar city with a track record for wealth: a truck and van in every two-car garage, the attached house almost an afterthought. Those who could afford to live on acreages, with space to spare, inevitably acquired adult toys: a motorcycle, boat, camper, or quad parked inside a Quonset, waiting for a vacation. A hot tub usually graced a large three-tier deck; maybe an above-ground swimming pool in back just for the hell of it. No sales tax in Alberta: the Canadian dream.

Frosty would tease these outsiders, with their quaint dialects and choppy accents. "You talk funny. You from *Newfunland*?" They sent cheques home, sealed with oil-stained fingerprints, bragging about their newly furbished riches: an Arizona condo for the winter months when temperatures dipped below freezing; the Sunday brunches at the Hotel Macdonald overlooking the

North Saskatchewan River, and, of course, the eighth wonder of the world — the West Edmonton Mall, the largest in the world. It even had a roller coaster, an indoor artificial ocean, and an ice rink. People could enjoy the mall, any time, any season.

Adeen had to admit that, although the consumer was king in the city, it wasn't all about money, at least in Edmonton. It had seemed unlikely to her at first, but Adeen discovered that the city was a haven for the arts. She didn't get to enjoy any of it, unfortunately, but she was comforted by the knowledge that her new hometown provided sanctuary to artists, writers, theatrical types, poets, and musicians who devoured the scene on Whyte Avenue, with its quaint bars, restaurants, bookstores, and art galleries, shades of New York's Greenwich Village. It seemed that whatever stirred the creative soul was acceptable.

Naturally, like everyone else in the city, Adeen was keenly aware of the rivalry between Calgary and Edmonton. The oil barons had transferred their wallets, bulging with hundred-dollar bills poking like hankies from Hugo Boss suit pockets, and relocated their offices to Calgary. Adeen had to laugh — on weekends you could see these cowboy capitalists pretending to be the romantic heroes of the westerns everyone loved in Alberta. They sent their business suits to the dry cleaner to be pressed and dug out their weekend garb: oversized cowboy hats and matching boots; a bandana to shield against gusts, rain, and sunburn; and chaps for good measure, protection against imaginary cacti as they rode the plains on their horses, one of their new hobbies. Edmonton might be the capital, but — the oil barons sneered — Calgary was where the money was; Calgary was where dreams came true.

It was certainly not Adeen's vision of an ideal city, but it did offer both a pioneer and urban sensibility, fossilized in its cowboy trails and canyons where dinosaurs once roamed. If you took a road trip to the tiny hamlets or villages scattered around the province, you'd discover folks stuck back in the past: Saturday night bowling, pool hall shenanigans, a movie maybe — *Fatal Attraction*, or some other Hollywood flick — a stopover at the A&W, and a quick fuck in the woods en route home — standard behaviour under a midnight dark.

Between the towns and villages, though, there was the wide-open space, the vaulted heavens that the literary types wrote about until they ran out of superlatives. The sky merged with the land at the horizon and the weather was a constant and persistent elemental force. Truly awe-inspiring, those brutal winters and menopausal summers, overwhelmed with both hot and cold temperatures.

Whatever part of the province she visited, Adeen observed how everyone did their best to ignore the Indigenous people. *Let the Natives fend for themselves* seemed to be the popular sentiment. Governments broke their promises, their treaties. Politicians pretended amnesia. The problem existed back in Quebec, too, she knew, but it seemed worse, or at least more visible, in Alberta.

And then there were the poor. The homeless camped in cardboard boxes along the river valley or slept stretched out in bus shelters close to the food bank. It broke Adeen's heart.

When she mentioned any of this to Frosty, he would ignore the problems she pointed out and declare with pride, "Alberta, it's *mah lafstyle*; Edmonton, it's *mah home*."

ADEEN

I didn't want to come to Alberta, but my best friend, Mona, was already here and convinced me this was the place to be — a place with a future, a place for Irene to thrive. So I came.

Mona and I would take these Sunday drives. We'd zip through little hick towns, more like villages: Hanna, Millet, Killam, Stettler. I noticed a pattern that I've never seen anywhere else. Every main street dead, like its citizens stayed indoors preparing for an invasion of aliens; everyone in church if it were Sunday, or tending to the fields the rest of the week. Teenage girls with bellies out to there. Should have been in school, but there they were, loitering outside the pool hall or bowling alley waiting for their boyfriends, or you'd see them walking along the gravel sidewalk pushing hard on strollers, usually in twos, as if they belonged to an exclusive club for teen moms. I'd watch them. I know what that's like. Guess there's not much else to do but fool around in a four-by-four town. I swear, every place had a bowling alley, a pool hall, and a Chinese restaurant — always a Chinese restaurant — and, oh yeah, a post office. Sometimes there'd be a hobby shop stuck out amid all the quaint buildings, where grannies bought their wool to knit afghans or socks or where they'd learn to quilt. And all of these places carried an identity. Enter Mundare, and a large Ukrainian sausage greeted you; Vulcan, with its nod to *Star Trek*, displayed a flying saucer; and Vegreville boasted a humongous pysanka — an Easter egg, if you're wondering. I guess even towns need an identity, recognition. The cemetery is the most interesting place. There is history on those tombstones.

After surveying the place with Mona, Montreal was starting to look a whole lot better. I was thinking of going back but Mona persuaded me to stay. So I did. But Edmonton definitely took some getting used to. The trick I learned to keep from losing my way around the city was to focus on a familiar landmark. First day on my own downtown, I had a panic attack. Felt the buildings closing in on me like I was in a Marvel comic book — Superman to my rescue. Didn't know where I was. Turned a corner and saw Holt Renfrew so found my way to the bus stop. Otherwise, the search party would still be looking for me. I never strayed too far from Holt's.

Even when I didn't get lost, I still felt out of place. People ridiculed my accent. I didn't know I had one. They thought I was a Newfie, but coming from Quebec and having learned street French, my pronunciation was off. It confused people. Holt Renfrew, I pronounced like the French: *Ronfrew*. Frosty's family would laugh and try to correct me. I rebelled. *Ronfrew, Ronfrew, Ronfrew.* I thought they were the ones who spoke with an accent. I felt lost in a different way. I didn't know where I belonged. Not Montreal. Not Edmonton.

It took a while, but I started to get used to this place. It sounds impossible, but I never ever saw a rainbow or a real live elk until I moved out here, so that's something, and on a clear fall night, the northern lights put on quite a show in all their hallelujah glory.

There is a beauty here, for sure. It was a nice change getting up in the morning to read the paper and not being reminded that again Quebec was going to separate from the rest of Canada. Yeah, I guess it's in the papers here, too, but not as much. Besides, I mostly just look at the comics and the crossword puzzle these days. The front-page headline on my first day — "Deer in Headlights Crossing Road Near Ellerslie" — made me laugh.

Anyhow, that's the story there.

FROSTY

rosty is in back hosing down the dust and debris from the cement path that skirts the Complex Arms and spills onto the tenants' parking stalls. Whenever he does any yardwork at this end of the building, he always whistles or sings an "old-timey" western ditty to occupy his mind, distract him from the drudgery.

"Told the Swanks I needed a power washer if they wanted me to keep their property nice lookin'. My wrist can only take so much. Do they listen? Naw."

"You talking to yourself again, Frosty?" The leather-skinned, bearded ex-hippie from the sixties' Summer of Love leans over the balcony rail from his third-floor apartment to spit a glob of brown phlegm, which lands on the roof of a parked van.

"Told you, Payton, stop with the tobacco chewin'. You're wreckin' my work here, and I don't want any complaints from the tenants about you again."

"It's Rosemary's van and she don't care. Give it a wash while you're at it."

"Payton." Frosty aims the hose at him.

"Praise be, Jehovah. He is awaiting me," he exclaims and then disappears inside his apartment.

Frosty now turns his attention to the front and is on his knees scraping a section of the sidewalk with a penknife. The Swank Property Management Group wants that burgundy stain removed pronto. "Doesn't look good for us," his boss said. A repeated rinse with the hose and the offending mark is now a lighter shade of smudge, the colour of a clear rosé.

Frosty Whitlaw was born in Mirror, a town with a population under five hundred, little more than a pinprick on the map of Alberta — now you see it, now you don't — that required a magnifying glass to verify its existence. He fled on his seventeenth birthday and never looked back, not even a curious glance.

Today, although he is now on the cusp of entering his mid-years, he still has the same cockiness, the same swagger of his youth, a cowboy about to mount a wild bull at the Calgary Stampede or exercise a racehorse during his stint as a stable boy in Phoenix.

Certain no one is watching, he sneaks a full blast of water to the roots of the nearby birches, which border the public property line. He is protective of the trees, the last ones standing and likely to meet a sad fate when the Swanks renovate and build an extension to the four-floor walk-up he and his wife, Adeen, manage.

Frosty squints, inhales the quiet of the day. He lets the sweat from his forehead carve a mark down his cheekbones to his jaw. A fall of water flows slowly around his chin, down his Adam's apple, and settles on the already damp neckline of his worn-out white T-shirt. It's a souvenir from their Vegas honeymoon, shows Elvis Presley with a high collar concealing a sagging chin, silk scarf around the neck to trap the perspiration, microphone near his open mouth. Frosty sporadically dries his face with the bottom half of the now stained T-shirt until a border of grey dampness outlines the hem.

He keeps his slightly crooked left hand hooked in the back pocket of his jeans and directs another dose of water to the rosé stain. May take more rinses, he figures, but this will do for now. A rainstorm would help. He scans the heavens for the possibility. The sky is without colour.

He straightens his back to examine the weeds flourishing with wild abandon in the next lot and to the north, where the world seems to tip off its axis. Nothing but parched land bare of vegetation. Worn-out dirt paths meander along the border of Mill Woods into the Pits. Sidewalks and unpaved roads crack like an old leather saddle in the heat of the sun; thirsty trees and shrubs, no longer green, already a faded tan. Wind chimes from balconies remain silent; no breeze to conjure any sense of motion.

He gives his mouth a wash and gargle with the garden hose then spits out the mixture. So hot! He sprays more water in his hair, his face, his now shirtless chest, and shakes himself like a horse after a good soak in a lake.

"Hey, Frosty."

It's Shy Shylene — on the right day, or the wrong day, depending on how you look at things, there's nothing shy about her. She is snapping her fingers as though she is listening to jazz.

"Hey, Frosty." Her voice accelerates, the snapping increases in tempo. "Hey, hey, Frosty." Snap snap snap. She suffers, for lack of a better word, from a mental affliction. *Unbalanced* is Frosty's term for her condition. The tenants measure her daily disposition by her behaviour toward them, which can range anywhere from normal to dangerous to normal to anti-social to normal to depressive to normal to overly friendly and back to normal. On the cloudy days, she is inert, gloomy, vacant, aimless, and confined to her apartment until her meds kick in. Today is sunny for her. A good day.

"Whatcha want, Shy?"

"Be a sweetheart and tell Adeen I have some clothes for her I'm giving away." Snap snap snap. "Hardly used. All designer labels and oodles of shoes."

"Tell her yourself."

"She's not home. And when are you coming up to install my new air conditioner? The instructions are all gibberish and I'm suffocating up here. I'm getting irritable. And you know how I am when I get irritable."

"Go take one of your pills and take a shower to cool you down," says Frosty and he directs the hose up at her as she is momentarily distracted.

She yelps, laughing and screaming, "You son of a gun. I'm going to get you."

Shylene leaps inside her apartment and reappears with one of those Super Soaker spray guns and blasts him in return.

"You asked for it, Shy." He chuckles.

They are in a water war now, back and forth, until Frosty can't help noticing the wet outline of her tiny braless breasts.

"Gonna get you," he says, taking aim at his target, and she springs back inside again without a snap, waiting for Frosty.

ADEEN

Okay. Call me crazy. Everyone else does, so join in the chorus. Maybe it's because I have so much fatigue; the unbearable fatigue of living. But I swear it isn't that. That summer everyone and everything seemed to be dying. The land was parched and coughing like it was trying to rid itself of a malignancy. The press described how many of the elderly, those living alone, especially in the rural areas, died from dehydration. No one cared for them. Forgotten.

I can recall sitting slouched over the kitchen table, my chest a shelf for my loaded head — how else to describe it? Wounded by a migraine. Anyone would think I was drunk. Uncontrolled dizziness set me off balance, an invisible magnetic force tipped me toward the bathroom. I was alone even though my ten-year-old daughter, Irene, slept on the floor amid her paper dolls. Happy land. No one to help if I cried out. Help! Help! And Frosty, nowhere in sight.

I remember a dog barking outside as though he wanted to alert someone about my despair. Hormones can create havoc on a woman's psyche, especially at certain times of the month. You know what I mean. I was a heavy smoker, two packs a day; kept my hands busy and my appetite in check. A harmless crutch — I told myself that's all it was because most days my life was like crawling through a London fog.

Then I started to guzzle down mugs of that dark rum with cola to begin the day. Should anyone drop by, they would think I was drinking java. Get it? Did I tell you I drink a lot of coffee? Went down smooth. Smacked my lips, it was so good — like a remedy for an imperfect life. An elixir. *Here's to life*, I would salute. Didn't keep much alcohol in the apartment, except for a six-pack of beer hidden behind Irene's bedroom door in case I got a yearning. Sometimes I'd make a trip to the Liquor Mart. Nothing like that hard stuff. Don't look at me like that. I mean, come on!

Anyhow, Frosty never went there. That's a lie. He turned a blind eye. He had his own problems. His tastes ran to mari-a-jua-na. This was not the life I had planned when I came out here from Montreal.

In the middle of this heat wave I was like a robot — somewhere between waking up and sleeping. Another scorcher. The verticals covering the open patio door remained static. Blasts of hot air settling into the cluttered living room did nothing for my sulky mood. A portable fan going full blast barely dried the perspiration from my face. No relief in sight that summer. I was cranky. Alberta turned me into a cranky bitch.

Frosty came in to change his wet shirt saying he was going up to help Shylene. That girl put on a good front most of the time. She had a recurrent manic-depressive illness. Everybody seems to be taking something these days to get them over the bumps of living. She's another tenant that'd been there since the Complex Arms opened its doors. She mentioned her affliction early on in our relationship and we just connected. I guess because

I'm nonjudgmental and just accept people, warts and all. I understand. She had no control over her mind. But none of us do, right?

Later Frosty told me that by the time he got to Shylene's apartment, she'd had a mood swing — sullen, morose, apathetic, lethargic. Didn't say much. Her depression could last for months sometimes. Thought I'd give her some time before going up to check out those clothes. Prepare myself for whatever was in store. If she was giving away things, meant she was aiming to go on a shopping spree. Manic rising. Again.

Apparently, as Frosty was installing her window air conditioner, she sat there on the couch staring into space. Before leaving, he asked if she needed anything else, and she jumped, startled as though someone caught her doing something illegal. When she got down like that, all of us let her be. Didn't know what to do about Shylene. She had no close family as far as I could tell. Wasn't about to throw her out into the street. And she paid her rent on time. No complaints.

I figure there's something wrong with all of us, so who am I to judge? Nobody's perfect. Let's have some empathy. When she was in her manic phases, she had men coming and going, a party every night. Told her I would look the other way when her male companions came for a visit. She didn't know what I was talking about.

Shy Shylene. Yep. Like many women, she carried her business like her sadness — hidden. We were friends. She meant no harm. I tried to help where I could, but even I was getting tired of those constant mood swings. I feared what may happen to her.

Anyhow, that's the story there.

THE TENANTS

rene, Adeen's daughter, is ten years old, but her mental disability makes her seem more like a two-year-old, meaning that sometimes she can be as difficult and demanding as one. Right now she is asleep, curled up like a snail on the living room floor. Her shoulder-length blond hair, styled in a Shirley Temple mop of loose ringlets, conceals the right side of her pretty face. Pages ripped from a *Sesame Street* colouring book blanket her legs; headless cut-out paper dolls and discarded photos from the lingerie section of a Sears catalogue are scattered around the room. She is snoring like an out-of-tune trumpeter swan and every now and then shudders as though flying through a nightmare, or is she somewhere in a winter dream? Irene extends one arm in the air, a ballerina ready to plié, but changes direction with a sudden whimper and plops the arm to her side, rubs her armpit, and resumes her slumber. The care and feeding of Irene is a twenty-four-hour marathon for Adeen and this brief interlude in midafternoon is a luxury. Adeen shuts her eyes and savours every second of peace. The portable fan on the kitchen table whirls in a steady stream of air, blowing the cigarette smoke toward her daughter.

"EEEEEEeeeee." Irene is awake now and yawns with a loud groan, her tongue flicking, mouth smacking like a toothless infant after eating a bowl of Pablum. Her howls are intense, her appetite fierce. She is a needful baby sparrow impatient to be fed. There is drool in the corners of her mouth and she is now crying, a scattered mewling that Adeen recognizes but ignores. Instead, Adeen opens the patio door, steps outside, slides the door shut, and massages her temples to reduce the ringing from the scream of Irene's high-pitched voice. She grips the balcony railing with determination and needs to catch her breath, or maybe to find strength for another round of Irene.

Adeen is disoriented from the drinking and the frequent migraines. Rum with coffee eases her pain. So simple to just fling oneself over the balcony, fly away, and push the restart button to a new reality. *Dear God, let's get it right next time!* Her life has come to this: a developmentally disabled daughter, a self-absorbed wannabe cowboy poet for a husband. She is the one managing everyone's lives, custodian of an apartment building with an assortment of diverse tenants who also rely on her generosity and compassion. At least she and Frosty live rent-free, his excuse for not seeking better employment.

Irene, Frosty, and the Complex Arms, with its cargo of eccentric tenants, tax her stamina and vitality. The stable residents who originally signed long-term leases are like family. She's their Mother Teresa, their confidante and adviser, to whom they confess all their transgressions. Adeen can keep secrets, and they take advantage of her goodness and vulnerability. She thrives on others' neediness, though; attracts them like bees to the hostas under the birch tree in back. It is a distraction for her own broken spirit, and it gives her a temporary sense of self-worth.

"Mommaaaaa. Mommaaaaa."

"All right, all right. I hear you." Adeen snaps her focus back to Irene, who is now in full-blown tantrum mode, scrunching up torn pages from the Sears catalogue and hurling them against the patio doors like baseballs into a practice net. Moments like this, Adeen will reach out and cling to her daughter, arms in a complex restraining position around the girl's waist as though Irene were still a stubborn three-month-old kicking up wind for attention.

"Oh, Irene. Come and give your momma a kiss."

Irene, confused, violently shakes her head side to side with increasing vigour and speed, the ends of her ringlets whiplashing against her cheeks, adhering to the cracks of her dry lips. She unfurls herself from Adeen's grip and reaches for a black marker lying on the floor and scrawls graffiti lines and circles against her mother's veined cheeks and ruddy nose. She sniffs the peppermint scent and licks at the markings like melting ice cream, her wet tongue lapping Adeen's face with doggie-like kisses.

"Stop it! Stop it!" Adeen subdues her long enough to whop the side of Irene's head then catches herself. "Sorry, sorry, baby."

Both stare at each other, stunned, as though they were strangers. Irene returns her mother's blows. The smacks escalate back and forth, a slapstick scene from the Three Stooges, until Adeen yanks the long blond curls and punches her daughter with a violent hand against her back. Irene's head jerks backwards, and she's on her knees in a supplication of screams and whines.

"No. Nawdy nawdy." Adeen, almost in tears, shakes her index finger at Irene, who slaps the wagging finger away from her face.

A disturbance in the hallway interrupts their scuffle and Adeen rushes out, leaving the door ajar and a bewildered Irene among her broken crayons, scented markers, and cut-up paper dolls. She is a forgotten nuisance for now. Adeen trips over Derrick, Zita's ten-year-old, who is shouting, "Bubbe down! Bubbe down!" and points to the knot of people in the foyer. Frosty, who had just come in from the yardwork, is kneeling over a body. He sees Adeen and yells, "Get some orange juice."

"Oh, for heaven's sake! Not again! Where the hell are her damn kids?"

An agitated Adeen returns, leaving a liquid trail of juice in the hallway for the mice to lap up. She halts beside Mrs. Lapinberg, spilling the liquid this time over the old lady's blue, fresh-from-the-hairdresser hair as she passes the drink to Frosty, who has propped up the elderly body in a sitting position.

Mrs. Lapinberg, who lived next door to the Whitlaws on the first floor, was diabetic, had a heart condition, and was prone to fainting spells if she forgot to take her medication, a weekly occurrence by Derrick's count. The poor woman lived alone and bothered no one. When she left her apartment, it was to sit on a bench at the bus stop in front of the Complex Arms and talk to passengers as they disembarked: students, other seniors, and young mothers with toddlers. Her son, Barney, visited weekly and accompanied her to the hair salon. Sometimes they would take a detour through the park nearby to rest in the playground and observe the children at play.

"You loved the swings the most," she would tell him while he puffed on a Montecristo No. 2 with a thoughtful nod. He would let her ramble on, acting like a used-car salesman who, desperate for a sale, pretended to be interested in what potential customers shared with him. Although she was eighty-two and suffered from numerous conditions, her mind was razor sharp, still there.

"Must you smoke those vile cigars, Barney?" She would fan the smoke away with her purse, exaggerating a cough like a patient dying from tuberculosis, but he would always ignore his mother's requests, toss an ugly stogie in the sandbox, and light another one. She would clean up after him, as she always did, retrieve the dead cigars, and chuck them into the nearby garbage can.

"Barney, the children. The children …"

And he would always say, "Ma, you didn't have to do that," and she would reprimand him like he was twelve again, caught smoking behind Mr. Schmidt's hardware store in Bruderheim.

Barney never had the decency to escort his mother to her apartment after one of their jaunts. He'd sit in the car chewing on another unlit cigar and wait as she struggled to make her way with her cane to the front door of the building. He was that kind of son. Once in the lobby, Mrs. Lapinberg would ring Adeen's doorbell and Adeen would come scurrying to guide her home.

"Where's that moron?" she'd fume, and Mrs. Lapinberg would say, "He takes after his father. May he be resting in peace wherever he may be."

It was not unusual for tenants to find Mrs. Lapinberg sprawled outside on the cement walk, inside the doorway, in the corridor, or even in front of her own apartment door. "Bubbe down! Bubbe down!" Derrick, like a town crier, would alert the building whenever Mrs. Lapinberg had one of her episodes.

They were both loners, she and Derrick, becoming a team over the summer months — adopted grandmother and grandson. They looked out for each other, held hands, and waited for the ice cream man to roll down the street on his adult tricycle with its stash of various summer lickings in the icebox behind the bike. The annoying bell lured kids like baby mice racing toward cheese in a mousetrap. Still, Mr. Softie was music to everyone's ears that summer of intolerable heat, when everyone and everything seemed to be dying.

"You sure you can have ice cream, Mrs. Lapinberg?" Derrick would tug her cotton floral skirt. She took so many pills for so many health issues that she wasn't sure herself.

"Pshsst!" she would hush him. "I can have once in a while. Don't tell Barney."

Adeen would often find the boy and his bubbe sitting on the front step, each licking a purple Popsicle, their favourite flavour.

The tenants shrink back to give Mrs. Lapinberg breathing space.

There's Jack, dressed as his alter ego, Jackie, in a silken blue Japanese kimono, decorated with spatters of paint from a morning spent creating another watercolour portrait of dying flowers, lilies this time. He was returning with his mail — an assortment of bills, his monthly dose of art magazines, and the *New Yorker* — when he felt the swoon of a large package dropping behind him. Mrs. Lapinberg had just entered the lobby and was reaching out for Adeen's doorbell when she became disoriented and fainted.

Zita, Derrick's mom, who lives on the second floor, saw Mrs. Lapinberg go down, saw the body splayed on the floor like an art installation gone wrong.

Shylene was scooting down the stairs to see what was keeping Frosty when Mrs. Lapinberg tumbled, right there, like Mother Mary at her son's crucifixion.

Rosemary was returning from her daily visit to the outpatient psychiatric clinic at the Royal Alexandra Hospital downtown when she was confronted by the mob of tenants.

Payton, the Jehovah's Witness, servant to Jehovah, keeps tolling his bell in sync with Mr. Softie's ice cream truck as it passes by, sounding the alarm that the end is near, or that it is the last chance for one of Mr. Softie's Popsicles or for Mrs. Lapinberg to repent and save her Jewish soul, if not her son's.

"Everyone, get on your knees," Payton orders, but no one obeys his directive. Instead, all eyes gawk in silence at the downed body.

There is a concern for an old woman who is beached in the lobby with such predictability.

Cody, the teenage boy who lives on the fourth floor with his father, Wayne, skips down the stairs with a punk beat and leaps over Mrs. Lapinberg as though he were jumping a hurdle in an Olympic meet.

"Show some respect," Adeen calls out in a commanding, no-nonsense tone of voice, "or I'll tell your father."

But Cody is oblivious to the commotion blocking his exit; his flashy boom box blares throughout the building as he manoeuvres his way out the front door, without even a polite nod to the unconscious Mrs. Lapinberg.

Jack adjusts his hearing aid and says to nobody in particular, "Kids today!"

Payton blasts his angry bell in Cody's direction as though he were conducting an exorcism. "You are doomed, son, doomed to the fires of hell, I tell you! Come back to be redeemed."

"Cut it out, Payton," Adeen says. "What did I tell you?"

Mrs. Lapinberg is now stirring, moaning, mumbling, "Sorry, sorry."

Frosty gives her a hand; her fingers spring to her forehead as though the brain cells are about to escape and she needs a moment to hold them back.

"I'm so embarrassed," she says, barely audible.

Jack returns to his apartment to complete his masterpiece of dying lilies. Zita drags Derrick upstairs for another dinner of canned spaghetti, his father still up at Fort Mac, not home for another week. And then there's Wayne, Cody's dad, just returning from work at the carpet warehouse. He missed the excitement. Rosemary has already disappeared into her apartment, but Payton continues sounding the alarm while Mrs. Lapinberg blocks her ears and says, "Make him stop, Adeen. Make him stop."

"Frosty, I've been waiting for you," Shylene has nuzzled beside him and whispers from the side of her mouth.

"I heard that," Adeen says to Shylene as she guides Mrs. Lapinberg back to her apartment.

"It's still uncomfortable in my place, Adeen. Frosty said he'd adjust my new window air conditioner because he didn't get it right the first time."

"Sure."

Shylene ignores the comment and lopes up the stairs. Everyone can hear her slam the door.

"I'm so sorry, so sorry to cause so much trouble." Mrs. Lapinberg is on her feet now.

"No trouble. I'll call Barney and have him come over."

"Oh no, dear. Then I'll really be in trouble."

"All right, Mrs. Lapinberg. Do you want to come over for supper later?"

Frosty is standing nearby, consuming the dialogue.

"Oh, thank you, Adeen. That would be lovely. Just don't tell Barney I fell again."

Everyone has scattered like cockroaches to their usual living places, and life resumes. For the moment, any more drama has been averted for another day.

Mrs. Lapinberg, in a tremble of profuse sweat, is determined to stand firm against the assault of age, despite swollen ankles heavy like matzo balls.

Frosty picks up the half-empty glass of orange juice, shakes his head, and turns to Payton, who says: "The end is near. The end is near. Be prepared."

"Fuck off, Payton."

ADEEN

That was the core of them. My tenants. Good people all, carrying their quirks and human frailties to my doorstep. I gave them what they needed: love, companionship, even food and drink. A bed sometimes if I found them on the street in tatters. I didn't tell the Swanks. They'd have fired us for sure. And I would never have heard the end of it from Frosty.

Tenants came and went, but those stuck to me like Velcro. Unshakable. I guess they all had their reasons. It sure wasn't the building. Oh, it looked new from the outside, but it was constructed in a hurry, below standards, like a lot of things out here. Pop-ups, I call them. One minute there's nothing there, then they appear. Out of nowhere. Of course, it doesn't take long before they begin to fall apart. Every ten years or so it seems these buildings have to undergo major repairs. I could see already where there were water stains on some of the ceilings on the top floor even though they were plastered with stucco to conceal any moisture leaks. But still, whatever savings at the start, the Swanks would have to pay in the end. Do it right the first time, I say. What do they care? They can declare bankruptcy and move on. Write off the Complex Arms. Well, I'm just saying. May not happen.

Nothing lasts here in Alberta from what I can see, not even marriages. People live in buildings that are like temporary shelters. Then when they make enough money, they move on up to new developments: Beaumont, south of here, or St. Albert just north of Edmonton, where the hoity-toity live. Pretty there, but it's pretty here, too. They talk about the crime rate in Mill Woods, but it's all over, even in St. Albert. Guy got shot the other day over a drug deal. Small paragraph in the *Edmonton Journal*, but if it had happened in Mill Woods, well, the headline would read that we're living on the south side of hell. What do you expect from a community with a population of almost one hundred thousand, the size of a small city?

There were lots of problems. A tiny piece of siding goes missing from a corner near the balcony and never gets fixed. Sloppy work. So in the winter months, ice melts and causes damage to interior walls. Everything is cheap aluminum; nothing like the solid red brick or stone in Montreal that lasts for centuries.

Frosty told me that because of the cold weather here, the bricks would crack after time, so aluminum and stucco are the way to go. Complain to the Swank Property Management Group and they just nod their heads, *Yeah, yeah, we'll fix it,* and then they conveniently forget.

I tried to keep my tenants comfortable. Maintain their apartments, maintain their lives. I couldn't just turn my back on them. My tenants had fragile spirits.

Anyhow, that's the story there.

THE NEW TENANT

rosty waits until Payton's bell fades into nothingness and then checks his mailbox since he is right there in the lobby. The building settles into a sigh of relief that all is well after another day of Mrs. Lapinberg, or is that the sound of Frosty moaning and groaning over the influx of bills and circulars that now spill onto the floor?

"Damn you," he says, stooping over to gather the junk mail.

A raspy voice from behind accosts him. "Who do I see about the vacancy?"

His eyes flash toward a saucy young girl whose luminous, milky-white skin is now casting a moonlit glow in the dim lobby. She is leaning against the entrance door, one hand fisted on her hip, poised in faded denim overalls, the fabric clipped, chewed, leaving a fashionable fray of threads at midthigh, like minishorts from the sixties. Frosty is soaking in the freshness of this tart-looking girl. A sideways glance down her open bib reveals she is braless, shirtless, and blessed with substantial bouncy breasts. A straw cowgirl hat perches over the fluff of bleached cotton-candy curls that coil at her ears like commas. She knows men find her almost impossibly irresistible. She is radiant, a sexy portrait from a bygone era recalling courtesans lingering by the "batwing" doors that separated them from the "proper ladies" passing outside the dance hall saloons. She is that youthful Marilyn Monroe in *Bus Stop*. That old black magic has everyone still in a spell.

"That would be me, Frosty Whitlaw, or my wife, Adeen Whitlaw. Here she comes now."

Adeen has just left Mrs. Lapinberg when she spots Frosty chatting with temptation. She approaches the duo, her face a scowl, ready for battle.

"You got dirt on your face," Frosty interrupts to avoid any embarrassing confrontations.

Adeen's immediate reflex: hand to face. Any pending skirmish now doused.

"Oh, oh, leaky pen. I was writing the grocery list earlier." She remembers Irene's marker attack and smudges the offensive markings with her fingers, leaving a blush of Gothic black that accentuates her cheekbones further.

"MOMMAAAA" echoes throughout the hollow hallway. All eyes are on Irene's sliding Bermuda shorts, now hugging her ankles, a long midi T-shirt hiding her diaper. She stands at attention for a moment, a palace guard waiting to be relieved from duty. Poke her shoulder and she will sway to one side as though asleep. Suddenly, she awakens in a spooky, horror-film kind of way, hands in constant motion. Ping pinging, her fingers flick, and then the clapping.

Adeen forgot she had left the door open.

"MOMMAAAA. MOMMAAAA."

"You better take care of Irene and get your face cleaned up before people take to talkin'." Frosty points with his chin in the direction of his stepdaughter.

"Who's the chick?" Adeen says nodding toward the possible new tenant, who is now fidgeting with impatience.

"She's interested in an apartment. I'll take care of her," he says in his best western drawl.

"I bet you will."

Brushing by the girl as he moves toward Adeen, Frosty manages to just skim his hairy arm over the girl's chest. The prickling sensation penetrates to the follicles of each hair, like erotic electrical currents.

"You got the keys?" he asks Adeen.

"Who's the retard?" The abrasive cowgirl is unsympathetic and curt.

"That's my daughter and her name is Irene."

Already she has rubbed Adeen the wrong way. Adeen is no longer embarrassed by Irene's public tantrums or displays of infantile behaviour, and she is prepared to defend her child against every slight, real or imagined. Everyone in the building looks out for Irene and Mrs. Lapinberg.

"If you feel uncomfortable with my daughter and her mental challenges — because they are challenges — you can find yourself a cardboard box and live in it. She has other talents."

"Like what?"

"She paints abstract art. She's a genius, really. That's what Jack, another tenant, who paints, told me."

"I suppose one man's art is another man's wallpaper."

Adeen glares. She really doesn't want this character occupying Jan's available apartment but the economic boom is now a bust and vacancies are plentiful. Property managers are luring new renters with various incentives. Edmonton is a city of transients, but luckily, there is a stable group of tenants in the building; some, like Mrs. Lapinberg, Payton, Jack, and Zita are permanent fixtures, who've lived there since the Swank Property Management

Group bought the Complex Arms. But the market is beginning to change.

"We're full."

"Now, now, Adeen. You know that ain't so."

"I'm being honest here, okay. I like to get these things out of the way pronto. You have a problem with my daughter?"

"Whatever."

"All right." Adeen sighs. "What's your name?"

"Blue Velvet but everyone calls me Velvet."

"Blue Velvet? Now that's a blast from the past."

"Blue Velvet Coburn is my full real name," she says, emphasizing each syllable like a note on the musical scale.

"Really?"

"I know it sounds made up, but my parents were hippies and my mom was pregnant with me at this outdoor concert in Sault Ste. Marie, Dick Clark's Caravan of Stars, I think. Her water broke when Bobby Vinton came onstage."

"Yeah, Bobby Vinton would do that to any girl," Adeen says.

"Apparently, I slid onto the ground. They were sitting on a slope far back from the stage, and just as he started to sing 'Blue Velvet,' I decided to make my appearance. My mom said it was like he was the midwife. She was his biggest fan and hated that my early arrival made her miss his concert. I don't think she ever forgave me. It was in the local newspapers the next day. 'Baby Born While Bobby Vinton Sings "Blue Velvet."' I was going to change my name, but what's the point? It's a conversation piece, right?"

"Okay, Velvet. Frosty, you go take care of Irene and bring me the keys. I'll show the apartment."

"Ah, come on, Adeen." Frosty is sulking like a two-year-old.

"Frosty."

"Shit."

Nonetheless, he obeys, walking back to the apartment in that halting manner familiar to cowboys who have sustained leg injuries.

"You from the Soo you said?" Adeen turns to Velvet.

"Yep."

"Guess you know that the Soo is the lousiest place in all of Canada to get a lift if you're hitchhiking. Got stuck there once myself."

"I don't hitchhike."

The two wait in the muted light of the corridor studying the linoleum floor and the turquoise walls needful of thicker insulation. What to say? They can hear the muffled conversations, raised voices arguing in a diversity of languages, music from various cultures, and a variety of cooking smells.

"Now what's taking him so long? Christ!"

"Maybe I should check out other buildings first." Velvet is on the brink of finding an exit when Frosty sticks his head out the door and slides a set of keys down the hallway toward Adeen. Show off! He is in a race as he shines the floor with his good leg, gliding, braking at Adeen's feet. The keys win by a head. His racing days are a distant memory, but he still insists on playing "horsey" at every turn of a moment. "Heck, Adeen," he would always say, "if you can't have fun once in a while, what's the point of livin'."

"Keys win."

"Frosty, for God's sake."

"For God's sake what?"

She centres her attention on Velvet. "The heat's getting to him."

"I hear you. No air conditioning in the building?"

"Sorry. With the amount of hot days we have here, not worth installing air conditioning. You'll have to get one of those portable or window fans. That's what some of my tenants buy."

"Velvet's thinking of looking at other buildings, Frosty."

He's positioned himself with a good side view of Velvet's breasts. "Lucky you found a vacancy in the Complex Arms," he says. "Everyone wants to live here — free rent first month, utilities included, bus stop just outside the door, walkin' distance to schools, a mini-mall with a Petro-Canada, a convenience store, a physiotherapist, and a daycare 'round the corner, if you need one. Need one?"

Velvet shakes her head. "No kids."

"Yep, too much trouble they are. Cute when they're babies, but if they have somethin' wrong it's hard, especially when the kid's not yours." Frosty is a slur of mumbles, shoulders slightly hunched, hands in his back pockets, nervous bow legs twitching side to side.

Adeen is doing her best to keep her mouth shut until they are alone, and then she will blast him, full steam ahead.

"You know, if it hadn't been for the tenant who fell off the balcony, we'd be full," Frosty says.

"Frosty."

"A tenant fell?"

"An accident."

"Irene okay?" Adeen is keen on changing the subject.

"Yep. Cleaned her up and she's watchin' *Sesame Street*. You know, Adeen, I can show Velvet the —"

"Bet you can."

"And what am I supposed to do? Watch *Sesame Street*, too?" Frosty's mouth is scrunched in a fading shout as Adeen and Velvet climb the stairs to view the vacant apartment.

"What about that air conditioner for Shylene? That should keep you busy."

Adeen is jiggling a handcuff of keys that looks like an overloaded charm bracelet. "It's on the fourth floor in front. No elevators in this building, but I look at these stairs as my Stairmaster.

Get my exercise that way," she says over her shoulder, Velvet coming up the rear.

"Oh, that's fine."

They reach the top floor and both are panting. "Didn't realize I was so out of shape," Velvet says.

"You'd be surprised how we can let the body go. Hey, what do you do for a living by the way?" Adeen inserts the key in the lock.

"Just got in town. Start looking tomorrow."

"Oh? What you good at?"

"Waitressing."

"I'll keep my eyes open. Hope you don't mind, but your neighbours are a dad, Wayne, and his teenage son. Divorced. Something wrong when a father gets custody of a kid, don't you think? Cody parties when the dad's away. Any noise complaints, give to me."

"And the other side?"

"Jack, a retired principal. He's the one I mentioned before who thinks my daughter is a gifted artist, and she's only ten. Anyhow, now he paints all day. Awful stuff but I guess, as they say, art is in the eye of the beholder. Does these watercolours of dead flowers in memory of his mother. That must have been some relationship! Says his paintings mean something. Well, what could dead flowers mean except they are dead? Harmless fellow, though. A character, but nice."

Adeen swings the door wide open. "Ta-dah!" The smell of fresh paint, vinegar, and bleach assaults their noses. "Immaculate. And look how bright the rooms are."

"Can we maybe open a window?" Velvet is feeling light-headed.

"Can do."

Adeen ambles toward the balcony, draws the verticals to one side, and glides the patio door open. Splashes of sun dapple into the living room through the tall birches across the road and hang on the walls like abstract art.

"Spotless and a good view. Look — you can see downtown Edmonton from up here."

Velvet joins her on the balcony.

"They're almost done with the Whitemud Drive over there. Will get you straight across the city in twenty minutes, they say. Edmonton is growing. Well, not as much as Calgary. But we have class. Lots of poets here. Frosty writes poems. Thinks he's Charles Badger Clark in chaps — one of those American cowboy poets who recites his stuff at rodeos and festivals. No money in that, but he likes to stand onstage and recite "America by Heart." Keeps him out of mischief. I used to be impressed when I first met him.... Anyhow, ever been to Calgary?"

"No, but my boyfriend's played gigs out there. Prefers Edmonton."

"Musician?"

"Supposed to meet him here."

"Yep. Cowboys, rednecks, punks, and transients hungry for a fast buck, find them here. Almost sounds like a country song." Adeen begins to sing, "Here here, cowboys, punks, rednecks, transients too many to feed, make a fast buck Fort Mac, awaiting your big fuck. Oh ... s'cuse me."

"That's a bouncy little tune," Velvet says.

"Oh, we get crazies here, too. Sometimes I think the Complex Arms is a loony bin!" Adeen faces Velvet as though she just remembered the cowgirl was there. "One bedroom, you said?"

"Yes, that's fine."

"Am I talking too much?"

"No. It's okay."

Both rest their eyes somewhere into the far-off space where sky meets land.

"I think I want to see other apartments in other buildings if you don't mind."

"Don't know where else you would find an apartment with such a view. You'll find out yourself, sure enough. See that land over there? Beautiful."

Adeen points to a sad spot across the unpaved road, beyond the sagging fence, far over the hump of sun, where a familiar dryness coats the barren fields awaiting further development. Over to the east, a rusty pickup truck, mostly ruined after too many years of unpredictable weather and neglect, sleeps on its side, the driver's door, windows, and windshield riddled with holes as though someone had used the vehicle for target practice. Half-submerged behind tall prairie grasses and wild flora — wild rose, Canada thistle, brome grass, and switchgrass — the truck appears to be in a slow sink. Beyond the slope, next to an abandoned farmhouse with its weathered grey complexion, rotting barns lean in an arthritic stoop like an old man teetering on the brink of collapse. To the west, the smog from forests burning up north near Grande Prairie hover over outlying regions, thin out, and creep into Edmonton.

"Wonderful scenery. You can sit out here and meditate and listen to the birdies argue. Relaxing. Some nights late autumn, you can even see the northern lights. Haven't seen anything until you see those northern lights. Quite a display. Worth the rent for that alone."

They both return their attention to the blank sky, still without a fleck of cloud, just a blur of white concealing rain.

Adeen takes a deep breath, exhales. "Okay. Plus first month's rent is free."

No response from Velvet.

"Can you smell the smoke?" Adeen inhales. "Awful thing. Everything is dying. Every summer a forest catches fire. Payton, one of our tenants, he's a Jehovah's Witness, says it's the end of the world. Armageddon is coming. Again. A summer from hell is what he predicts. Nobody has seen anything like it. Oh, he won't bother you by the way. Just a bit peculiar."

Both are welded to the spot, uncertain what to say, what to do next. Adeen finally twists her body to face Velvet.

"So you want this apartment or not?" She is jangling the keys again, a nervous habit; something to break the silence.

Velvet has been patient, polite, drumming her fake white fingernails on the balcony railing, her forehead a furrow of indecision. "Haven't made up my mind yet."

"You'll like it here. Some of my tenants, they're like family. Like at Christmas, we get together and sing carols on every floor and end of this month, just after Klondike Days, we're throwing a block party, a barbecue in the courtyard below. Now that's a good reason to rent here. With all the tenants contributing, best food ever and it's free."

"I don't need a family."

"Everyone needs a family, someone. Just saying that we have a great bunch of people living here if you have any worries. It's a safe building. We all look out for each other."

They're about to head inside from the balcony when Adeen sees it.

"Oh, damn! Thought they would have gotten rid of the kid's tricycle."

"Your husband said a tenant had fallen?"

"Down there." Adeen points directly below. "Jan and her little girl, Nina, both hit the pavement hard, right there. You can still see some of the brown stains. Frosty tried to scrub the blood off after the cops said it was okay, but we couldn't scrape it all; waiting for a hard rain to erase that shit. May have to recement that patch."

A ferocious silence spreads between them again. Velvet is absorbed by the stain; can't look away.

"Mary Poppins parachuting in an open umbrella. That's the way I see Jan. Lovely girl. So young. Yep, yep, yep. I should have followed my gut. They weren't here a week when we heard this banging, crashing of furniture, crying and horrible screams. Frosty and me, we ran up here and the guy was just running past us, down the corridor like an escapee from the remand. Almost tripped me, and there she was, Jan, in the hallway, crying, snot running down her nose like she was a kid herself, and the little one, only a toddler, hiding behind her mother's ass. I'll never forget the look on Jan's face, teary eyed and her saying how he had wrecked her life. But don't you think we wreck our own lives? I mean, she decided to live with the creep, so her responsibility and no one else's. That's what I say."

"You say a lot, Mrs. Whitlaw."

"Call me Adeen. When you are the manager of an apartment building, well, let's just say, it goes with the territory. Do you want to hear more?"

"Sure. Might as well."

"Anyhow, we went inside and the place was a holy mess. He had smashed the terrarium, broken glass everywhere, and this lizard running loose around the carpet. The guy didn't look mean when he rented the place. Seemed like a nice family. But then, what's the definition of nice or even normal? What's the definition of family, eh? That's what I want to know."

Velvet is pushing the tricycle back and forth with her foot.

"Not a regular occurrence here by any means."

They again lean over the balcony in a silent acknowledgement to where Jan and Nina had landed.

"An awful thing. An awful thing. Jan died but the kid lived. She saved the toddler. Made herself like a cushion for Nina. Husband is out on bail waiting for a court date. Nina is living with her grandparents somewhere in England. Husband's friends and Frosty taking his side, saying that it was an accident. She was drunk, Jan's husband told the cops. Bullshit. Jan didn't drink. Her husband threw her over. I just know it."

Adeen turns away, reaches with anger for the tricycle. "So I need a deposit if you plan on renting the apartment."

"I thought first month's rent was free."

"Yeah, but I still need a deposit. You can leave any time, but I need three months' notice."

Velvet takes another look at where Jan and Nina had fallen and then averts her face in horror. She shuts her eyes as though that gesture would erase the scene of such cruelty witnessed on this balcony.

"You okay, girl?"

Velvet nods as they re-enter the living room, Adeen carrying the tricycle by its handlebar. "Everything in the apartment has been sanitized, so no worries."

Velvet is still mulling over her decision.

"Okay. Includes utilities for a one-year lease."

"You got yourself a deal." Velvet shakes Adeen's hand.

ADEEN

Where people are concerned, I'm intuitive. I didn't want National Velvet or Velvet, whatever she called herself, as a tenant, but I gave her the benefit of the doubt. I mean, she was from the Soo. I would expect the same if it were me. Anyhow, I planned to stay out of her bleached hair. Should have followed my gut feeling. Just no good vibes came out of that feeble brain of hers. I mean, she went around braless for heaven's sake. I knew I'd have to keep Frosty on a short leash, that dog.

But the Swanks would have thrown us into the street if they ever found out I had rejected a potential tenant. We lived rent-free and that was a saving. The Swank Property Management Group wanted low-maintenance occupants who paid their rent on time, didn't cause any trouble. I told them nothing. Plus, they wanted the building in pristine condition. Guess who did most of the work. Oh sure, Frosty could do repairs, but some days he had problems with his wrist and leg on account of when he got hit crossing Whyte Avenue after a merry night of drinking at the Commerce Hotel. A lot of times, I did the tough jobs. Guess I'm grateful he isn't in a wheelchair.

I don't know. Lately, I just been wanting to run away and live with the wolves. At least you know where you stand with them. Plus, they take care of their elders, which I'll require in my old age. But where would I have gone with a daughter who spoke in sounds and a cowboy for a husband who thought he was Charles Badger Clark?

If someone had asked me when I was a kid, "Adeen, what do you want to be when you grow up?" I would have said I wanted to be an artist, paint portraits, not be a caretaker of an apartment building, attending to needy tenants and evicting mice. Oh, those mice. No pets were allowed in the Complex Arms, but ten-year-old Derrick had these mice in a cage, a birthday gift from a friend. Actually, the friend's mom wanted to get rid of the critters and he asked if he could have them as pets and so I said okay. How bad could it be? "Just make sure they stay in their box," I said. Well, one got loose. Eeek! Frosty set traps. I had a soft spot for Derrick but ... Rosemary almost fainted in the hallway when she saw it.

No, I wanted to be a social worker. I guess because of Irene. The one I had after Irene's birth was so kind and generous. I wanted to make a difference somewhere in this world. I don't know. I grew up in the fabricated, idealistic world of the sixties. We marched in the streets of downtown Montreal chanting love and peace slogans, tossing pennies at the homeless who huddled around Metro stations waiting for a miracle of food. Jesus dividing the loaves and fishes so everyone could eat. No Jesus. I was one of those innocent flower children who burned her bra and wore sheer, tie-dye skirts and peasant blouses. Yeah, I was a hot chick; nothing like Velvet though. So many possibilities then.

I wrecked my life. My fault. I chose my life, just like Jan did. No one forced me to sleep with my boyfriend; no one forced me to move here, even Mona, my decision alone. Only have myself to blame. We are responsible for our lives. Do I sound like I'm trying to convince myself? Convince you? One night and poof, like that, everything changed. "You made your bed. Now you can lie in it," my mother used to always chant at me, like her life was any better.

But I had my tenants. Frosty said I intruded on their lives but, you know, when shit happened, I was the one they came to for the fixing. I was like a den mother there, and besides, it reminded me that my life was decent enough compared to some of them.

Anyhow, that's the story there.

GOODNIGHT, IRENE

Adeen closes Irene's bedroom door with a gentle twist to the knob. It is always a victory to see Irene settled and in bed. With no air conditioning, the unbearable heat in the apartment makes caring for Irene an almost impossible task. The series of impulsive tantrums and exhausting pursuits that inevitably occur when the heat rises always results in Adeen on the verge of tears. Over the years, however, Adeen has discovered a solution, a last resort that has become a bedtime ritual. She sings "Goodnight, Irene." This repetitious folk lullaby, a natural sedative, always manages to lull her daughter into a peaceful sleep for a few hours.

Adeen tiptoes past Frosty's six-foot-four frame, outstretched on the second-hand corduroy couch, a rescue from a fleeing tenant. Soiled bare feet dangle over the edge; he has been snoozing since Adeen returned from showing Velvet the vacancy. He is now stirring.

"Did she take the apartment?" he mutters drowsily.

"Oh. Didn't mean to wake you up."

"Can't sleep none how." He sits up, ruffling his hair with his fingers, but the front curls insist on springing back onto his forehead.

"Yeah, took a while. Velvet, what a weird name! Reminds me of those garish Presley paintings done on black velvet, the ones you see in those cheap motels on the way out of town. Anyhow, I convinced her that the apartment was a bargain. She liked that she could see the sky and downtown from the balcony. 'Like home,' she said. Mr. Swank should be pleased that I signed up another tenant, filled up that difficult vacancy. And considering the economy, it seems to me this might be a good time to ask for a raise."

"When she movin' in?"

"She signed the lease and is moving in tonight. Needs a place real quick, she says."

"Blue Velvet Coburn sounds like the name of a rock band. Think that's a real name?" Frosty says in his usual soft drawl as he heads for the fridge and a Molson. Adeen follows and both seat themselves at the kitchen table. Adeen is digging into a salad bowl of chipped ice.

"People name their kids after anything these days. It's the trend. So yeah, I believe her."

"You told her about what happened up there?"

"Yep. Showed her where they landed and everything. Didn't seem to bother her one way or another. She seemed hesitant at first. Don't know why. Tried to sell her on the benefits of renting at the Complex Arms — close to everything, you know the drill. Going to look for work tomorrow after she settles in, she said."

"What kinda work she lookin' for?"

"Waitress jobs. Hope she's not a troublemaker."

"Adeen."

"Yeah."

"Stay out of her business."

"Not crazy for the bitch, so not to worry."

She slides two mini cubes of ice inside her mouth and starts to mash them like a dog gnawing on a bone, her left cheek out to there with the crush. Frosty is laughing.

"What's so funny?"

"You still have your clown face."

"Oh, I haven't had a chance to wash up."

She scoops more ice into her mouth as though she were preparing for a shortage and fixes her eyes on Frosty, who is shuffling toward her with a tender awkwardness. He massages the back of her neck, strokes her hair, damp with the humidity of the day, brushes back her moist bangs. "You got time for me?"

Adeen is somewhere else now, talking to air. "You know what I did today, Frosty."

"No, hon, what?"

"I hit her. First time I laid a hand on Irene. Scared me half to death. All that rage and then, wham, she hit me back, and we were in this duel like the Three Stooges minus one and it scared the shit out of me because I have never ever laid a hand on Irene, even when she'd crap in her pants."

"Maybe it's time to put her in one of those institutions where they can take care of her." He releases the ponytail and lets her hair flutter through his fingers. "She's ten now, and it's gettin' harder and harder for you … and for me. Maybe go some place nice, Jasper maybe, and not have to worry 'bout her."

"No. I promised when I had her, I would never put her into one of those nasty places. I saw *One Flew Over the Cuckoo's Nest* and vowed that would never happen to Irene. And besides, who's going to take care of this place? Someone has to be here all the time."

"Those are just poor excuses, Adeen. We are replaceable and the Michener Centre in Red Deer, I hear it's a fine place. She'll have plenty of friends there and good care."

"The Michener? They used to sterilize patients for God's sake. Did awful things. Eugenics, they called it." Adeen is shaking her head. "I can't."

"That was years ago. Things have changed. We can at least check them out, no?" He is fondling her inner thighs, his hands riding to her crotch. Adeen feels numb. She is busy swallowing the crushed ice cubes.

"Frosty, you knew when you married me that Irene came with the luggage."

"Yep, and I've honoured that deal, haven't I? But things change. I love Irene like my own daughter, but you don't see what she's doin' to you, hon — to us. Look at your face."

"I'll go shower before I forget."

Adeen runs into the bathroom, studies her reflection in the foggy mirror. An image bounces back: a gaunt woman, her already sun-dried face a canvas of wrinkles, and a body on the cusp of middle age. How did this happen? She is crying as she steps into the shower and turns on the cool spray of water. Lathering her face, hair, inner thighs, someone's hand, not hers, is guiding the soap in the dark creases of her body. Frosty is rinsing her small breasts, her back; his head leans over her shoulder to kiss the crook of her neck. They both share the shower, let the water pulse away the soap and grind of the day. Her face tilted upward, she is giggling and gulps water. In dealing with the minute details of living, Adeen had forgotten how much she loves this man.

His mouth is on hers now, sucking the wetness from her lips; an entanglement of tongues. She presses her compact buttocks hard against his pelvis. He guides her out the shower stall and both tumble onto the cool damp tile floor. She is laughing now, and he is riding her in a slow rocking motion, gaining speed, moving faster and faster, a human pumpjack, up and down, up and down, and she is saying, "Frosty, Frosty, Frosty, stop, stop."

And he is saying, "Not now, hon, not now, not now." And then the bronco rider halts, heaves his chest, raises his arms in the air like he had just been declared champion at the Calgary Stampede, and collapses, his face resting on her breasts, gasping for air, his heart fluttering.

"Neeee. Neeee." Laughter, a standing ovation. Adeen and Frosty face the open bathroom door and there is Irene, applauding their sorry efforts.

ADEEN

I tried to teach Irene so many things that were simple for other children in her age group. I worked hard with her. I wanted her to experience a classroom setting, thinking that maybe through osmosis she would learn a thing or two. I enrolled her in the Catholic school nearby, which had a special-needs teacher working with mentally challenged students. Age-wise, Irene was always much older than her classmates. But mentally? She was still a baby.

In grade one the class was preparing to receive their First Holy Communion. With loving patience, I showed her how to cross herself so that she could receive Holy Communion with the other kids in her class. Every day, every day, we would practise. I would slowly guide Irene's hand to her forehead, chest, left shoulder, and finally right, and Irene, looking puzzled, parroted my movements over and over for months at a time until one day, there it was. I cried out, "Yes, yes, Irene, yes, yes, good girl," nodding and crossing myself, too, and Irene just kept repeating the gestures, jumping up and down, up and down, shaking those hands as though she had just touched a hot stove and was trying to cool them. Irene didn't have a clue what she was doing or why, but she liked getting dressed up in her white veil, dress, stockings, and shoes. She looked lovely and even mimicked the other children when it came time to receive the body and blood of Christ.

I am a lapsed Catholic from a long time ago and have no use for any church or their hypocritical, self-righteous believers. Pious flaw-flaws, Mother St. Mary Ronald, my fifth-grade teacher, called them, not realizing that she herself was one of them. But I led Irene to Catholicism, a religion I could at least monitor just in case there was a heaven. I didn't want my daughter to languish in limbo where all nonbaptized babies wait in line until the gates of heaven open up to them, if that ever happens.

It took months of patience to get Irene to cross herself, but she did it, and for that brief moment, at least, both of us felt some joy — Irene for her accomplishment and me for the possibility of a future for my daughter. No expectations, but there was always a glimmer of hope.

It makes me smile to think about that time and Irene's happy dance for this small success. Of course, everything she learned by imitation was soon erased from her mind. The next year I had to pull her out of school because, after a while, even the special-needs teachers couldn't handle her.

What happened that night made me wonder if I could handle Irene anymore. Frosty was mad as hell. I was just embarrassed. First time that ever happened. Irene wasn't a baby anymore in terms of her physical self. She probably thought we were playing a game of wrestling. She liked to watch wrestling matches on TV every Saturday night. She just clapped whenever they went down. Funny, I mean odd, that she got so much pleasure out of watching two people harm themselves, even if it was for entertainment.

After the bathroom humiliation, I seriously considered Frosty's suggestion. I spoke to Mona to get her take on things, and she agreed with Frosty. We went as far as arranging a tour of the Michener, but I just wasn't ready to give away my daughter, even though it was only an hour's drive from here. Instead, I made up my mind to be more vigilant. Frosty was losing patience with me. My marriage was tottering like a drunken whore on stilettos. I had so much on my mind at that time, my brain hurting with the migraines. Do you understand?

Anyhow, that's the story there.

MONA

Summer light glides early across the prairie. The sky is already a jazzy fusion of pink and purple threads, the bashful sun just emerging. It is barely dawn. Crabby crows hide in weeping birch branches; smaller birds, chickadees perhaps, are gossiping in the corners of the lilac bush oblivious to danger. *May Be, May Be, May Be,* they seem to say. Another replies: *8:30, 8:30, 8:30,* as though it has organized a flock meeting in a nest and is reminding the other birds that all should be in attendance and on time.

Adeen reclines in the lounge chair on the balcony, entertaining the first beer of the day, and massages her hot cheeks with the chilled brew. The squawking, querulous birds (whatever happened to the 8:30 meeting?), the distant piercing wail of the train and rhythmic bump of wheels over tracks, the waste disposal men in their gigantic bulbous truck in back — all signal another day, and Frosty has yet to return from an all-nighter. The humidity is unforgiving, even at this early hour.

After the bathroom fiasco, Frosty fled, ran away again like a naughty child, his usual coping mechanism. She had become accustomed to his petulant behaviour and no longer worries about his whereabouts. He always returned because where else could he go and who else would love him more than she? Frosty was a good stepfather, showing patience when required, but now, even he found the situation intolerable.

Adeen's mind skips to another place, and time.

Irene. It had been a difficult delivery. A moment too long in the uterus and a deficiency of oxygen left the baby damaged, with partial facial paralysis, a shrivelled mind, and a language of sounds. Irene's father had blamed Adeen, said he would always feel imprisoned by an obligation to a woman he no longer loved and a child he didn't want. So he had vanished from their lives, Irene not yet one.

"You little tramp," her drunken mother had shrieked when Adeen broke the news, "you weren't supposed to follow my life. I wanted better for you. I wanted better." The drama queen had collapsed to her knees, weeping, hurling the empty beer bottle at her daughter.

Adeen would forever feel torn by guilt, by the burden of raising a child with too many challenges. "Perhaps if I hadn't gotten drunk that night."

"Perhaps you should stop blaming yourself," the kind young social worker had tried to soothe her.

At the advice of her school counsellor, Adeen completed her final year in high school — in the D class, the dumb class — and graduated with the highest marks in typing and steno. Still, as a single mother, she could foresee no future in Montreal, a city in a province on the brink of separating from the rest of the country. She was not fluently bilingual, a requirement for any job. At interviews she would always say in French, "*Mais je comprends bien la langue.*" But it was never good enough.

Her widowed mother, emotionally frail and dependent on alcohol to steer her own life, disowned Adeen the morning of Irene's birth. With no emotional support, no social life, Adeen had wanted to end it all, drink herself to death, stick her head in an oven, rip her skin with thumb tacks, cut her wrists — she was good at theatrics, like her mother — but no one noticed her plea for help, not even her case worker, who observed food in the fridge, a spotless subsidized apartment, and clean clothing for Irene. Enough to report a passing mark.

And then Mona — their friendship dated back to kindergarten — had coaxed Adeen to Edmonton with money for airfare. There Mona was already an established hairdresser with her own home salon in a new development called the Evergreen Mobile Home Park, located on the northeast side in a wooded ravine on the outskirts of the city. She convinced Adeen it would be an ideal environment for Irene to thrive — fresh air, greenery, farm animals, family events, children to play with, a close-knit community. Adeen wasn't so sure that it was the ideal situation, but it was a good, practical place to be, at least temporarily. There was no future for an anglophone in Montreal. At least here, out west, as history had revealed, there was a sense of entrepreneurship, possibilities, and adventure, if nothing else.

"You know I love Irene, and since I work from home, I could babysit when you're at work. Housing is cheap here and you can get your dream house eventually. Opportunities galore and the men are men, not walking ads for Calvin Klein. Come on, Adeen, you have nothing to lose. Edmonton is where it's at, girl. And if you don't like it, you can always go back. I won't stop you."

A house. She had never lived in a house. Her nomadic childhood in a series of tenements, public housing in Montreal's slums — the Pointe, Little Burgundy, Saint-Henri, the East End — had resulted in a dispirited existence. For Adeen, a house symbolized stability, safety, a home, a loving family, a future for Irene. It was a plan and, indeed, with nothing to lose, nothing left, she saw Mona's offer as the proverbial lifeline. She grabbed it.

On July 1, 1982, Adeen, a single mother with five-year-old Irene secured to her like a dog on a leash, arrived in Edmonton, a city in the throes of an economic boom. Apartments were scarce and expensive; jobs plentiful. The world seemed to be migrating to Alberta.

They temporarily settled with Mona in her tiny mobile home in the Evergreen Mobile Home Park, and at midnight the three rose to their feet on the small deck with glasses of Mouton Cadet, and iced tea for Irene, and sang "O Canada" as they watched the fireworks explode into a prism of colours. Adeen pretended the display was meant only for her, a welcome celebration to a fresh beginning; a standing ovation for a decision well taken. "Thank you. Thank you," she bowed to the pyrotechnics. At first Irene was frightened by the kaleidoscopic flash and explosions bursting into the abyss, but nonetheless, she followed her mother's lead and also bowed as though she were greeting royalty. Everyone dissolved into laughter and clapped at the spectacle. And then Adeen met Forester (Frosty) Whitlaw.

"EEEeeeeee. MOMMAAAA."

Adeen flips the empty can behind the lounge chair. *Who cares where it lands*, she thinks. She can clean up later. A stream of water pulses from above; a waterfall splashing against the wrought iron railing. She looks up.

"Hey, Payton, is that you spilling precious water?"

"Sorry, Adeen, but it's so hot, just trying to cool down the patio here so I can go barefoot."

"How many times have I said you can't do that? Now it's dripping all over Zita's balcony."

"Bet she'll enjoy the shower." And he hunches over the railing.

"Payton. Leave Zita alone. She's probably napping. This heat's hard on her with her pregnancy." But before Payton can reply, a heavy crash from inside the apartment interrupts their exchange.

Irene is seeking attention and, in a dishevelled sleepy mess from just waking up, stands pointing a finger directing her mother to the living room. "Neee. Neee."

Adeen, still in fatigue mode not having slept since ... she doesn't remember when ... sprints inside. Irene, skipping, hopping like a summer hare in the middle of busy traffic, bursts into sudden applause as though her handiwork deserves an encore. Adeen already sees the downed patio verticals, Irene cackling with joy, alternately shaking her fingers and clapping her hands hard. The window coverings lie in a heap of noisy aluminum on the floor like siding meant for the city dump.

"Irene, come here, baby. Come here." It takes every effort for Adeen to restrain herself from hitting the child.

Irene looks for her standing ovation, *bravo, bravo*. She beams, *look what I did*, becoming hysterical at the mention of her name. It's not working. Her daughter is in a frenzy, spinning like a circus dog in performance, begging for a treat — praise.

Adeen reaches out but Irene pulls away.

"Neene."

The living room is now a slippery racetrack. A game of tag ensues. In her excitement, Irene had soiled the salmon-coloured carpet, a trail of urine to be dealt with later. They chase each other in a circle of *catch me if you can*. Adeen halts with an unexpected abruptness and collides with her daughter. She scoops up the corded skipping rope lying on the floor and ties Irene's hands behind her back, as though she were at a calf-roping match at a rodeo. Irene is braying now until she is finally reduced to submission. Adeen lets Irene simmer and runs to the medicine cabinet, returning with a bottle of pills. She is attempting to force open Irene's clamped mouth. Irene chomps on Adeen's fingers like a famished infant. Irene is banging the side of her head against the floor while Adeen muscles her down with the palm of her hand and shoves a sedative down her throat, folding Irene's lips shut like a sealed envelope. Irene has no choice but to swallow.

The doorbell rings. Adeen waits until Irene surrenders completely, lies motionless. The ringing is continuous, accompanied by urgent knocking. Exhausted and dispirited, Adeen crawls to the door, sobbing uncontrollably. Her sanity is drifting; she is falling into a stupor, a dark place of detachment. Her doctor had prescribed an antidepressant for these wild scenes, but Adeen has never favoured solving problems with drugs. Of course, she is quick to ply Irene with similar medication to handle her erratic mood swings. She is considering going to a happier, peaceful place herself; either her or Irene. It could never be Irene. Something had to give.

There seems to be a rhythm to the knocking now, as though several hands have joined to drive the door open. She is in no rush to deal with a tenant's demands because there are always complaints: leaky pipes, clogged toilets, no heat in winter, no air conditioning in summer, and last week Rosemary asked her to evict the two mice who had set up camp under her dishwasher.

"I'm coming." Adeen sounds winded and carries the exhaustion of someone who just completed a workout at Gold's Gym and needs to wind down.

"It's me. Mona. Open the frigging door."

Adeen is wiping her eyes with her knuckles. "All right, all right. Said I was coming." Mona barges inside the apartment in a fury of impatience.

"How'd you get into the building?" Adeen says.

"Someone buzzed me in…."

"Who?"

"Don't know. Someone —" And then Mona is taken aback by the sight of Irene curled up on the living room floor, wrists tied behind her back. "What happened here?"

"I couldn't control her. Had no choice."

"Bad choice." Mona bends over to untie the skipping rope but Adeen interferes, slaps her hands. "Let her be. She needs her sleep. And me too."

"I can see that, but Adeen, when did this start happening? She's tied up like —"

"Don't judge me, Mona. It's the only way." Adeen is now heaving uncontrollable tears.

"Sweetie, you need a break." Mona is hugging her. "There, there, everything will be fine. Why don't I take her off your hands for a couple of weeks, huh? She always liked Evergreen. Maybe she misses her friends there and the petting zoo. She's all cooped up in here and with the heat and everything … I can take her to the pool or the children's centre like I used to."

"Maybe. I don't know. Let me think about it."

"Of course."

"Okay. She's yours."

ADEEN

What would you have done in my place? I needed a break. I know, I know. I could have put Irene in one of those places, but she is still my flesh and blood, my responsibility. But Mona, so kind and loving, somehow she knew how to control Irene. She was good like that. Why do the bad mothers get the difficult kids? Mona married once and that was enough for her. No children.

Let me tell you about Mona. She worked for a while as a file clerk for this inflatables company — you know, those businesses that manufacture balloon cartoon characters to advertise products and attract motorists. There's always an inflatable sitting on some rooftop, like a car dealership, for example, trying to lure customers into their showroom — a dangerous distraction for anyone driving by, in my opinion. Anyhow, Mona was not good at her job; always misfiled everything. But the boss fell in love, married her, and took her home where she lived unhappily ever after. The guy was mucho wealthy. You're either rich or poor here or on the way to either — no in-between. I can't blame her for marrying the guy. He set her up with her own beauty salon in the basement of this gorgeous mansion on a hill overlooking the river valley. He even financed her beautician studies. Mona thought she had found her true vocation, if not true love.

Two years into the marriage, the guy started seeing someone else — standard behaviour here — and they divorced. He wanted a child and Mona couldn't deliver. Why are men such bastards? Anyhow, Mona was no pushover and demanded a settlement or she would take him to court and expose him for the bastard he was. He gave her enough money to buy a mobile home in the Evergreen Park and she moved her shop there.

She wasn't a beauty by any means, but there was something about the way Mona carried herself, strong and confident, that attracted the guys, and her thick black hair was always a draw, a real asset. She hadn't really been tempted since her divorce, though, and she vowed she'd never marry again.

I reminded her she came out ahead with an alimony that provided a roof over her head and a business of her own, doing what she always wanted. She was one smart cookie: reliable and a true friend. So when she said she would take Irene off my hands, I wanted to shout hallelujah! Freedom at last, for a while.

Anyhow, that's the story there.

ZITA

Zita's mother crammed the corners of her daughter's suitcase with frozen homemade Italian meatballs in Ziploc bags. It was her way of showing love.

"I have no room for them," Zita pleaded, but Marietta persisted and found a way to make everything fit.

"*Dolcezza*, you don't know how to pack. Here, I show you."

She rearranged the luggage as though she were rearranging her daughter's life. Marietta reminded Zita not to forget the Italian sausages. "Do you have everything?"

"Yes, *Mammina*, I have everything."

There was nothing more to say; nothing more to do.

Earlier that day, after breakfast, Zita had caught Marietta sitting on the back porch tossing bread crumbs at the pigeons that landed on the neighbour's garage roof below. She detected anger in the way her mother hurled the pieces of stale bread at the unsuspecting birds.

Older now, Marietta still resembled a Modigliani portrait: serious brown eyes squinting against the light of day, the sixty-year-old skin barely creased, yet the cheeks a robust red from too many broken capillaries. She had spent too many young years in the Mediterranean sun gathering crops of grapes and *misticanza* in the fields of Sicily. Her throwing hand was still strong notwithstanding the loose "chicken" skin hanging below her upper arm.

Zita had phoned for a taxi and now waited in the living room. It was not yet noon and already the sidewalks of Toronto's Little Italy slithered with humidity. She separated the shabby lace curtains in search of her ride, and pressed her cheek with a fierce intensity against the window screen, leaving a cross-hatched hive of squares against her skin. Her mother's doorbell was unpredictable, needing repair, but Marietta feared the landlady would increase the rent if she dared complain. So she lived alone with a broken bell, ears always half-cocked for possible footsteps, interruptions to her isolation and loneliness. Derrick had stationed himself on the cement steps below, sentry for any vehicle remotely resembling a yellow cab, easy to spot from afar. His *nonna* had spoiled him with gifts and money but now he, too, was anxious to return to Edmonton. The air here was suffocating. He could barely breathe from the sweltering heat.

Zita was not the daughter Marietta wanted her to be and Marietta was not the mother Zita needed her to be. Zita suddenly felt trapped, claustrophobic in this hollow shoebox that was her childhood home. How she wanted Marietta's praise, acceptance, love. Why was it always so difficult? The rebellious Catholic daughter was a disappointment and must be punished.

In a moment of anger, her mother had discarded all photos of the family's existence from the living room's sideboard. Where once there were displays of her Sicilian parents, Zita in a veil of whiteness clutching an onyx rosary for her First Holy Communion, an assortment of girlhood photos, Derrick's baby pictures — an hour after birth, first Christmas, first steps, first grade, second, third — there was nothing now. A family in disarray; a family abandoned. That was the year Zita moved with her husband and son to Edmonton.

"I won't see you again." Marietta had never forgiven her.

"I'll call you every Sunday, *Mammina*. I'll come and visit."

Marietta didn't believe Zita was leaving Toronto until she saw the moving truck; didn't believe it was for a better life, a job for her husband, a future for her son. She took it personally. Zita tried to assure her that she still loved her, but truth be known, she had fled to psychologically separate herself from her mother's unpredictable and abusive control, which always pulled her down. Shifting her life to another province allowed Zita to recover her sense of self. As expected, Marietta ignored her daughter's Sunday calls, but eventually she relented and Zita heard her mother's voice.

"You should be here with me and not in Edmonton."

Zita had pleaded, "What do you want me to do? Divorce my husband, forget I have a family and come live with you until you die? And then what?"

Marietta had spat back, "You family. Everyone selfish. No one think of me. I live alone. We no do that in my country."

And Zita, her adult child, had broken down again with guilt, a planned manoeuvre on her mother's part that always worked.

"You can come here and visit. It's not far," Zita suggested.

"I no like to fly."

"What do you want me to do? What do you want me to do?"

Zita's anxiety and confusion frightened her mother, causing Marietta to retreat, loosen the reins, but soon she was back to her typical pattern of behaviour. Nothing ever changed.

"Never mind, never mind, it be all right. Everything be all right," her mother chirped as Zita, now feeling like a dirty rag, accepted defeat.

If Marietta had her way, Zita would have been glued to her heart and lingered there until death pulled them apart.

A year after she left Toronto, Marietta sent Derrick a birthday card and wrote a note to Zita in Italian: *As long as I am alive, you are my heart.* The disposable daughter had tossed it into the recycling bin wondering if Marietta knew its meaning.

On this scheduled first visit since the move to Edmonton, Zita had not yet announced her second pregnancy. Her condition was obvious, but either Marietta was in denial or she thought Zita had just put on weight; a daughter's joy shattered by a mother's myopic oversight. Here she was sticking out like a hot-air balloon, but no questions were asked. *Are you pregnant? Do you feel the baby moving? Let me touch your stomach. Do you feel okay?* None of that.

And yet before Zita married Howard, before Derrick's birth, her mother was known to compulsively complain to her church friends that she would never be a grandmother.

"Hello, *Mammina*."

"What's the matter?"

"Well, good news. You can tell your church friends I'm going to have a baby and it's a boy. We're calling him Derrick." Zita was being flippant but only silence at the other end had greeted her. "Are you happy for me?"

And then, "Shit. What kind name Derrick? Mario better."

Zita wept in her husband's arms. "Why does she always do this to me?"

"Don't let her get to you. You know there's no pleasing her."

Years later, seeing Derrick at play with his grandmother, Zita reminded Marietta of her descriptive comment.

"I never said shit. What you say. Such a liar."

"How can you still look God in the face every Sunday, *Mammina*?"

"I was worried about you. You were too old to have a baby."

And now she was pregnant again and not a peep.

Where was the taxi? Zita entered the kitchen, opened the fridge for a container of lemonade. She poked her head into the freezer — nothing but Ziploc bags of frozen meatballs and preserved jars of tomato sauce in case World War III was declared. She was overcome with a sudden nausea, stomach cramps. The baby kicked. She and Derrick had anticipated Marietta's fondness for all things Italian. Every type of meat, fish, or pasta was smothered in her thick aromatic tomato sauce, and after a five-day binge they both pleaded indigestion, craving an unhealthy Canadian hot dog topped with ketchup, mustard, relish, onion, and coleslaw.

Today was rigatoni day.

"I don't want pasta every day, Mom! Gross!" Derrick had said.

"Be polite and eat, or she'll feel hurt."

"But I can't eat any more."

"Okay, then give me yours and be quiet about it." And Zita shovelled his rigatoni with the hot tomato sauce onto her plate.

The day they had arrived, the table was already an overflow of every Italian delicacy under the sun. There was no time to unpack — everything would get cold.

"*Nonna*, you make the best meatballs."

"You like? You are so big now. You were so little when you left your *nonna*. You miss? *Nonna* love you."

Guilt. "Don't do that to him, *Mammina*."

"I do nothing."

Derrick nodded, the tomato sauce and butter spilling over his chin. He had won over her heart again.

"Eat slowly," Zita scolded, "and chew, don't slurp."

"Let him be. He love his *nonna*. I can see."

Food. In Marietta's world, food equalled love. It was her equation for life. Her home carried the flavours and smells of Kensington Market, with all its spices and herbs and cheeses. Stacks of Italian sausages and *capocollo*, ciabatta, cucumbers, dill pickles, tomatoes, grapes, potatoes from her garden, and large tubs of minestrone soup in the basement freezer waited for the next disaster; mountains of meals to consume, erupting volcanoes of love and other emotions.

"Eat, eat," she would say. "Everything taste good." To refuse was to hurt. Zita didn't want to offend her mother but at some point both she and Derrick had enough.

The rest of the visit was a mishmash of gossip and complaints.

"The landlady. You should see!" Marietta gasped and in hushed tones said, "She's dying. Cancer. *Si.* She wants to sell the duplex and then where I go? I pay two hundred and fifty dollars. Never mind, I get a room. Nobody cares." And she pinched the top of her nose with thumb and index finger, shutting her eyes as though she had just been asked to solve the problems of the world and needed a moment.

"*Mammina*, we love you. I told you to come live with us in Edmonton." Zita rested a reassuring arm, only to have Marietta shrug the weight off her shoulder.

"And I told you what will I do there? I am too old."

Her butterfly fingers fluttered about her face waving at imaginary flies. Marietta had lost sense of her bearings and was staring beyond, outside the kitchen window, as though she just spotted an apparition. Her eyes had forgotten Zita's presence. The small fan on the table, which separated them, was the only noise — a steady breeze blowing airy kisses that disintegrated into the humidity.

Zita wanted to ask her so many things. First, she wanted to say how much she loved her — out loud — but she was afraid again. Afraid Marietta would turn away, insult her, distract herself with grating cheese or boiling water for the pasta. She couldn't look at her mother; instead, she picked at half-polished nails.

"And how's the choir?" Zita interrupted the strained silence.

The butterfly fingers again. "Big shots! I don't go anymore. I'm no good enough for them. They no call."

But Zita had heard her many times on the phone, turning down invitations to picnics, to dinners, to church socials.

"My daughter and grandson here. You know how it is. They only come a week."

There is that silence again broken by the steady hum of the fan.

"You get the news there in Calgary?"

"Edmonton, *Mammina*, and, yes, there is civilization out there."

"Ah, Calgary, Edmonton, all the same." She supported her head with knuckles cupped under the chin, Mediterranean eyes piercing like lasers. "You will be back."

"No, *Mammina*."

"*Si*, you wait and see."

"No, I'll come visit again, but I'll never come back."

"And where I go? Who take care of me?" She suddenly propelled herself out of her seat.

"*Mammina*, we've been through this already."

"I have to make the *capunata* sauce. We have fish tomorrow." And with a sulky pout she opened the fridge and returned to the sink loaded down with eggplant, celery, and capers.

"*MAMMINA!*"

It was always the same. Zita scrutinized her mother standing above the deep, antique sink, washing the vegetables, torso dancing rhythmically to the task at hand; breasts swaying; hands flaying. Such attention and pleasure in preparing a meal; Zita thought she should be so lucky.

"Mmmmmmmm, the saucie be so good. So delicious, *sì*!" Marietta dropped the ingredients into a wide saucepan and continued to sing without missing a beat. "Too bad you not here tomorrow to taste." Tra-la-la. Guilt trip.

A shuffle of feet downstairs; the door opened and Derrick yelled, "Mom, the taxi's here." Marietta still rooted to the back stairwell watching the pigeons compete for bread crumbs.

"*Mammina*, it's here. We're leaving," Zita called out.

Organized chaos. Marietta helped her daughter with the luggage.

"Remember to put the meatballs in the freezer as soon as you home." An awkward moment. She kissed Derrick on his head and said, "*Nonna* love you." She slipped him an almond Hershey bar, her eyes distorted with moisture from the tears and sweat. Zita hesitated, not knowing again what to say, do, but Marietta was still her mother after all, so she leaned forward and hugged Marietta, kissed her cheek. "I'll call you Sunday like always, okay?"

As quickly as it was done, Marietta pushed her away, erased the kiss with her arm as though it were dirt and ran inside tripping over the last step. Zita stared beyond her mother's backside, spun around, slid next to Derrick in the back seat of the cab.

"You okay, Mom?"

"Did you see that?"

"Yes," he nodded. "Why did *Nonna* push you away?"

Zita rolled down the window and let the breeze caress her face, dry her eyes. She had forgotten how unbearably hot and muggy a Toronto summer could be.

In Edmonton, the taxi pulled up in front of the Complex Arms. The driver was removing the luggage from the trunk when Zita heard her name. Adeen was sitting on the bench in front, Irene in a game of skipping rope on the cement walk. *Home*, Zita breathed. Adeen was waving for her to come over. "Zita! Zita! I have mail for you."

"I have something for you, too." Zita hurried toward Adeen, reciprocating the gesture. Derrick lagged behind, carefully carrying the food tote like a ring bearer at a wedding.

"I didn't forget," and Zita opened her suitcase and removed three Ziploc bags of Marietta's meatballs.

"No, you didn't!" Adeen unzipped the package and removed the foil.

"It's the real deal. My mom's meatballs are the best. Still frozen. See. She uses Italian sausages. No ground beef for her. And some of her baked ciabatta." Zita handed her a plastic grocery bag.

"Oh, but your mother meant it for you and your family."

"We had plenty. Believe me, Derrick and I have had enough. Plus, she gave us her *capunata* sauce, so not to worry." She pointed to the food tote that Derrick still gingerly carried.

"Oh, my! So tell, tell. How's Toronto?"

"Meh. Overrated and underfunded. The Small Apple. Changing, that's for sure. Lots of different immigrants coming in. Getting expensive. Tearing down old houses and building new ones. Where will the poor go?"

"I thought there might have been a glimmer of hope that things had perhaps improved." And then she wanted all the news about the trip. "And so your mother. She was happy to see you and Derrick? Yes?"

"Don't know. She barely said goodbye. Day before we left she said she probably wouldn't see us again, that we won't come back. And poor Derrick, she smothered him with these ugh wet kisses and gave him chocolate bars. She's such a hypocrite. Criticized me for marrying an Englishman, and now Derrick is the love of her life."

"Was she happy you're pregnant again? Surely, she must have been."

"Didn't say. She just kept feeding Derrick, and he just kept asking me when we were going back to Edmonton."

"You mean you didn't tell her?"

"No. Didn't get a chance. She thought I looked healthy. All that weight."

"I'm so sorry, Zita. Never mind. This is where you all belong anyhow." Adeen patted her stomach.

"Everything okay here while I was away?"

Adeen mentioned that she should be on the lookout for their new tenant, and shared the story of Velvet's birth at a Bobby Vinton concert in the Sault while he sang "Blue Velvet."

"Wow! That must be embarrassing for her."

"Seems fine with her. So, no, you didn't miss anything, Zita. Some things just don't ever change. Boring, like watching canola grow."

Zita was laughing now. "Ah, come on, she made that up."

"Don't think so. And I don't like the way Frosty keeps his eyes on her. Makes any excuse to go by her apartment to see if she needs anything. She's just as bad. Here's your mail."

Adeen walked briskly into the blazing sun; Zita waddled after her, and Derrick was still hanging on to the food tote. They reached the cool interior of the building. Adeen clasped the packages close to her chest, the smell drifting by her nose. Marietta was renowned for her scrumptious baked goods, especially the bread. Adeen dug into the exposed heel of the ciabatta as though it were a burger and devoured half the loaf as though she had been on a hunger strike until Zita's return.

"So glad you remembered the bread."

Frosty was never fond of any foreign food, preferring Alberta beef and potatoes, and Spam sandwiches for a snack, which set him straight for the day. So the meatballs and tomato sauce and ciabatta were all hers to enjoy. None for Irene, as Irene would take a mind to playing with the meatballs.

Adeen helped Zita and Derrick with their luggage to their second-floor apartment and reflected on everything Italian. She longed to get into her kitchen and shove the frozen meatballs with their sauce into the oven and chew on more ciabatta. *Zita, so thoughtful*, Adeen thought. Like a good daughter.

Today is Zita's thirty-fifth birthday, and in Marietta's world any birthday is an excuse for more than a party — a blessing from the Pope would be in order, or a certificate of longevity, a minimum requirement. By evening, not having heard from her mother, a daughter's worry turned to panic and so, as always, she phones. That familiar voice — buoyant, insouciant, expectant.

"It no Sunday. Why you call?"

"Are you okay, *Mammina*? I was worried."

"*Si*, I okay."

"Well, do you know what day is today?" Zita hesitates, thinking perhaps Alzheimer's has finally taken hold of her mother's mind. She could forgive Marietta for that.

"*Si*, I know. Your birthday."

"You know! You know! And you didn't call — didn't even send me a card! You never forget." She feels the baby's light kick, rebelling against the noise of the world yet to be experienced.

"*Si*, I know. Everything *merda*."

"You didn't forget?"

"I have done enough for everybody. I have to think of myself."

"What are you talking about? What are you saying? I'm your daughter. How can you do that? It's like I wasn't born! Oh God! You don't know what you've done. You don't know what you've done," Zita is screeching like a demon.

Marietta is calling her daughter's name now, trying to get her attention. "Zita, Zita, you too sensitive."

But Zita is gone. She needs to repeat it, repeat it, say it out loud. It hasn't quite registered — you didn't forget, you didn't forget, you knew and you deliberately didn't acknowledge it, didn't acknowledge it, didn't acknowledge it ... and with that realization, the back of her throat suddenly releases such a moan, ascending into a howl, full throttle ahead now, words hiccuping from a blubbering mouth, sweat melding with the tears and snot like a baby's desperate cry for mother's milk. "You don't know what you've done, you don't know what you've done, you don't know what you've done," and her mother's consistent reprimand, "You should be here with me, not over there. Never mind your husband and son."

Zita has lost control, deaf to a mother's sudden soothing words. "You too sensitive." Something has left her body, snapped, staccato thoughts, words, escaped memories, a daughter's indignity, and her response:

I/DON'T/EVER/WANT/TO/SEE/YOU/AGAIN/I/
DON'T/EVER/WANT/TO/SEE/YOU/AGAIN

Zita has dropped the phone, collapsing on the couch, blood seeping through her sweat pants. She is hysterical, frightening herself with the unremitting rage of loss — a lament, a piercing wail heard only at Irish wakes, or from women in the last vestiges of labour, before the urgent push, the first hurrah of birth and the final severing of the umbilical cord.

———————

It is after Mona had driven away in her van with Irene still asleep in the back seat that Adeen hears the manic scream, someone in harm's way, in pain, someone being beaten, robbed, killed? *The building is going to hell*, she thinks.

Adeen follows the noise of distress, which seems to originate from Zita's apartment. Derrick is running down the stairs, two steps at a time, and crashes into her. He's in a panic.

"You have to help my mom. I don't know what's the matter."

"What happened?"

"I don't know. She was on the phone with my *nonna*. She started to scream and yell and threw the phone down. Come see, Mrs. Whitlaw."

"Where's your dad?"

"Fort Mac until the weekend."

Adeen rushes in and there is Zita flat out on the couch, frantic, wailing.

"Zita, Zita."

Adeen attempts to shift her to sit up, raising her knees, sliding her legs onto the floor. Zita is now slumped against the cushions, head back, eyes closed.

"Is my mom going to be all right?"

Adeen feels the glue-like substance in the palms of her hands and when she looks down, a spread of blood had seeped through Zita's rear end, staining the couch.

"Mrs. Whitlaw," Derrick crouches against the armchair. "Your hands."

And she sees the thick burgundy clots creeping around her fingers and palms like an abstract painting pouring pain.

Adeen hovers over Zita, pushing her bangs away from her forehead. "It's going to be all right. It's going to be all right." And she reaches for the phone on the sofa table and calls emergency.

"She doesn't love me ... doesn't love me," Zita's voice grieving.

"Yes, she does. She ... you know some mothers just don't know how to show it, is all. It'll be okay." Adeen is wiping Zita's face with a found terry cloth hand towel. Zita has passed out.

"Yes, yes, it's going to be all right."

Derrick is half-hidden behind Adeen.

"Is my mommy going to be okay?"

Adeen extends an arm and he is encased in a huge hug as though every squeeze would push out a sorrow, make it fly away.

ADEEN

Stillborn. A girl. Barely five months. Zita wanted a sister for Derrick. Funny, women who want babies don't always get them. She blamed her mother for the miscarriage. What mother would forget a daughter's birthday, a life she bore; the soul of a human being? I didn't know how it was going to turn out, but Zita was hurting. What was the matter with Marietta? I should have stayed out of it, but Zita's husband said nothing and did nothing but work, as though if he worked hard enough, stayed away, everything would fall into place. Men are not emotional creatures.

I've always said, it's the ones who shouldn't be mothers who seem to be the fertile ones. Look here. They've been on the news. This woman so overwhelmed by her life she drowned her two babies in the bathtub. Said she looked away a minute and when she turned back, they were underwater. And this one: after she gave birth, she pushed her car into the Mississippi and drowned all her kids. Four of them. She survived. Everyone thought at first it was an accident, but then the girl confessed. Said she had been feeling blue since her last one and it wasn't her fault. Feeling blue. Postnatal depression, they called it. Even with all the problems Irene had given me, I couldn't ever, you know, get rid of her. Can you imagine? I couldn't even kill an ant. Let them be. No harm done. Even animals protect their young. From what Derrick told me about mice, they take better care of their babies. They lick them clean of any unfamiliar scent. Okay, sometimes they get carried away with the licking and eat one, but it's always done out of love, not intentionally. Animals, unlike humans, are not cruel unless they are attacked. There is a purpose to everything. But I guess when you're mental, you have no control.

Now, I told Derrick to watch out for his pets. He had my permission to have a couple of mice from the pet shop but don't bring in any of those field mice, I told him. Rosemary, she was a senior with a dying husband — they lived on the second floor — she swore she saw one of those critters come from under her dishwasher. I told Derrick that if I saw one I would be furious. I would set traps. I can be brutal when I want to.

Anyhow, that's the story there.

MRS. LAPINBERG

"You missed the commotion here. Zita miscarried." Adeen is raising her voice. "Where you been?"

"Adeen, why don't you stay outta everyone's life and stay quiet."

Frosty slumped into the apartment with angry wide strides, banging the door behind him, the wall hangings sitting at a tilt from the force.

"You are part of my life, Frosty, and as your wife, I have a right to know. Look at me." Adeen spits the words out. "You're never around when I need you."

Her hair a tangled mess, a result of just waking up from a nap, she grabs the back of the padded plastic kitchen chair, flings it at Frosty so the back hits the linoleum floor, leaving a dent the shape of an exclamation mark. Weariness rumbles between them. He springs for the bedroom in a rush as though he's just remembered an appointment that requires a fresh shirt. This summer has been a turning point in their relationship. Adeen faults the miserable heat wave that seems to be infiltrating every nook and cranny of their lives, causing tempers to short-circuit.

A staccato, light knock and Frosty is shouting, "Come the fuck in." Mrs. Lapinberg pokes her head in the doorway with Mrs. Antoniuk behind her, another senior who lives in the Complex Arms. With an uncertain temerity, Mrs. Lapinberg says, "Excuse me. I hope I'm not disturbing anyone."

Frosty brushes past her in such a huff he almost collides with the frightened Mrs. Antoniuk, who is now cowering meekly behind the door.

"Where you going?" Adeen's temper is still out of control.

"I'm sorry, dear."

"It's okay, Mrs. Lapinberg. Normal conversation here. Come on in."

"No, dear. Don't want to miss my *General Hospital*. I'll be out of your hair in a stitch."

"Did your son come by last night?"

"Oh, yes, and that's what I came to see you about. I'll be leaving end of the month. I know I'm breaking my lease, but here's a cheque for the remainder of my rent. Barney found me a lovely seniors place in Sherwood Park close by to where he and his family live. He said we'll be able to see each other more often and the grandkids are just so pleased, isn't that nice, so ... oh, here, I almost forgot. I started to clean out some drawers and I'd like for you to have this. I remembered you liked it."

Mrs. Lapinberg presents Adeen with a decorative plate, an antique of some value that Adeen had always admired on her tea visits.

"But don't tell Barney. He doesn't like it when I give things away."

"I know. Please keep it, Mrs. Lapinberg. I wouldn't want you or me to get into trouble with your family again."

"No trouble. I'm still his mother."

"Oh, Mrs. Lapinberg, we're going to miss you so much." Adeen reaches out for a hug and can feel the comforting squish of droopy breasts like the pillows on her brocade settee, and the scent of Evening in Paris.

"Well, I'll be out of your way. Imagine, me always fainting away like that. You and Frosty have been so kind to me. And the other tenants. Such a nice building. I haven't told Derrick yet, poor boy. Waiting for the last minute. He's such a sweetheart. He should really have friends his own age."

"Oh, Mrs. Lapinberg." Another hug.

"You and Frosty, come visit me at the new place. Promise?"

Adeen nods, knowing that will never happen. Mrs. Lapinberg's son will sever any friendships his mother ever made.

Mrs. Lapinberg's loneliness was apparent to everyone but her selfish children. The family did not appreciate Adeen and the other tenants looking out for their mother.

"I'll tell Barney to leave you my new address."

"You are too kind, Mrs. Lapinberg. Will you be joining us for the neighbourhood barbecue at the end of the month? We can also make it a farewell party for you. I know people here would want to say a personal goodbye."

"That would be so nice, my dear. Can't remember last time anyone gave me a party. I'll bring my knishes. That okay?"

"Yes, Mrs. Lapinberg, but I hope that's not too much trouble for you."

"No, I can still make them. Not as fast but keeps me busy."

"Well, okay, and thank you again for the plate. It's so beautiful. I'll put it up here in my china cabinet for safekeeping."

"Oh, don't put it out until I'm gone. My Barney might see it and think you stole it."

"Mrs. Lapinberg, are you sure you want me to have this?"

"Yes, my dear."

"All right. I'll put it in the cabinet drawer. For safekeeping."

Mrs. Lapinberg was already at the door when she looked back over her shoulder to say, "Yes, for safekeeping. We must all feel safe, mustn't we?"

Adeen can hear the shuffle of old slippers across the hallway. She proceeds toward the open door where Mrs. Antoniuk, who has moved herself back into the hallway, patiently waits.

"Something wrong with toilet. Overflow. I cannot fix."

"Frosty is out right now but I can have a look. Maybe it just needs a plunger."

"Maybe."

Much later she studies Mrs. Lapinberg's plate. *Must be worth something*, she thinks.

Fatigue overwhelms her again. She is always tired these days. She collapses on the couch for another little nap, just a little nap, five minutes is all, and she dozes off to the cacophony of birdsong that sounds as though they are arranging another rendezvous, somewhere in the branches of the elm tree. *8:30, 8:30, 8:30. Be there*, caw the black crows.

ADEEN

Mrs. Lapinberg. Sweet, sweet, sweet lady. She became frail like a lot of people her age. I don't know. I do know that she should not have been living alone, so I was glad to hear Barney found a good seniors home for her care. We treat our pets better.

Never liked the way her family manhandled her. They rarely saw her, except when they needed her to sign cheques. She should have been living with one of the kids; at least Barney would come around sometimes, but that Arlene, her daughter, youngest, I think, rarely saw her. She lived in wealthy Glenora, pretentious little snob. Mothers and daughters. Yeah, special breed of a relationship. Zita told me she had banished her own mother, not from the misery of being her daughter, but from the rage of being a dispensable daughter. Sigh!

Maybe because the daughters are mini versions. No. I mean, Irene is nothing like me. I don't know. Hidden under all those tantrums and stubbornness, maybe there's a part of me in there somewhere. Maybe her father was the crazy one. Certainly doesn't come from my side of the family. We Irish may like our Guinness now and again but we take care of our own. Yes, indeed.

I would hear Mrs. Lapinberg moaning, crying sometimes when her kids came over. I'd crush my ear against the adjacent wall and listen hard. They would always be arguing, and sometimes I would hear the sound of slaps, like one of the kids hurting her. I wanted to run in and ... I did the first time it happened. Knocked on the door and knocked until Barney finally let me in. I guess it gave them time to normalize things. He looked ruddy and winded; perspiration was streaking down his cheeks like he had been moving furniture on a hot day.

"I was wondering if I could speak to your mother," I had said. And he just shrugged his shoulders like he had a parrot perched there and wanted it to fly away. He said that she was asleep and couldn't be bothered. But I could hear her stifling a sob or two from the bedroom.

"You okay, Mrs. Lapinberg?" I had called out, and the sobbing stopped.

"Just brought her some ice cream. She likes ice cream," I had said. Had to give an excuse so I didn't look nosy, right?

"Her fridge is full of ice cream," said Arlene. I was surprised to see her there. Guess she needed money for her expensive lifestyle; must have been desperate to come all the way here to see her mother. Acted like she was the perfect daughter sometimes. Such a hypocrite. Showed affection to her mother in public, but God knows what she did when they were alone.

"Just wanted to make sure she was okay. I'll just leave it here," I said and left the container on the coffee table.

"My mother's fine," so said Arlene. And she showed me to the door.

If you ask me, I think there was some elder abuse going on there, but I stayed out of that one ever since Barney threatened to tell the Swanks that I was stealing money from his mother's purse on those afternoon tea breaks. It was a lie, of course. Mrs. Lapinberg would forget that she had this generous habit of giving Derrick money to spend on childhood pleasures that his parents denied him — comic books, toys, candy — and sometimes that left Mrs. Lapinberg short of cash for her own needs. I would admonish Mrs. Lapinberg, but she seemed to get such pleasure seeing Derrick so happy. I have everything I need, she would tell me. Such a good heart. Barney had no proof but blamed me anyway.

I did intervene another time, actually. "I'll call the cops on you," I threatened Barney that one time. "The walls are thin and I can hear, you bastard. You touch your mom ... if I hear her cry one more time ... I'll get my friends after you," I yelled.

He wanted to strike me, but I surprised him with a karate kick to the groin.

"Don't mess with me, bud," I said. I looked brave but shook scared.

He left in a holler with me shrieking so the whole building could hear, "It'll swell up for a couple of days, bigger than it's ever been. Your wife will be happy." I can still see him there bent over clutching his balls, his face a hostile mask of pain, cursing with swear words I had never heard before. How does that song go? "I Am Woman!"

What did you want me to do? I couldn't stand by and have someone beat the shit out of an old lady. I couldn't let him lie to the Swanks about something I didn't do. I don't steal. She had told me about spending money on Derrick. "I love to spoil him," she'd say. "He asks for nothing."

With that last episode, her fainting in the hallway again, well, it seemed they finally realized Mrs. Lapinberg was unwell. Can you tell I was worried about her? She was like my grandma that

I never had. We make substitutes in life. Such a sweet dear lady. She'd lost a lot of weight since moving in. I worried about her. I said that already, didn't I. I worried about all my tenants. I was just an old flower child who still wanted to save the world. How difficult could that be, right?

Anyhow, that's the story there.

FROSTY AND ADEEN

A soft breeze rattles the bedroom verticals, cools her exposed feet and ankles from the heat of the day. End of July, the other side of summer, autumn in queue, daylight shrinking into dusk, so deep her sleep, she doesn't hear Frosty come in. Now she'll be up all night.

He's sitting on the balcony nursing a Molson, smoking his Player's, coughing and spitting phlegm over the railing. Adeen is now by his side.

"Maybe it'll rain. Feels like something coming down."

"I went for beer. That all right with you? Shit." He's looking up at her with a guilty defensive expression daring her to think otherwise.

"I didn't hear myself asking."

Adeen is combing his thinning hair with her fingers, and he's attempting to disconnect the touch by shifting his head side to side.

"Mona came 'round to take Irene off my hands for a couple of weeks. It's my nerves. Sorry, Frosty. My fault. Don't mind me." And the fight is over. Until the next time.

No reply from the lounge chair, just a suckling of beer, an infant yet to be weaned. Frosty has a thirst. To annoy Adeen, he forces a prolonged artificial burp until he is out of air.

"Must you?"

"Mr. Chen came by while you were asleep to give their three-month notice. He and the missus buildin' a house in the Meadows." As Frosty says this, he slams the empty Molson can on the railing. Another burp. The can wobbles, bounces a beat before smacking the pavement below, and then comes a familiar voice.

"Hey, watch it there, Frosty. Could have hurt someone."

"Sorry, Payton."

"God in Christ forgives you."

"Yeah, yeah, yeah. Stop with the sermonizin'." Frosty pops open another can from the six-pack by his side and slides back into the comfort of being Frosty.

Adeen has taken a seat on the other patio chair, searching the horizon for answers to her messy life, then says, "They deserve it. Came all the way from China with nothing. Not even speaking English. His restaurant must be doing well. Did you know she got a job with the feds when she came here? Imagine, working in the filing department and hardly knowing a word of English. She told me that was how she learned the language, how to speak it and write it. Never mind all the misfiled client files and government documents." Adeen is chuckling. "Smart one, that Chen."

"Yeah, well, some people they get lucky. Asians like to gamble and you know how these foreigners are with their big families and money matters. They all camp under one roof."

"That's so cliché, Frosty. You know that's not true. At least they show something for their hard work. And it's family."

"What you sayin', Adeen? I don't work hard enough?"

"Why do you take everything so personally? I don't want to fight. Anyhow, Mrs. Lapinberg is also leaving, end of the month, and she paid up what's left on her lease. Plus, I had to call a plumber for Mrs. Antoniuk's toilet because it overflowed and a plunger didn't do the trick, so there's a shitty smell in her bathroom because you weren't here to help."

"You coulda waited."

"An emergency, Frosty. Now her floors will need disinfecting." She is sniffling, struggling to arrest tears, which Frosty considers a human frailty.

"My allergies have been bothering me," she says as she hunts for a tissue.

His simmering anger is clouding his thinking to the point where he wants out but reverses his decision and lowers himself back into the lounge chair. Instead, he says, "Goin' to the casino tonight. So if you don't see me 'round, you know where to find me."

"Casino? You promised me, Frosty."

He slaps his knees and rises. "That's it. I'll be back later tonight. You're drivin' me crazy."

"You're drunk, Frosty. If you're going to the casino, don't bother coming back."

The slam of the door, then welcome solitude. She listens as his footsteps fade down the hall and out the front door, hurls a worn-out cushion against the wall; feathers fly like so many snowflakes but these don't melt.

"Christ. More work. Stupid."

She's familiar with this scenario. Of course, he'll be back. No doubt. Full-blown tears now slide down her cheeks, curve around the precipice of her chin, and meld with the perspiration already dampening her T-shirt. She suppresses anger with tears, a measure to purge loneliness, pain. "It's desirable for survival," her social worker once told her. "Don't hold back; tears cleanse the soul."

She calls Mona to check on Irene, but there's no answer. She makes a mental note to call later. They're probably out at the park. She finds the vacuum and cleans up the mess of feathers on the carpet. "Asshole," she mutters to herself. "What did I ever see in him. Won't cry ever again. Ever. All cried out."

ADEEN

I had only been in town a couple of days when a small, family-owned construction business in Edmonton hired me as an office administrator. The city with possibilities, indeed! My first time out and I landed a job. Flush with confidence and unspeakable joy, I received my first paycheque. I divided my money: rent for Mona, a pittance for my savings account, and a shopping splurge. Just this one time. And just for me.

That Saturday I walked into one of those western apparel shops in West Edmonton Mall — you know, the largest shopping mall in North America, where you find everything under one roof, including the kitchen sink. Anyhow, I was looking at those fringed, cowhide jackets, thinking of buying one for Mona as a thank you for her hospitality, when this dude walked up to me and said in a voice deep as the valley, "Need a hand, ma'am?"

"A hand?" says I.

"Help," he says. "Can I help you choose a jacket? These are for men. Ya lookin' for somethin' for your man?"

"Oh, no," says I.

I tried to ignore his tight butt in his faded jeans as he led me to the women's section. I kept thinking of the movie *Midnight Cowboy*. You know, where Jon Voight is wearing that buckskin tan jacket with the foot-long fringes on the sleeves. I mean, really, coming from Montreal, what was I to think? You see those types somewhere on the Main or at a costume party. I tried not to laugh out loud so I just smiled. Nonetheless, I did find him rather attractive, this captivating nonchalant hunk of a buckaroo, a bolo tie around his neck and a pronounced belt buckle that could have doubled as my compact mirror. I looked at his hands — hands say a lot about a man — and couldn't help noticing how calloused they were, his well-bitten fingernails so unlike those of the Quebecois men I used to date, with their manicured, varnished nails and Armani suits from Eaton's menswear department. It looked like this cowboy had spent his days working on the range. Seemed to be out of his comfort zone selling western wear.

After he rang up my order, jackets for Mona and me, he said, "Just about finished my shift. Name's Frosty. Wanna have a bite?"

Oh. My. What a voice. His cowboy way of speaking gave me goosebumps. Reminded me of Ben Cartwright on that TV show *Bonanza*.

I had a distrust of men, instilled in me by my own father's abandonment of me at the age of five and later my high-school boyfriend, Irene's father, deserting his duties. They always leave, don't they? So many single moms out there. Still, Ben Cartwright persisted and I couldn't resist. What harm was there in a coffee with a cowpoke? He took me to the food court nearby, ordered two cups of coffee and a plate of Chinese food for himself. Said he hadn't eaten yet. At the cash register, he made an apologetic fuss about his missing wallet.

"Probably left it in my jacket pocket at work," he said, with that sheepish dimpled grin of his. He made a grand effort of patting his shirt and jeans pockets this way and that, as though a wallet would reappear by some miraculous intervention. He wore his jeans so tight there was no room for anything thicker than a thumb. The only bulge I noticed was the one below his polished belt buckle. In any case, that day I paid for our order. It was one of those things. Some invisible force drew me to him. I should have left right then and there. Instead, I stayed. I blame my foolish decision on a craving for male attention, companionship, a father for Irene. Love. Perhaps. Maybe it was his melodic voice. Who knows? I was lonely. It had been a while since there had been a man in my life. I mean, Mona is a wonderful friend, but even Mona is looking for some rich guy to take care of her. Again.

"My treat next time, okay?" he had said with an apologetic look that said *Please?*

I didn't intend there to be a next time. "No big deal. It happens," I said.

His twinkling, deep brown eyes stared into mine then slid up and down, side to side, taking in as much of me as he could see. "You got a gorgeous mane. Sorrel, like my Boss." He was trying to redeem himself. Pathetic when I think of it now.

"Your Boss?"

"My horse. I call her Boss. Like the sound of it. Come here, Boss, and let me ride you, I say to her. Always makes me laugh."

"I don't know horses. I'm from Montreal. We drive cars." Tried not to sound sarcastic, but I couldn't resist.

"Well, you'll have to come 'round and see her. I live near Tomahawk. Rent some land and a trailer from this real nice widow, Mrs. Ruby Garnet, but one day I'll have my own spread with prize-winnin' thoroughbreds. My dream. And yours?"

I just stared into space as though I had to sort out my memory files to choose the best dream, and then, as if someone had just nudged me awake, I said, "My dream? I guess a father for Irene, a house would be nice. I've never lived in one. We've always stayed in rentals, my mom and me."

"Irene?" He just stared at me.

"See, I have this daughter …"And then I just took a giant breath and, in an avalanche of words, everything unravelled: the complexities of being me, moving to Edmonton, Mona's generosity in accommodating us, and the challenge that was Irene. This bit of information was intentional. Get it out of the way fast, I thought. It had always been my experience that at the mention of Irene and her mental problems most men would excuse themselves to the washroom and never return, but Frosty surprised me, waited until I had finished, reached over to press my hand and said, "You're so brave. If I can help in any way …"

I ordered more coffee, and the afternoon lapsed without any thought to anything of importance, and my life with Frosty was set in motion.

He spoke little about his past, only that he was born Forester Whitlaw, the eldest of five boys, on his grandfather's farm in a tiny hamlet somewhere near Stettler. Forget the name now; it was that memorable. "Close your eyes," he said, "and you'd be out of there in a spit" — and he faked a spit in the air for emphasis — "long before you could whoop up dust quick on the road out. Ain't nothin' there … but cowpies."

His dialect and bad grammar, heightened by his baritone western twang, added to his appeal. Later, he would confess to writing poetry, which boosted his attractiveness even more. A cowboy poet! In between his noisy slurps of coffee, which I ignored, he described a typical prairie childhood: shooting gophers, fishing, farming, and helping his grandma with her garden.

"Know how I came to the name Frosty?"

I was going to ask. Related to Frosty the Snowman, maybe? But I kept my mouth shut and picked a packet of cigarettes from my purse. I was still smoking then. Figured I was there for the long haul. I decided to give him a chance. I had nothing better to do that afternoon and besides, his eyes and dimples were difficult to ignore.

"Got one of them things for me?" he said, pointing to my smokes.

So I slid the package of Du Mauriers over to him.

"Winters here, you'll find out soon enough," he said as I lit his cigarette, "are harsh."

He blew coils of smoke at the ceiling as though he were savouring every molecule of nicotine. He told me I might want to head on back to Montreal at the first sign of snow.

"I know snow," I said. "This is Canada after all. Like that Quebec guy, Gilles something or other, who sings 'Mon pays, c'est l'hiver.'"

He didn't know Gilles something or other or the song. Some Canadian, aye. Anyhow, don't think the western provinces know anything about the east except how Trudeau screwed them with the National Energy Program.

"My country is winter," I translated.

"Yeah, but nothin' like here," he had said. "Starts snowin' end of October. Kids wear their snowsuits over their Halloween costumes, and the white stuff doesn't let up until sometime in June." He didn't let me interrupt. What a hog! Should have seen it then.

I didn't believe him about the snow stopping sometime in June. Malarky. He still hadn't said anything about how he got the name Frosty.

"Well, never you mind," he said. Instead, he told me how a man could freeze to death just poking his nose out the door, get wet fingers stuck or freeze burnt on doorknobs. Rip the skin right out from under you. And then, get this, he said, "Make sure you keep your tongue in your mouth, at least when you're outside." He laughed like a maniac and that made me uncomfortable. I felt my body move the chair slightly farther. At this point I wondered if I should just leave.

"My grandpa, Forester, when he was a kid, instead of riding his horse, Radiator, to school in the winter, would run beside him and keep warm under the horse's breath. By the time he got to school, there was a mess of frosty white eyelashes and eyebrows from the freeze of the moisture, and that's how everyone came to call Grandpa Frosty. My parents named me after him. Poor folks."

I was going to say, *How can someone so handsome with such a fine voice be such a bumpkin?* It was beyond my big city understanding. Were they all like him here, I wondered? Even the farmboys I knew from Saint-Donat and Saint-Bruno would be considered sophisticates next to this cowboy who called himself a poet.

He told me I could call him Frosty, like his friends, or Forester. I thought this name was strange, too, as I came from a world of Marcels, Michels, and Maurices, but at this point, newly arrived to this godforsaken place called Edmonton, everything was weird. If I had the fare, I would have scrammed out of here and right back to the mountains we called high-rises.

I told him I would call him Forester because we weren't friends.

And you know what he said as he took another puff on his ciggie — or shall I say, MY ciggie? "Could be with time we can become friends. Maybe more. What say?"

I ignored him, said nothing, and then he invited me over to his place on Saturday to meet Boss.

I checked my watch and gave this big yelp. "Holy shit," I said. "You're going to be late getting back to work. Boss will probably can you. I mean your work boss."

It's like he didn't care. Then he confessed he'd quit that day and was to start work at Northlands Raceway the following Monday morning grooming the horses. He has this love affair with horses.

"I always was a wrangler," he said. "Not a trainer."

Didn't have the brains, I guess. He just liked taking care of them and watching them race. When I asked why, he said they were forgiving. Made a bet now and again just for fun. I should have raced right out of there for sure. What is it they say about hindsight?

He took another puff of the cigarette and said, "You know how you can tell a rich rancher from a poor one?"

"Beats me," I said.

"By the number of horses in his corral. The more, the richer. Yep. That'll be me one day. Make all that money in Nashville with my songs and spend it all on breeding horses, preferably winners. Stick around," he said.

I was speechless. What could I say? I'd just met the guy. We all have dreams, I guess.

Frosty contemplated the palms of his hands and drew my gaze there. They rested on the table as he continued, "Wanted to be one of those jockeys once, you know, but, well, I grew too tall."

He had a rustic "aw shucks" kindness and romantic sensibility that intrigued me, pulled me into his world. It didn't seem to bother him that I was the mother of a child with a disability. I liked that. That won me over immediately. We left the food court, he scooping up the package of my Du Mauriers from the table and shoving them into his shirt pocket. Frosty said he would ring me up and he did. I told him, "No funny business." He swore it would be just a visit, a "gettin' to know you kind of Saturday" at his place.

Anyhow, that's the story there.

HOW IT BEGAN

They made a date the following weekend. Frosty said he would pick her up; introduce her to Boss and his dog, Twister; then drive her home at a decent hour after a barbecue of steaks.

"Didn't get a chance to go into town for groceries so have to make do with hamburgers or hot dogs. All right with you?"

"Oh, sure. I'm not fussy," she said. "I'll bring some wine if you like." A cheap date. She was worth more than hamburgers and hot dogs, but with Irene part of the package in this relationship, she couldn't be too particular.

"That's okay, got some beer in the fridge."

"I guess beer goes better with burgers anyhow."

She hated beer; eventually, it would grow on her and become her elixir. But that day, with the defiance of a woman who read too many magazines touting a cosmopolitan style of living, she brought Mouton Cadet for the ride. A night out, that's all it would be and then she wouldn't see him again. It wasn't as though she had anything else planned that evening, so she scratched off the date on her life calendar as an adventure.

She vowed to play it safe this time. Her high-school boy-friend had made the same promise that night, "I'll be careful, Adeen, don't worry," and Irene happened nine months later. After the birth, her doctor prescribed birth control pills, just new on the market, liberating women's libidos. Her blood pressure climbed to dangerous levels so she discontinued their use, resolving instead to lead a healthier, albeit celibate, life.

Frosty agreed to be a country gentleman, and Adeen believed him. She'd decided beforehand to drop him after this first date but brought along a box of condoms, just in case temptation overcame her. Mona, whose strength was in her intuitive power where men were concerned, was skeptical about a long-term relationship with this hound-dog cowboy poet and sensed his neediness. "If you're looking for a romp under the stars with Roy Rogers and nothing else, then go for it. Have fun. You deserve it. But anything serious, Adeen, take it slow, girl."

The ride to Frosty's, up hills and down into valleys, revealed a spectacular show of unspoiled canola fields on either side. The road seemed to deliver an undulating countryside stretching into eternity, a runaway spool of magical reddish-gold thread playing with her imagination. There was an incomparable beauty here, for sure, but there was a monotony to it; nothing like the Laurentians that always left her speechless, especially in autumn, the trees loaded with the colours of Mars.

"Mona was right," Adeen said. "The so-called mountains in Montreal are just big hills when you look at this." Her arm reached out the open passenger window as though to touch the Rockies beyond this side of paradise.

"I'll take you to Jasper one of these days and you can see close up," he said.

"Nah, that's okay. I like to look at them from afar."

The blazing sun eventually dissolved into dusk. They stopped at a gas station to use the facilities, to refuel both the truck and themselves. Adeen purchased a carton of cigarettes, soda, and bags of chips to sustain them until they reached their destination.

"Can you turn on the air conditioning?" Adeen yielded to the heat wave after a fruitless marathon of fanning herself with a Post-it notepad she snagged from the dashboard.

"Broken. Been meanin' to get her fixed but it's never been this hot."

Adeen, her hair in a loose ponytail, stuck her head out the window, whipping her head this way and that to catch the breeze. She held back her bangs and let the gentle breeze blow-dry the wetness from her forehead.

"Nasty. Summers here have been warmin' faster than a bowl of soup boilin' over a campfire." He leaned his head back against the seat and removed his cowboy hat to scratch his scalp, revealing a white demarcation where the brim shaded his forehead and where the sun burned his face.

Eyes fixed on the meandering road ahead, he said, "You religious?"

"No, but I'm spiritual."

"Makes us both then," he grinned.

When Frosty pulled up in front of what appeared to be a used RV, she could only stutter, "You. Live. Here?"

"Romantic, ain't it?" he leaped out and helped her from the truck. Her short legs did not agree with anything higher than a convertible.

"Year-round?"

"It's what you call a fifth-wheel trailer and measures thirty feet, eight inches. Has all the amenities of home: sleepin', showerin', dinin', cookin', and entertainment. Has lots of space for storage, and big enough. What more does a man need?"

The trailer was stationed in an open field that bore the ambiance of a deserted campground in the off-season. A horse, she presumed it was Boss, relaxed in the nearby pasture under the shade of a lodgepole pine.

"I thought you lived in one of those solid mobile homes."

"Naw, this is more rustic. It's parked, so it's solid." He could see her disappointment and said, "It's only temporary until I have enough money saved for a ranch house on a couple acres of land. A bit tight right now, but, hell, I'm young and healthy."

Adeen, speechless still, at loose ends, trailed behind the lone cowboy poet. One sorrel in a corral; *he's not rich*, she thought.

"Like it?"

But before she could answer, a dog charged out of the doghouse and almost ploughed into her.

"You have a Lassie dog!"

"Twister's his name. Part collie, part shepherd. Here, boy. He obviously loves you," Frosty said as he pulled a biscuit from his jeans pocket to steer Twister away from Adeen.

"You always carry dog biscuits?"

"Yep. Can't let a dog go hungry. Here, boy.

"Show you the inside. You'll be surprised. And then I'll give you a tour of the place once I unload your bag. I'll have you meet Boss."

While the exterior seemed somewhat weathered-looking, the interior was something else entirely, not what she expected. Clean, neat; a small kitchen area to cook and eat; a couch that unfurled into a bed; a private washroom and an area for storage completed the floor plan.

"The master bedroom, or livin' room, sits over the truck bed up there and with that large picture window in back, you get a panoramic view of the land."

He set her bag of produce on the compact counter and laid the Mouton Cadet in the fridge, which carried the requirements for the barbecue and nothing else.

"Don't like to overload the fridge 'cause I'm not always here," he said. Before she could respond, he was guiding her outside. "Come here and meet Boss."

Besides the RV, corral, and doghouse, there were no other buildings in sight. Tall lodgepole pines sheltered the fifth-wheeler. In the distance a house was barely visible, a square box with a sharp triangular roof, perched on a hill.

"Who lives up there?" Adeen pointed.

"That would be my landlady, old Mrs. Ruby Garnet. It's her property. Since she become a widow five years ago, she rents out the trailer. She and her husband, when they retired, would hitch their truck and just hit the country roads. She said it was so freein' to just drive around and stay in warm climates when winter turned ugly. I do chores for her when she needs doin' and she lets Boss graze in her corral."

She stroked Boss's head, repeating, "What a lovely horsey, what a lovely horsey," then held strands of his mane against her head to compare hair colours.

"Close," she said, "but I think mine is more auburn." First time she had come head to head with a real live horse. Boss nuzzled her.

"Aw, he loves me, too," she said.

"Animals sense a good person. Atta boy." Frosty patted his neck.

She began to understand his pleasure in the beauty of these animals, this immeasurable verdant land. On the way back, with Twister lagging behind, they detoured to pick saskatoons by the side of the gravel road. She savoured their sweetness, not minding that they left her hands smeared in an abstract coating of inky juice.

"Have you ever eaten anythin' so tasty? So, you bake?"

She shook her head. "Afraid I haven't had much practice. Not a bad cook. I can do spaghetti and eggs. I mean separately."

He paused to study her as only a cowboy could.

"What's the matter? Something on my shirt?" she scowled, pulling the neckline away from her neck.

"Nice muscled breasts, like Boss's."

Another missed opportunity to take her exit right then and there, but she was still intrigued by this cowboy who lived under such secluded conditions with only a horse and dog and a sky with no borders. So, out of curiosity, she remained. For a bit.

That evening he grilled burgers on a firepit and as dusk rolled into night, she drank her Mouton Cadet; he, his Molsons. She listened to him recite poetry. His.

FOR ADEEN

yur hair is like a forest fire
wild in all its fierce flames.
yur eyes, a mystery in
blue and green and something else.
yur skin translucent
pure like winter snow,
speaks my love.
I am yur dove.

"Ah, that's nice," she struggled, searching for the appropriate kind words. "I like the imagery for sure. And the last two lines rhyme." She was trying to restrain herself from giggling.

"Really? Maybe one of these darn days I can sell some of my poems to Nashville and they can make them words into songs. Then I'll be rich and I can buy us a ranch."

"And more horses," she said.

"What's a life without dreams, huh?"

"You are rushing things, Frosty. I don't know you and you don't know me. It's our first date. Don't know if you noticed."

"What's there to know? The first time I laid eyes on you, I just knew." It sounded as though he were describing Boss.

"Knew what?"

"That you and me were meant to be. Hey, there's a song right there."

She got up and brushed the dry grass and dirt from her jeans. "I think I better leave now."

"Not staying the night?"

"No, changed my mind. I told you, this was just a visit."

"It's a long ways back. I promise not to do nuthin'."

"Can you call me a cab?"

"A cab? Not here, honey pie. You'll have to walk."

"So I'll walk. See you around, Frosty. It's been swell, like they say in those old movies."

Alberta days ring warm, but at night, cool moonlit breezes fan the land with a dapple of branches swaying under the watchful eyes of insomnious owls begging the question, *Who? Who? Who?* Frosty accompanied her into the darkness of the highway.

"You're goin' the wrong direction. It's this way if you're headin' for home." His voice raspy in the darkness.

"Going to that house up that hill with the light."

He smiled and headed back to the trailer and waited and waited by the firepit. He and Twister. Didn't take long before Mrs. Garnet pulled up.

"This yours?" she said.

Adeen flung open the truck door and climbed down.

"I convinced her you were a good man and she should remain here for the night at least. Not figuring on getting a coyote at her. You're plenty. So here she is, Frosty. All yours."

"She said you were a gentleman so better not make her a liar," Adeen said.

He just grinned as Mrs. Garnet waved goodbye. Twister barked and pranced around on hind legs like a circus dog, pirouetting as though he were glad to see her again and wanted a treat.

Frosty made a bed for her on the hammock and he took to the sleeping bag. He honoured his promise.

Midnight.

"You cold?" he said. "I can hear you shivering all the way here."

"I'm not used to this camping out in the wilds of Alberta."

"Got more blankets." And he joined her on the hammock.

"Maybe we should sleep inside like civilized people."

"But you'll miss the experience." And his chilly hand searched her breasts for warmth.

"I knew this would happen." She slapped his hand away and sat up.

"Just tryin' to warm up my fingers," he said.

"Really? You gave me your word."

He leaned back onto the hammock with a loud sigh of surrender as she inched her way near the edge. They both scrutinized the sky, now an indigo blue, lit by a billion stars. Summer was on its last legs as it manoeuvred its way to the other side of the solstice. They searched for the early possibility of the northern lights without success. He pulled his long cowboy arm from under the blankets and waved his hand across the expanse of sky and said, "This here is mah home."

The gentle squeak and sway of the hammock lulled them to sleep, the only night sounds.

ADEEN

A year later, on a warm September day, we married. Have to tell you that Mona became hysterical at the news of our engagement, but I ignored her. "You'll be sorry," she said.

I didn't want to let her down, but he was such a sweet cow-poke, wrote poetry and dedicated these little notebooks to me, and Irene loved him. That last thing made him a keeper, you know. And no one has ever loved me like him. No one.

"Do you love him?" Mona's daily bombardment of questions aimed to slip me up, to make me reconsider, but I always replied that I loved that he loved Irene. "Yeah, but do YOU love him," she would repeat and repeat. Honestly, I just didn't know how to define what I felt.

According to Mona, that wasn't enough, but it was my life. She tried to make me feel guilty by reminding me not to come running back to her, complaining about Frosty, because Irene and I would be on our own.

She'd complain about his lack of hygiene, but he worked in the stables at that time and carried the odour of horse manure, so what would you expect? "Love has no scent," I would say in defence of Frosty.

I liked that he had a soft spot in his heart for all those horses at the racetrack, and he treated them with such respect. It says a lot about a man — that he loves animals and children. I admired his compassionate, kind nature. He was so naive at times. I mean he barely finished high school and wasn't into travelling or educating himself. Just wrote poetry about being a cowboy and all things western.

He later told me his interest in writing poems came from his grandmother's love of words. To compensate for his childhood fear of the dark and confined spaces, she would read to him until he fell asleep. His parents were going through a rough patch financially, so they parked him on his maternal grandparents' doorstep for a year until things got better. Frosty told me he still remembered falling down a shaft into a dry water hole, pitch-black, crying, and Bogart, the family dog, apparently kept circling the well and barking nonstop. I guess to alert someone. His grandfather got tired of the ruckus and came out to shut the dog up. But smart Bogart just kept on yipping and yapping. The grandfather thought he heard a whimper, leaned over the well, and there was Frosty curled up like a doughnut in tears. Poor kid, he was only four. As a teenager, he started to write about the experience for therapy and said he loved finding the words to express his feelings. I mean, that was different.

I finally answered Mona so she would stop bugging me. "Yes, I think I do love him. He has some fine qualities underneath that stink." She told me to buy him some Old Spice and maybe she would come to the wedding. Best friends. What could I say?

It was the perfect prairie day to get married. We both wore white cowboy boots and hats and I carried a bouquet of wild roses that withered as we said our "I do's." Frosty probably picked them by the side of the road just before the ceremony. I looked like Dale Evans to his Roy Rogers. All that aggravating fringe dangling from under our sleeves got in the way, especially at the wedding table whenever I reached over for a bottle of wine. Something would always get knocked over. Mona thought we would burst into "Happy Trails" just before we cut the cake, which was shaped like a dark chocolate thoroughbred, with figurines of a bride and groom on top a saddle. Mona took photos to mail friends back in Montreal. "They won't believe this," she said. Was this the western way?

It was a simple outdoor affair at his brother's ranch, the way I wanted it. Nothing fancy. I take all responsibility. Should have asked for a reception at the Hotel Macdonald downtown, but I've always been a cheap date, as I said, so now I was a cheap bride. Denton, second brother in command after Frosty, had six horses loitering in the corral behind his low-lying ranch house. Compared to his four younger siblings, who had yet to strike it rich, Denton was a success; his family held him up as an example of what luck, hard work, and perseverance could accomplish. Others attributed his wealth to crooked dealings and a violent temper. He was not shy about solving his money troubles with a revolver.

When I was introduced to Denton, he bragged how Albertans are self-reliant. No handouts from government. There was a problem on the farm, everyone chipped in and helped. Really? No subsidies? But I didn't go there. It was my wedding day, so I tried to steer serious discussions to safer subjects that wouldn't turn into a fighting match. I couldn't help noticing how Frosty flirted with every cowgirl at the party and how he drank until he passed out. Red flags, which I ignored. A sign of things to come, obviously. I suddenly had a yearning for all things Montreal. Maybe Mona was right about Frosty, but she was the one who had wangled me to move out here. Okay, I made the choice.

Not a good choice, given that there were a lot of other items on the bad side of the ledger. I can't forget that first sighting of

Denton's crazy third wife and their peculiar-looking two-year-old daughter, a sad waif with a pathetic face like a character out of *Les Misérables*. The wife was giving us a tour of the ranch when we passed the kitchen window, and there she was, this elf of a child staring vacantly past us through a dirty pane, the remains of something burnt, smoke having settled on the glass surface.

"Why don't you both refresh yourselves in the hot tub while I get us some pork chops on the grill," the wife slurred her words. "We spend a lot of time in there, me and Denton, drinking champagne, wondering how the poor people live." A raucous laugh spit out of her raw throat. I wanted to smack her one, so startled was I by this ignorant woman. She could use lessons in how to keep her house clean and care for her daughter like any decent mother.

I know it was wrong to measure all Albertans against the Whitlaws, but they were an odd bunch. Are there no normal families out there anymore? The Wild West would never be my way of life, I knew that for sure. I couldn't relate to the conservative mentality, where money ruled the day. Good Lord! I should have turned my back on the wedding and just left. So many chances to walk away from this cowboy, but I remained stubborn. I wanted to prove Mona wrong.

I agreed that Denton's home would be appropriate for our wedding. No cost to us. *How generous*, I thought. El Cheapo is more like it when I look back. Of course, there was a catch. His family — mother, father, and all siblings — lived on the compound nearby, neighbour to neighbour. Ready-made help available whenever Denton needed it. I was yet to find out that Denton made arrangements for Frosty and me to live on the compound also, a small plot of land assigned to us; a sort of Alberta-made *Dynasty*. I wasn't going to have any of that. Almost like a religious cult, without the praying and Kool-Aid.

Anyhow, I settled for a dollar-store wedding. Would my marriage follow the same path? Wasn't I worth more? But at that time I just wanted to be loved, and Frosty loved me and Irene, so I overlooked the other failings. Nobody's perfect, and besides, I was happy.

We wrote our own vows and declared them in the middle of a golden canola field, the sun bursting with pride in shades of tangerine and burgundy behind us. I mean, Frosty being the poet and all, he insisted. I walked away wearing a wedding band from Woodward's. Mrs. Garnet and Frosty's crazy mother helped set up a barbecue reception, and all the men donned western gear and do-si-doed past midnight in the barn, where loudspeakers blared country music: Alabama, the Judds, Waylon Jennings. You get the picture. Probably scared away half the wildlife. The women guests, I swear, all looked like they were related to Tammy Wynette or Dolly Parton, and they all advised me to stand by my man. *Out here*, one of them told me, *men are men and women are glad of it.* Whether they were or not was a moot point.

It was a day of wonder, where everyone, including Irene, looked like a photo shoot for *Western Living* magazine, everyone neat and clean; nothing fancy. Mona grudgingly acted as maid of honour. She was still my best friend, after all. Frosty's brothers attended, the youngest serving as best man.

Eventually, the music died and the wedding guests departed; a handful of Denton's restless friends and immediate family members remained behind to sober up before driving home. They shot at empty beer cans poised precariously on several fence posts in back of the house, the beams from parked trucks, vans, and the porch light illuminating the makeshift shooting range against the backdrop of night. Hee-haw!

Too much drinking obliterated any human decency. Frosty's drunken siblings vied for attention as Denton dared his brothers to arm-wrestle or jump over the bonfire, and always it was Denton who took the lead clearing the licks of flames, while everyone else would chicken out and just watch. When everyone eventually settled down to a peaceful moment around the fire waiting for daybreak, the prairie night exploded with yelling and screaming, their mother raging about how her father, Frosty's ruthless grandfather, had repeatedly beaten the cow. After a while the mom's eyes would glaze over, but then she would start again: "He beat Daisy with a stick because she wouldn't milk when he said so …" On and on her voice whined, her emotions rising until she was in a near frenzy. Frosty had to calm her down with a slug of bourbon. *Get her to a therapist,* I thought. We should have eloped. Married quietly. But I was looking for a caring family. Were there not any out here who, even if they might not be the Waltons, were close enough? Was dysfunction the order of a prairie day?

A momentary lapse in judgment. Too late, I was now Adeen Whitlaw. I thought of Irene. I was doing this for her and all doubts erased themselves. I wondered what my own mother would make of my marriage to Frosty. I could hear her: *Trash. You know what we do with garbage like you.* She made me crazy, made an emotional girl like me want to kill. I shrugged off my fossilized childhood and remembered to seize the day. *Carpe diem,* as they say. Live in the moment, Mona would tell me. Joy today. Let me taste it before it rots, shrivels, and dies like a forgotten apricot in a fruit bowl. I did the best I could. Honestly.

Anyhow, I refused to live in Frosty's trailer, and to prove his all-consuming love for me and Irene, he accommodated my wishes and boarded Twister and Boss with Denton. While searching for a place to live, we came across an apartment building, the Complex Arms, in Mill Woods, and so our married life began. We opened a savings account for our dream house. One day I rushed home after an evening walk, excited to have passed a new neigh-bourhood being built across several blocks down the road from us. I loved the show home, a bungalow with bay windows, attached garage, and a small lawn. Perfect.

"Come see, Frosty," I said. "Found our dream house. It's gor-geous." I would drag him there for a view, make a detour on our family walks in the evening, the three of us, nodding by our future home, me pointing to Irene and the house and saying that will be ours one day. And Irene would jump up and down in her happy dance, clapping her hands harder and harder as though that would please me even more. Frosty would squint, drag on a ciga-rette, case out the area for the nearest liquor store and say, "That's not what I had in mind. An acreage, somewhere with privacy, no nosy noisy neighbours."

"But it would be a start, Frosty," I tried to convince him.

He had other things in mind.

Irene took to her stepfather immediately, but my exuberance slowly faded as the years wore on. Frosty continued to work in the barns at Northlands Raceway, grooming and feeding the thoroughbreds, but the occasional bet eventually escalated to a compulsive habit that developed into an outright fondness for gambling. He managed to live a rather rudderless life, keeping his addiction secret until one day the bank called and repossessed our lives. I was stunned. We both wept while he begged forgiveness and vowed abstinence from his temptation.

I remembered my wedding vows, for better or for worse, so I gave him another chance, but his compulsion to visit casinos periodically reoccurred without my knowledge, finally exhaust-ing not only our bank account, but also my spirit. Yet I never left him.

———————

After he bolted out of the apartment that night with the threat of going to the casino, I waited up for him until daylight seeped through the half-drawn bedroom venetians and the chickadees and swallows woke up the neighbourhood with their usual arguments about one thing or another.

"Shut up, you stupid birds. I'm trying to sleep. I hate you," I screamed at them. I lay back on the bed, studying the dancing shadows on the walls, never realizing until then how our apartment could use a fresh coat of paint. In fact, the entire building could use some freshening up. Cheap contractor material. Walls never primed. MDF for kitchen cupboards. Nothing lasts here, for sure. I wanted to sneak upstairs, knock on Velvet's door, and find Frosty there. It would be the last straw, but I guess I really didn't want to know; instead, drunk on too much beer, I wobbled to the balcony with the achy back of needing a new mattress. With a large coffee cup in hand, I slouched over the railing with an unsteady grip and splashed some of the brown liquid below.

The quiet made me momentarily think of Irene. I wanted to call Mona, see how she and Irene were getting along, but I erased that thought. Best not to know. Mona with her loving assertiveness knew how to handle Irene, keep her occupied, but then she didn't have any distractions like a lazy husband or an apartment building to manage mostly by herself. Easy for her.

I meditated on the unoccupied farmland before me and how it always overwhelmed, distracted me from my problems, especially in the early morning when everything lay slow and low, no one creeping, being loud and obnoxious. I would reach out to my innocence, my youth spent in the gritty streets of Montreal with their rackets of pedestrian traffic, patois of language, a mix of French and English and something else. The Parisian boutiques with their designer clothes, the gourmet restaurants serving poutine on fancy plates, and the dance clubs I relished but never favoured because I was the mother of a child who required too much care. *You made your bed, now you can lie in it,* my mother's tired refrain, inherited from her own mother, and her mother and … settled into family myth. It never left me.

I wondered what would have happened if I had stayed in Montreal. Life's questions left unanswered. The road not taken. Got that from a poem somewhere. School, I think. It had stuck with me. No point looking back. A teacher once told me that all paths lead to where you were always meant to be.

By now I should have been living on an estate, an acreage — at least soaking in a hot tub, Denton's wife's words bounced back, *I wonder how the poor people live.* I guess it was never meant to be. I was always angry and I didn't know why.

After the death of Frosty's wealthy grandmother on his father's side, all the grandkids received a small inheritance. Except Frosty. At every family event, they would all suck up to the old lady. Even Frosty's mother whispered to me at our wedding, "Be nice to Grandma and she might leave you something, wink wink." For me, this went against all my values and basic principles of kindness, honesty, and integrity taught by the Catholic nuns. I was gobsmacked by that kind of talk. Frosty was the worst of the lot. At her funeral he read a poem he'd composed as part of the eulogy, an attempt to redeem himself in her dead eyes, but Grandma wasn't listening. She lay in her expensive mahogany coffin, a Madame Tussaud wax figure with a forced smile, the sagging skin folded under her chin and neck like a botched facelift. She surprised the family and left Frosty's portion of the inheritance to me. After all, I was the reliable one: hard-working and level-headed. Frosty was a bewildered cowpoke when he tore open the letter with the will from the estate lawyer. I told him there must be some mistake, but there it was.

Frosty claimed that since I was his wife the money belonged to him also. We argued. Looking back, I think this was the beginning of the end for our marriage. Money always changes the dynamics of a relationship.

"Whose name is on this piece of paper? Aye? Aye?" I shouted. "She left it all to me." The twenty-five-thousand-dollar inheritance was enough for a down payment on a house, was mine to do with as I pleased. So close to my dream of home ownership.

He broke down; a grown western hunk of a man, on his knees begging for an inheritance that was not his to take. "What did you do, Frosty, that she left nothing for you?" He didn't reply. It was left for me to find out.

Anyhow, that's the story there.

ROSEMARY

Five years ago, Rosemary Androski stood in front of her rural classroom, opened her mouth like a guppy and not a word escaped. Diagnosis: a nervous breakdown brought on by the death of the last of the men who had molested her when she was a child. There were three. A year later her husband, Walter, suffered a stroke. With his encroaching dementia and her need for counselling, the Androskis decided it was best to sell their farm in the Peace River and relocate to Edmonton so both could receive the medical attention required.

Her daily trek to the psychiatric outpatient clinic at the Royal Alexandra Hospital became routine. A noonday visit with her therapist, shopping at the Mill Woods Town Centre, which always invigorated her, a cup of coffee, a forbidden chocolate doughnut in the food court, and then home. The day nurse remained with Walter until her return, but his care and feeding at night fell to Rosemary. Despite her own emotional fragility, she learned to live without a decent conversation from the man she married fifty years ago. Like Irene, he now spoke a language of sounds. The things Rosemary missed more than her beloved farm, her five sons who rarely visited, and her position as a rural school teacher, were friendship, companionship, intimacy, and unadulterated sex — all things that Walter could no longer provide.

The bus driver drops her off in front of the Complex Arms. The folded doors open in a double-edged sigh. She dismounts in that unhurried pace that characterizes the elderly. Tall and big-boned, she holds her seventy years in a regal posture of defiance against the gravity of age. In her youth she vowed never to become one of those cranky old ladies with their eyes searching the ground for pennies or craters that might cause a fall. So her head is always held high, nose in the air.

Rosemary swallows her breath and hiccups. Heartburn accompanies all the other assaults of old age. She lingers on the sidewalk until the bus rounds the corner and is out of sight before she exhales, preparing for what she will find inside — Walter asleep, nostrils plugged with tubes tethered to an oxygen tank. He is eighty after all, and ill with a menu of chronic diseases. Rosemary wonders why people live so long if they can't take care of themselves. "I'll kill myself before that happens to me. It's so inconvenient for everyone, isn't it?" she once confided to her therapist.

Her arthritic knees are bothering her today, so she shuffles like the blind. Despite her care, Rosemary manages to twist her ankle on the lip of the cement walk and she falls, scraping her knees and the palms of her hands. The contents of her Safeway bag — a litre of milk, bread, bananas, and a half litre of Ensure for Walter — scatter before her like runaway bowling balls. She used to be so strong. So healthy.

After she methodically gathers the downed groceries, she stalls a moment and stretches her torso to either side, revving up her legs to start moving again. She shuffles with determination toward the building, and by the time she reaches her apartment, she is walking upright again, head still held high like Queen Elizabeth inspecting the Welsh Guards at Windsor Castle.

Even with all the windows open, the interior of the two-bedroom suite carries the claustrophobic odour of illness, the hefty melancholy of the dying.

"Is that you, Rosemary?"

She turns her head toward the voice; Adeen exiting Walter's bedroom.

"Barbara had an emergency at home so she asked me to stay until you got home. I didn't think you'd mind."

"Oh, dear. Barb is such a gem. I'll have to call her and see if she needs anything. Oh, dear, oh, dear. And how is my Walter today?"

Adeen updates her on his condition, trying to read a scribble of indecipherable notes left by the home nurse, but Rosemary is too busy to bother. She is soaping her bruised hands and knees with dish detergent and paper towels by the kitchen sink.

"He should really be in a hospital. Such a burden for you."

Rosemary ignores the comment. Adeen knows she should keep her mouth shut but it is not in her nature. "Don't be so self-righteous," Frosty always scolds her.

"Well then, I'll go but if there's anything you need, let me know, okay, Rosemary?"

"I'm here now, so you can go."

"Well then, goodbye."

"Goodbye and thank you," Rosemary says as Adeen discreetly closes the door behind her.

Now there remains only the sound of Walter's laboured breathing and the beeping from the heart monitor.

Rosemary puts away her groceries, except for the Ensure, and rummages through her bag, spilling the contents of her day onto the kitchen table: pills for her depression and anxiety, her active bladder, her sluggish blood pressure; a book, Jane Fonda's *Prime Time*; her change purse, a comb, a couple of Poise pads, and apartment keys. She shoves a Cozaar and Losartan for her blood pressure down her throat with an index finger as though she were about to induce vomit and gulps water from her water jug. She removes a teacup and teaspoon from the kitchen cupboard and pours the Ensure. Rosemary approaches Walter's bed, sets the cup on his night table, and listens, counting the intervals between breaths.

Adeen, or perhaps it was Barb, had tucked Walter in his bed, and he now appears to be asleep.

"Walter."

He answers in short snorts and gulps as though reaching for air.

"Walter. Adeen thinks I should put you in a home, but then what would I do? All alone in this apartment, what would I do without you?"

She curls a strand of his hair behind his ear and smiles.

"You can do with a haircut, Walter. You're starting to look like an old hippie."

She rubs his forearm, as though by a magical genie trick he will wake up and be the effervescent Walter she once knew.

"How does that feel? I know you aren't sleeping. Open your eyes, dear, and look at me."

Still no response.

"I brought you something to eat. I know you don't like it, but I found this new chocolate flavour. Chocolate was always your favourite, remember?"

He blinks as though preparing to speak, rolling his head slightly toward her, eyes black slits, and was that a smile or smirk, she wonders. She scoops a teaspoon of Ensure but he remains steadfast and moves his face away from her offering.

"Okay, Walter, maybe later." She sets the cup of Ensure back on the bedside table. Perhaps once it is warmed up, he might want to take a sip. Walter hasn't eaten anything solid in weeks, and every day he weakens, sleeping all day as though he were bracing to die.

He shuts his eyes again and she caresses his once muscular arm, strokes his bulky farmer's hand: square, rough with callouses, and fingertips stained from too many unfiltered cigarettes, now just a fragile attachment to his arm. With an impulsive need, she guides the useless hand to her breast and holds it there until he stirs. His eyelids flutter but he is still overwhelmed by fatigue. She releases his hand, letting it involuntarily plop by his side in its usual place. She finds her voice.

"I was so young when I married you, Walter. Twenty. And you, you an old man, in my eyes anyway, at thirty. I never thought we would last, but here we are fifty years later. Never told you this, but I knew you bribed my poor parents with money so they would let you marry me. You must have really loved me, or is it that you were just desperate for some help with the chores?"

And then she blurts: "I didn't love you then, Walter, but I have to admit that over the years I have grown rather fond of you. Maybe that's love. Is that possible? What about you, Walter. Did you love me? You never said it out loud, not even when we made love. I sometimes thought you just used my body like hired help."

She waits for a reply, some movement, but there is none. She bends over his bedside and kisses his forehead like he is one of her sons. The Mill Woods train whistles in the distance. A nightly lullaby, a comfort for Rosemary, reminding her of home and that she is not alone.

"I love you, Walter."

A faint wind breezes through the open window, lifting the hem of the flimsy curtains.

"Ah, that feels better. Maybe we'll get some rain soon. Remember how we used to sleep with our feet outside the covers so we could feel the cool sheets on a hot summer day. So hot today.

"Oh, almost forgot to tell you, dear, my therapist says I've improved so much, she wants to see me only every other day. Isn't that wonderful?"

Walter is breathing through his mouth, now wide open. Drool settles in the corners of his mouth.

"I guess I best leave you." She reaches for a tissue and wipes the spittle. "I'll just be across the way if you need me. Like always."

Rosemary enters her small bedroom, changes into the transparent black negligee she bought herself one Valentine's Day. She switches on the TV, clears her throat as if she were about to present a speech. Walter's bedroom is directly across the hall from hers and she keeps both doors partially open so she can hear his laboured sighs. Just in case. She slides a video into the box and slips under her duvet. It has become habit, the ending to another stressful day of confusion and exhaustion.

It isn't the nakedness of the couple copulating that arouses her, but their heavy panting, the way the young girl moans and groans, gasps for air to prolong the pleasure, the way her partner grunts with unrelenting desire.

Rosemary cranes her neck toward the open door, cocks her ear to hear Walter's breathing, the machine still beeping. Both are faint but she is too distracted to notice. She lifts her nightgown and touches herself. She is now moaning, too, a quartet in ecstasy and pain — Walter, the couple in the video, and Rosemary — a crescendo of breaths, rising, halting, rising, halting, then stopping altogether. She stifles a cry, removes her arm from under the covers, switches off the TV with the remote, and lies there.

The next day Rosemary doesn't remember when her life began and Walter's ended. A seamless death.

ADEEN

People's lives. I thought I had it bad. Rosemary's story was crippling. I truly believe Albertans who want to live as far away as possible from their neighbours carry secrets. Acreage living, and rural communities framed by acres of land away from anything, is the dream for many. At least that's what Denton's wife told me. This is how the rich live. The isolation would kill me.

If you have an addiction, a mental illness, something not right in your head, sure, keep your life on the privacy settings. There are exceptions, of course. I don't want to colour everyone here with the same black paint, but it's been my experience that ... well, what can you do when that's your introduction to a province, a city, a town? My initial impression of Edmonton — okay, don't hurt me — was that it was a place of much indecision and lethargy, bland as a vanilla bean. It took forever to get anything done.

Rosemary was both educated and smart. She was another one of my original tenants. She relocated from some sleepy rural town in the Peace River to access the psychiatric clinic here. You see, she was molested as a child. She was writing her memoir when we became friends. As I remember it, she was sitting on a bench near the bus stop, waiting for the 66 to take her to her daily appointment. Her doctor said putting her feelings down on paper would help her deal with all that pain and anger. She was looking for someone to type the manuscript and since I had worked as a secretary and could use the money myself, I said sure. There were nights when I would be typing and had to stop and weep for all the harm that was done to that poor child.

The molesters were all relatives. Can you imagine! What a screwed-up family. Screwed-up world is what it is. Felt like ripping up the universe and telling whoever created it to start all over and do it right the next time. Rosemary never finished writing that memoir. Can't blame her. I guess it was just too painful.

There was an incident that still haunts me to this day. Five-year-old Rosemary was sitting in a washtub. Her mother was giving her a bath when the father walked in from the fields for supper and started to whip the dickens out of the child with one of those beaded skipping ropes. Waves of water splashed, splashed like an angry ocean, the wet rope on wet skin, wet rope on wet skin, her punishment for disobeying curfew, overstaying at the playground, and the mother just stood there and said nothing like she was next in line. And then the mother finally cried out. "Stop! Enough!" Well, yeah, lacerations and blood in the tub would make anyone take notice and do something. Little Rosemary pretended it wasn't happening. She told me that's how she dealt with the pain.

I thought it a great coping device to bear life's agonies. I've done it myself several times, but not with her intensity. Times when Irene hurt me with her slapping and kicks, and I had to refrain from punching back, I just had one of those out-of-body experiences, you might say. My mind went somewhere else; someone else took over.

The first time Rosemary let me into her apartment to babysit
Walter while she went for her appointments, she showed me the
three molesters: her father, uncle, and paternal grandfather.

"How can you hang their photos on your wall?"

"They're family," she said.

I didn't understand. "But they hurt you," I said.

"I forgave them."

"I would have killed them."

Walter's stroke and his now full-blown Alzheimer's taxed
Rosemary beyond endurance. For example, he kept peeing in
the van's passenger seat whenever she took him for his medical appointments. I suggested she put him in an assisted-living
residence but she refused. I understood. It's like me and Irene. I
couldn't put her away either. You don't do that to family even if
they make you miserable.

It was early, dawn, when the wail of an ambulance woke me up.
The blare faded as it approached the Complex Arms. I looked
out the window and saw the vehicle parked in front. *Now what?*
Rosemary came stumbling out her door into the hallway bawling
her eyes out. "He's gone, he's gone."

I let the medics in and they tried to calm her down, guided her
back inside with me following straight behind.

Rosemary just stood in her apartment doorway as the emergency crew entered Walter's bedroom. I told her I would stay if she
wanted company. Could I call anyone? Her family, perhaps? But
she shook her head as though I had slapped her cheek a couple
of times.

"I'll call my son in Manitoba," she said. "He'll want to know."
I led her into the living room. "The other one up north," she continued. "He doesn't need to know. He's a bit slow and lives on his

own in the woods in a log cabin we built just for him. He doesn't like people. We gave him some land so he could stay near the old farmhouse. He wouldn't understand. He is mentally unwell. Not his fault. Poor genes. My fault."

It's always the mother's fault. I told her if she needed anything to let me know. What else was I to do? My tenants. Like I said, they are like family to me. Rosemary Androski and Mrs. Lapinberg, both like the grandmothers I never had.

Walter died in his sleep, a quietness she wasn't aware of until she brought him his Ensure next morning and he was lying there stiff as plywood, his oxygen mask by his face as though he had put up a good fight. I guess she had a sane moment to call emergency. That's the way I want to go. Quiet-like. In my sleep. I stayed with Rosemary as the ambulance drove off then helped her phone her son in Manitoba, the one with a Native wife and two sons.

At that point Frosty arrived from wherever he had spent the night, saw the open door to Rosemary's apartment, and burst inside. Asked what was going on. I said this was not the time to talk. Walter's dead. We had another argument the night before and I just didn't want him to touch me until he grew up.

I left Rosemary, assuring her if she needed anything to come see me. Don't think she heard. She was still staring out there somewhere into space like she was undergoing an out-of-body experience. At the same time her voice changed into something evil. "Glad that Kraut is dead," she hollered in this husky, unrecognizable voice, her mouth ugly in a twist of words. "Glad that Kraut is dead," she kept repeating. "Now I am free!"

People's lives. Crazy.

Anyhow, that's the story there.

WAYNE AND CODY

Mid-July. Another sultry prairie day. Adeen is outside sweeping the dust and grime that accumulated on the cement walk. Neighbourhood children play in the dirt or hopscotch on the side of the road. Some are immersed in pulling out quack grass, searching for four-leaf clovers, abandoning their skipping ropes, toys, and chalk. She is mumbling to herself in a self-imposed gibberish. A surge of wetness drips from her face, skis down her neck and seeps through her T-shirt at the neckline.

She is puzzled by the slow movements of an indigo-blue Toyota as it crawls then stops in the parking zone across the street. She noticed the van the last three days, always stationed in the same space. The driver hid behind oversized, movie-star sunglasses, contrasted by the lacklustre, dyed black hair, a sorry attempt to put a lie to her advancing age. The entire Gothic statement reminded Adeen of a witch.

There is familiarity in the look of this mysterious creature, and Adeen moves forward for a closer examination, dropping the broom on the lawn. The woman tosses a cigarette out the window. The street is empty, but Adeen checks both ways, nonetheless, because there are always crazies on motorcycles who race up and down.

"Hey, you! That's littering. There's a fire ban. I can report you." Adeen runs to pick up the smouldering stub.

The woman turns her head to face Adeen as if to say, *So report me.*

Then Adeen recognizes her. "Fern, is that you?" She is leaning into the driver's open window. "Fern?"

"Yes, Mrs. Whitlaw. That would be me."

"Wayne know you here?"

"No. I just want to see Cody."

"He should be coming 'round from work soon. How you been doing?"

"Better than I was when you last saw me. I've been clean two months now, out of rehab. Living in Vancouver. Take a day at a time."

"Yeah, that was pretty nasty business. Good for you."

Adeen is taken back to that moment in time when Cody was just twelve: his mother living her days in smeared convulsions of cocaine, dirty stringy hair, and unwashed mottled teeth; Wayne coming home from work to find his son patting his mother's forehead with a cold facecloth, urging her to wake up; and she, passed out on the kitchen floor from too much booze, too many men, too many drugs. The ambulance with its screaming siren signalled pedestrians and vehicles to get out of the way on the ride to the Misericordia. Adeen minded Cody, let him play with Irene and sleep over until his father returned from the hospital the following morning.

"She's going to rehab," he said. "We'll see how that goes this time."

But months later Wayne received custody of Cody and they never heard from Fern again ... until today.

"Mind if I join you?"

"No, come on in, Adeen, and we can catch up."

Adeen slides onto the passenger seat, the smell of nicotine and coffee already assaulting her headache.

"I'm surprised how much Mill Woods has changed." Fern is rummaging through her purse.

"Hasn't it though? Just keeps on a growing," says Adeen, her arm stretched out the open window.

A mutual courteous pause. Explanations unnecessary, both staring through the windshield on a deserted street, the sun glaring down on them like a klieg light. Fern readjusts the car's sun visors.

"Yep, have to feel sorry for the farmers." Adeen is making conversation to conceal her discomfort in seeing Fern again.

They observe the transit bus approaching, coming to a full stop in front of the Complex Arms. As it pulls away, Fern spots the back of Cody's knapsack, his boom box under his arm. "La Bamba" by Los Lobos spills into the cavernous light of a summer day and makes her smile. He will change his clothes, grab a bite as is his custom, and then head out for a late-night rehearsal with his band, the Icicles, at the Pits — not a club, but an undeveloped area with tall prairie grasses, near the swamp in Mill Woods, where they can play loud and lewd, set up their portable amplifiers, and blast their music until the gophers scram underground for cover from the racket. Cody is lead guitarist and writes all their lyrics; wants to be the next John Lennon.

"That's him. There he is!" Fern can't contain herself. "Cody," she calls out.

He's bopping up and down heading for the building when he halts and listens then resumes his dance moves. His mother is persistent and repeatedly shouts his name, Adeen joining in the chorus to get Cody's attention. He lowers the volume and shifts his body in the direction of the parked voices.

"Cody. Over here." Adeen is now out of the car waving wildly. "Come and meet someone."

He's on the edge of the sidewalk, somewhere on the lip of the street, uncertain what to do, and then his mother removes her sunglasses and smiles. "Cody," her voice urgent.

Instinctively, he races into the middle of the road, diagonal to the crosswalk, and heads for the Pits, where he can lose himself as he used to do whenever his mother had one of her "fits." Adeen and Fern pursue him with their eyes. No one sees the white truck as it speeds around the corner, curves onto the street, and hits Cody, spinning him into the air like a football hurled aloft for a last-minute touchdown. And there's Adeen and Fern running, shouting, stop, stop, stop. Too late.

Wayne, hysterical, frightened, sits motionless, rooted in the truck. "I didn't see him. I didn't see him. The glare. It blinded me. I didn't see." He points at the burst of sun that just ruptured his lifeline to normality. "My son," he says, his arms slack by his sides, nose running.

Fern is blanketing Cody's broken body, embracing him with her own numb arms, swearing at Wayne. "You killed him; you killed our son."

The paramedics brake near the body, jump out, and try to pry Fern away. Wayne now staggers toward her. She is being restrained by an officer.

"If you had only stayed away, he'd still be alive. It's your fault," he says. And his arms are flailing about, ready to assault her, but he is punched down.

"It's always my fault. Loser." She is drenched in torture.

"We need to ask you some questions, sir." The second officer escorts Wayne to the police cruiser.

Neighbours gather around the scene. Payton, Rosemary, Jack, Zita, and Derrick, who is crying, "Cody, what's wrong with Cody?"

Zita covers her son's eyes with the palms of her hands. "Come inside, Derrick. Come inside." His mother presses forward in a rush of protective custody, hurried arms wrapped around his shoulder like a prayer shawl. Derrick peeks through the crook of her arm where a sliver of light still lives.

And just as suddenly as dusk settles over the scene of the accident, everyone vanishes, back to their two-by-four lives until the next big thing. Just Adeen is left, now surveying the splattered blood, another murky spread of burgundy.

The mean sun sears the air, intensifying the stench of Cody's blood. Adeen studies the sky. *The rain, where is it?* She slips inside, arms herself with a mop and pail, and proceeds to erase this splotch of life.

ADEEN

Cody. The Pits. Oh, I will never be able to go there again. It was the place where the neighbourhood kids went to play, you know, shoot gophers, carve their names on tree trunks — a piece of utopia not far from here. Parents called the woods and fields the woodlands, but the kids christened their playground the Pits. Don't ask why. Cody said it was his backyard. The Complex Arms has only a courtyard and parking stalls for tenants in back. Couldn't play back there and the front was just a walkway to the bus stop and lawn. So Cody would always scram over to the Pits after school and meet up with friends.

In early April, still cool for the prairies, he took me there. We raced our second-hand bikes like mountain bikes. We could have walked, but it looked like rain that day and Cody really wanted to show me his secret place. Heck, rain never stopped anyone from doing anything here. I guess because we get so little of it. We rode down a wide hill into a marshy area, a deep valley to get to the other side. We used the boards placed there to ride across the wet marshes, and there it was, the Pits, a forbidden place full of adventure. Some kids had built a tree house from discarded wood, cutting fingers on the rusty nails that stuck out like fishhooks. It was a place to get dirty, escape behind the rows of trees, catch frogs in the valley, climb the chain-link fence to the graveyard on Ellerslie Road, a place to grow, a place to think, a place of solitude, a place for love. Everyone needs a room of their own. Even, what's her name, Virginia someone or other said so.

There, he pointed: a forest of trees with pathways in the middle, a discarded couch and armchair under a dome of dead branches. Yet beyond all that bleakness, there was an exterior pathway verdant with life and greenery and raspberry bushes. Things grew here, even children. The strangest thing. To me the Pits was just a dumping ground for rubbish — parts of broken-down bicycles, old tires, furniture — a burial ground for pets and fractured hearts. Junk really. Now when I think of the Pits, I think of Cody and that outer layer of road, which he called the pathway to hope. He wore the soul of a poet that young man. Frosty could have taken lessons from him.

This is where he played his music, where he wrote his songs and fell asleep on the threadbare couch, searching out the stars through the spaces of the overhead entanglement of dead branches. I guess, when you're a kid, you can see things that adults miss.

Concrete slabs all in a pile, tiny tombstones where they buried pets is what I saw. You entered through a bike path behind the new houses and navigated downhill to where you could catch the bullfrogs and tadpoles. "Feel the peace here," Cody would say. And I could. Later, I would come to the Pits alone and wander among the sloughs and prickly wild roses, careful to avoid the gopher holes. It was like looking across the ocean, an endless sea of existence — had to pinch my arm to make sure I was still alive. It was the noise of nothing that shifted me into a state of mind away from Frosty and Irene. I tried to explain to Cody once but he wouldn't hear of it. He already understood. I didn't have to say anything. Such maturity for someone so young.

Kids of all ages and backgrounds gathered here. No discrimination. High-school kids, well, you know high-school kids. Grad night parties, birthdays, every day was a carnival. No excuse required. Life was still a party. You'd find empty beer cans in a heap waiting for someone to clean up. Should have told Payton, my tenant, who collects empties, but not too many adults knew about the Pits, and besides I'd promised Cody it would be our secret. It was an exclusive club. Bonfires were a common sight, usually at midnight. Didn't matter the season. And lovers created hideaways, engraved their initials on the bark of nearby birches: DS + EJ encircled in a heart. I always wondered who DS and EJ were. Even Cody didn't know.

Developers were moving in and paid no heed to the graveyard, sacred ground, surrounded by a Save-On-Foods and Shoppers Drug Mart. Mill Woods was expanding. Malls were springing up everywhere. The Anthony Henday highway circled a path into Edmonton's suburban communities; the Pits was left untouched. For a while, anyway. You could still lose yourself in its maze of trees, shrubs, and wildflowers.

That April day — and it wasn't April Fool's Day, just saying — "Isn't this cool?" Cody said and motioned for me to join him on the ripped blue-leather couch. Removed his fleece hoodie and laid it down like a blanket. "Come here," he patted the scrappy cover and unlocked the sky. A flurry of red paper hearts tumbled over me like confetti in Times Square on New Year's Eve.

"What the hell," I said.

Cody had stencilled miniature hearts, cut them up, and flung them into the air. "What the hell," I kept repeating as though I was born with a limited vocabulary. I found myself lying beside him. Through the gaps in the overhead web of dead branches, we tracked a couple of robins as they built a nest from fallen twigs, preparing for new arrivals.

"Even Mother Nature knows to shelter their own. Humans should take note," Cody said, and then he turned over to his side, his face parallel to mine. "Mrs. Whitlaw, you know you are a beautiful woman," he said.

My eyes popped. Guess he didn't get out much, or was he teasing? "Give me a break," I said. But he continued to flirt until he leaned over and kissed me on the mouth. "Cody," I shrieked, "I'll tell your dad."

"Tell him what?" he said

He was sixteen, after all, practically a grown-up, he said, but I had never cheated on Frosty and wasn't about to start with this underage boy who could land me in jail; although, I have to admit, I was flattered. I blame his adolescent hormones. Had been a long time since anyone complimented me on my looks, except Payton, and that seemed a hundred years ago. I told him his Jehovah would not appreciate his committing adultery. That set him straight.

Cody's actions frightened me. I hopped on my bike and took off like a race car over the muddy wooden planks, over the broken walking bridge, and back to the Complex Arms.

"Hey, don't tell my dad, hey! I was only kidding." He yelled with a teenage desperation that echoed over the sloughs and meadows of the Pits.

I could hear his voice eventually fading to a low decibel, like the clicking of knitting needles. I didn't tell Wayne. Cody and I kept our eyes to ourselves after that. That's why it's so difficult to accept what happened. I loved him. Like the son I never had.

And Wayne? He didn't leave his apartment after the accident. One moment Cody was alive and sprinting over Mrs. Lapinberg's downed body in the hallway, and a day later, gone. July can be a wicked month. Wayne became a shut-in. Didn't go anywhere. Mental. Everyone goes mental eventually, don't you think? Humans are so fragile. Can't blame him. All the tenants tried to reassure Wayne it was a fluky accident, not his fault. I tried to help. Brought him food, took up his mail. Last week he said the carpet store gave him leave of absence until he was ready to return, pending an investigation.

It was in all the papers. A father killing his son. *Filicide* they called it. That's not what happened but, you know, bad news sells papers. It was a sad situation but then isn't life just one big sad situation after another? I kept my eyes on him as he spent his days sitting on his balcony, binge-drinking beer, his eyes red with the despair of loss. He kept Cody's dead boom box beside him even though it didn't play anymore. Cody's favourite song was "Only the Lonely," by Roy Orbison. That says a lot, doesn't it? Wayne didn't want any help. *Just leave me alone*, he'd say, so after a couple of days we all went about our business.

When I didn't see him on the balcony a week's worth of summer after the accident, I went up and knocked on his door. "Wayne," I shouted, "open up." But no answer. I asked Frosty to come help me, bring the spare keys.

"Leave the guy alone," he said.

We unlocked the door and searched all the rooms. Called out his name. No Wayne.

"Satisfied?" Frosty sneered at me. "Told you to stay outta other people's business."

"This is strange. He's never left his apartment since Cody's death," I said.

"Well," the poet cowboy said, "even murderers need sunshine."

I wanted to smack the life out of Frosty. "He's not a murderer," I cried out. "What's the matter with you?" And I hit him hard on the chest.

Then as we were heading back to our apartment, we bumped into Derrick, moving slow and sad carrying a shoebox. Could I come help him bury his pet mouse, Zooey? I had set up traps for the field mice and somehow Zooey got trapped. Derrick was inconsolable. Another death. We decided to take our bikes and head for the Pits, bury the mouse there with all the other critters. We heard a shot as we neared the area; thought it was a bad firecracker that didn't make it on that July 1 holiday, but Derrick said it was probably kids shooting at gophers. The older kids got a kick out of killing them. I asked Frosty once why they hated the gophers. They were so cute. He said something about you should see what happens to a horse if his foot catches in one of those holes.

So we get there, over the planks and into the valley we go, and in the middle under the dome of lacy branches lay Wayne. Thought he was asleep. I called his name but nothing. I ran toward him and turned him over and blood gushed out of his ears and mouth. He had shot himself in the head. His gun was on the ground beside his shoulder, and I remembered the one shot we heard earlier as we approached the Pits. Didn't have cellphones then, so told Derrick to run for help. "Get Frosty or your dad to call emergency and bring them here. Tell them we found Wayne at the Pits near the old couch and he's hurt."

"But my dad's working," Derrick said.

"Tell your fucking dad to stop working and spend some time with you and your mother for a change."

I'm screaming now and Derrick starts to cry. I'm not good with children. I can see that now. I told him I didn't mean to yell at him.

"It's okay, Mrs. Whitlaw," he said. "My dad always yells at my mom."

Oh, Derrick. I wanted to throw my arms around this boy and tell him to just be a kid, but he was already out of my reach, on his bike, stirring up a dust storm, and I was calling after him, "Just find Frosty."

No one but Zita to teach her son the ways of the world. Poor Derrick. He'd seen too much already. He just ran as though the boogie man was chasing him.

Wayne had left a folded note in cursive script. Couldn't help myself. I had to read it.

> *Goodbye.*
> *See you soon, Cody.*
> *Dad.*

That's all. Just that. I returned the note to where I found it near the gun and started to cry, and all I remember is the medics pushing me back and Frosty's arms circling my waist and his smashing Derrick's face against my hip to distract the boy from the lifeless body that was Wayne. Oh God! I couldn't look. This only happens in the movies. But what is real and what is make-believe?

The police didn't know how long he'd been lying there but it couldn't have been too long, they said, because the body wasn't stiff yet, the blood still warm. I mentioned the approximate time we heard the gunshot. "We all have an expiry date," I said, and it was Wayne's turn. I guess he wanted to be with Cody. The despairing state of loss, living without someone you loved, pushed him to do what he did. I know that. Love can do that sometimes.

I still tear up thinking about Wayne and Cody. We never did bury Derrick's mouse. I think it just sank into the muck as fertilizer under the dead black trees. Derrick witnessed enough misery that summer. Although I sympathized with Wayne's loss, I didn't relish the clean-up of more spilled blood. I'm only human.

Nobody heard from Fern again, either. The woman probably went back to Vancouver and purchased a bag of heroin. What else can a mother do when she can never do anything right? As for me, I had a barbecue to organize at the end of the month and another apartment that needed cleaning, so I filed the incident in the archives of my memory bank, where they all remained until further notice.

Anyhow, that's the story there.

PAYTON

ayton rummages through the Dumpster behind the Complex Arms. With his Bible tethered to his belt like a fancy tool for fixing whatever ails your body or soul, he winces at the sight of the discarded rubbish. A gold mine of cast-offs: an armchair that just needs reupholstering, a saucepan that could be transformed into a planter for growing herbs, old copies of *National Geographic*, and bottles that could be returned for coins to fill his empty pickle jar.

He is a man of the world, he will tell you. A former registered nurse, a former hippie, too, he is a man of faith now and always grateful for whatever bounty he receives from his Jehovah.

Although raised a Catholic, he followed his mother's precarious footsteps as she sampled various faiths, searching for the one that would carry her through the demands of married life and motherhood. Payton grew up with four brothers and two sisters in a transient environment, with parents who shifted their lives from one

Alberta town to another in search of gainful employment. The result was a dispirited family, short on affection, friendships, and proper education. Finally, they settled in Edmonton. His father eventually found a job as a city sanitary engineer, a fancy phrase for garbage collector. At seventeen Payton's life began to take a turn for the better.

Every year Klondike Days, celebrated during the last week in July, draws throngs of people to experience the era when Edmonton was regarded as the gateway to the North. Crowds litter the downtown's main thoroughfare, Jasper Avenue, to view the parade, with all its colourful streamers, floats, and inflatables, while marching bands, cowboys on horses, and the city's "world famous" celebrities — the mayor, hockey stars, parade officials, entertainers, Klondike Kate — are at the helm of wagons and convertibles. Clowns amble alongside and squirt water pistols, perform circus tricks, shake children's hands, and always, at every intersection, balloons are let loose into the giddy swarm of spectators.

Since childhood Payton had been obsessed with the summer fair, when Edmonton women would adorn themselves in Victorian costumes, corseted in layers of petticoats or crinolines to give skirts a beehive shape, and parade around the downtown core with open parasols against the hot July sun. The men styled themselves in nineteenth-century era double-breasted jackets and silk vests. Some would dress themselves as prospectors and march with heads down, still searching for the elusive nuggets of gold as advertised by Travel Alberta. The parade was always mesmerizing, offering escape for a neglected teenager with nothing to aspire to. He could be a clown, Payton thought. See the world.

Payton and his siblings would save their pennies from chores and collect bottles year-round — some things never change — so they could attend the fairground and take in the rides, the Ferris wheel being top on their list. They would play the games: hoop the bottles, ball in bucket, knock the cans, and, Payton's favourite, test your strength on the high striker — any prize for one win and Payton always won, walking away with a herd of stuffed animals because he had a good throwing arm from playing baseball with his brothers.

The best part was the food. Melt-in-your-mouth sweet cotton candy, corn dogs that have no right to be drenched in fried batter, and the homemade ice cream piled high with whipped cream. He loved to hang upside down on the Zipper and spill change from his pocket onto the sawdust floor then perform a search and rescue. The lineups for the rides, the fudge, and the roasted corn on the cob were bonus memories for a deprived middle child seeking love. It surpassed Christmas as a happy remembrance because every Christmas some family member would start an argument, which always escalated into a fist fight after the turkey dinner — too much booze, too many broken souls among all the siblings who vied for their parents' attention.

Klondike Days offered distraction, respite. Then, one year, they provided rescue, direction.

Throughout his childhood Payton remained rudderless, seeking guidance and stability, but then one summer while attending Klondike Days, he was introduced to a religion that replenished his spirit and provided answers to life's questions. He met a young woman named Johanna. A Jehovah's Witness.

She was poised outside the fairground gate, distributing magazines from her church, *Watchtower* and *Awake!* Her parents would round her up at the end of the day, but in the meantime she, being a dutiful Witness to Jehovah, worked hard recruiting individuals to the exclusive club, the Kingdom of God. Saving souls was her mission. She was forbidden to enter the fairgrounds, so there she stood on the outskirts, a quiet irritant in the faces of the noisy revelers. Temptation and evil lurked everywhere.

Payton had stopped to examine one of her pamphlets. A shy conversation ensued, and he was drawn into her world. It was easy. He wanted to be saved by someone and she convinced him that Jehovah, who is the Creator and Supreme Being, loved him. She had lifted her arms and invited him to Kingdom Hall to witness for himself, to feel the love, no pressure.

The small packed room contained a study group immersed in readings from the Bible, discovering God's truth. That knowledge, the leader told him, would save him. "You will escape Armageddon when the time comes. You will be one of the hundred and forty-four thousand souls resurrected to life as spirit creatures in heaven and be priestly rulers under Christ. Hell is the common grave of mankind, a place of unconscious 'non-existence.'" That's all Payton needed to hear. Here was a church he could support, someone who made all the decisions and excuses for him, and this religion would bring structure to his chaotic and desultory life. Everything had a pat answer: no divorce, no military participation, no homosexuality, no blood transfusions, no adultery, no tobacco, no drugs; however, drinking in moderation was acceptable. "Jehovah says I can't" was Payton's comeback should anyone ask him to do something he feared. This God finally gave him life's answers where his parents and the Catholic Church couldn't. And if anything was offensive or disagreeable, he could always point his index finger to the Bible and say, "It's against my religion."

Just one roadblock to overcome. That autumn he was registered for nursing school. How could he reconcile his chosen profession with being a Jehovah's Witness? His church elder reassured him that it was a matter of his conscience. He would be breaking God's law; however, he could care for a patient but not be the provider of treatments related to blood transfers. Payton was asked to write a short declaration for the church's record that he would abstain from administering blood and blood products.

So he and Johanna spent time studying the Bible, his face pressed next to hers, staring at the pages. He defined himself as a good person. This religion was easy. He was baptized and became a devout Jehovah's Witness.

Payton was most grateful to Johanna. He married her, and she bore him a son. He carried out his duties as a missionary and sermonized on street corners, in front of the main public library, on Churchill Square, hawking the magazines season to season, from Edmonton's bitter arctic winters to its short-lived but intensive broiling summers. His attempts to convert family members and friends failed miserably. Even his mother declined. Identifying herself now as an atheist, she attempted to convince him that the Witnesses were just another religious cult preying on the vulnerable, but Payton was adamant. "You will be banished," he accused her with a dissociated interest as though someone else were speaking.

"So you mean to say that if I needed a blood transfusion or I would die, you would let your mother die?"

His head rolled to his chest as though he needed a moment to prepare a response. He raised his eyes and, without blinking, said, "Yes."

After that, he estranged himself from the entire family and no one heard from him, not even after the birth of his one and only child, Francis. Every day he dealt with patients requiring blood transfusions, blood, the elixir of life, the blood of Jesus. He always carried the Bible with him as a reference manual. It gave him confidence to have a response to life's problems. He could reconcile his two lives, his profession and his religion, by detaching himself from the reality of the hospital, *this hell* as he called it, and invariably would summon another nurse to perform blood transfusions. Staff always accommodated his requests and left him in peace because he was otherwise a competent nurse.

His life had become perfect, but suddenly it changed. Johanna met a man outside a downtown bar where she was handing out the Jehovah's Witness literature. He was a tourist, a Catholic fisherman from Prince Edward Island, the antithesis of the western provinces. There, the ocean beckoned Jesus to walk on water, to divide the fish and scatter food among his followers. Here, the Rockies concealed the ocean and no one paid attention to the dying salmon in the Pacific. Christ, we need a miracle. A woman easily swayed, Johanna was vulnerable to this dashing Maritime man, converted to Catholicism, moved to be near the Atlantic, and became his bride. Her life with Payton, she realized, had been a boring seance of Bible readings and hawking Jehovah's publications.

While the Maritimer was exploring his own spirituality, she, a sheltered Witness, was exploring various aspects of life that had been denied her. Her fisherman taught her to tango and eat lobster, to read forbidden books, erotica, and to participate in sexual adventures, run naked on Cavendish Beach. In many respects, this fisherman was a question mark. Who was he but some handsome rugged stranger who brainwashed her to move with him to the other side of the country? She was desperate for excitement, a fresh beginning. This wasteland of wheat fields and oil wells had smothered her. At least there, in Prince Edward Island, she could breathe the salt air and kick the red sand — the West no longer held any attraction. She apologized to Payton. He was civil, and in some respects it was a relief for him, too. He was never a good father or husband, totally consumed by his religion, his own salvation. To outsiders, he carried the facade of a selfish Narcissus, a jellyfish without a backbone. That defined him completely.

Today, he receives a letter from Francis, who must be around twenty years old. His son wants to see him. Payton doesn't know what to make of it.

He stuffs the empties into an oversized recycling bag, lugs it back to his apartment, and sets it inside the doorway. His living room stinks like a pigsty, the decor is that of a warehouse for discarded objects he has found around the Complex Arms, a depot for the salvation of souls and their possessions. In preparation for Armageddon, rows of plastic milk bottles filled with water and containers of flour line the kitchen counter. *Always be prepared*, Payton's motto borrowed from his one year with the Boy Scouts. Piles of Jehovah's Witness literature clutter the living room floor, as though a procession of followers in rapture mode just marched through the apartment.

As Payton is leaving for the bottle depot, someone knocks on his door, the one papered with all the religious slogans. No one buzzed the front door to the building, so he presumes it is Adeen bringing in another garbage load of bottles for his harvest as is her habit. She is kind that way and always overlooks the messy apartment.

"Come on in. Door's unlocked."

And when he looks up, a tall, lanky young man sporting black horn-rimmed glasses with the look of Buddy Holly presents himself, a mass of dark curls tumbling over his forehead. There is a familiarity about the eyes, a reincarnation of his younger self on the doorstep.

"Yes?"

"I'm Francis."

Payton's face draws a pale shade of fright and discomfort. "Your mother sent you?"

"Actually, no. She's gone."

"Not surprised at all. Always followed anyone who blinked at her."

No words follow from either and then Payton says, "Want some water? Hot as a furnace today. Not like Charlottetown. Is that where you guys are living, with all those sea storms and washes to shore? Eat a lot of fish and lobster out there, do you?"

"Dad." Those words foreign to his ears; he doesn't recognize them, but indeed he is dad to Francis. "Dad."

"What is it, son?" Again, how odd the word sounds to his ears. *Son.* "Just like your mother, always beating around the bush. Get to it. I was on my way out."

Payton disappears into the nearby kitchen, washes a glass from the sink, pours cold water from a jug in the fridge, and hands the glass to Francis.

"What is it you want? Money? Don't have any. I'm a witness to God. You read the Bible, Francis? No, expect not. Your mother being a Catholic and all."

Payton opens the "Good Book," as he calls it, and reads: "Behold, I will throw her on a bed of sickness, and those who commit adultery with her into great tribulation, unless they repent of her deeds. Revelations 2:22.

"See, it says here a woman can't leave her husband, but your mother, well, she was … she was what you call … I couldn't give her enough."

Francis flinches, his face a study in embarrassment and animosity at the notion that his father dare speak about his mother in such a manner, a goddess from the ocean as his stepfather called her.

They sit there for five minutes, each scrutinizing the other, their clothes, their mannerisms, and their awkwardness. Like father; like son.

"What do you do out there, Francis, besides catch fish all day?"

"I help with the lobster traps."

"Ah, so you are a fisherman, too. Figures. Well, the Lord divided the loaves and fishes. When you can do that, I'll hold you up higher."

They continue to examine one another, Francis shifts his buttocks in the rigid black plastic kitchen chair.

"We going to keep staring at one another all day or do you have something on your mind?" says Payton.

"My mother didn't tell me a lot about you. Albert, her second husband, was devoted to her. They had a lovely marriage. And he has been a wonderful dad to me. Not religious even though he is a Catholic, but he loves me, and he's a kind and considerate human being. She never spoke ill of you. Just said she made a mistake. Assured me I wasn't a mistake."

"Not religious, aye. That explains it. No wonder she fell from God's grace." Payton reaches for his bell, which is always by his side, and sways it like a blessing, a tinnabulation of music without the drums.

"Redeem, redeem thyself. Ask for forgiveness." And then he stops. "So how's the old lady doing these days? She come with you?"

"Yes, in a manner of speaking, she did. She's with me now. Wanted to say goodbye to you."

Payton peers over Francis's shoulder to see if Johanna is hiding, ready to jump in and say, "Boo, I found you."

"Where? Where is she?"

"She wanted you to have this." Then Francis unbuckles his briefcase and pulls out a beautifully polished dark mahogany receptacle.

"Some of her ashes are in this box you gave her when you proposed. You can do what you want with it. The family came to disperse the rest of her ashes over the Three Sisters Mountains. She loved the ocean but she always spoke of the mountains, the place she called home. She wanted to be buried here. So we brought her home, me and my dad, Albert, we brought her home."

Payton again flinches at the word *dad*. It doesn't refer to him this time but some stranger, a fisherman.

"Where is … is … Albert?"

"Waiting for me downstairs."

Payton's fingers smooth over the glossy container, half the size of a cigar box, feel the indentation of her name engraved on the cover. Each letter seems to carry her essence: J-O-H-A-N-N-A. He remembers assembling the pieces with such loving care. After the divorce he searched for the box among the things she left behind, not realizing until now that she had taken it with her, that perhaps his thoughtful carving held some meaning for her.

"Johanna dead?"

"Aha."

"The Bible was right." He is pealing the bell again. "Behold, I will throw her on a bed of sickness, and those who commit adultery with her into great tribulation, unless they repent of their deeds." He silences the bell again and turns to ask, "She was sick with the cancer, I bet."

Francis just glares at this tiny pathetic man, who once played baseball with him as a young boy, whom he once called Daddy. He rises from the chair, readying himself to vacate this long-forgotten chapter of his life.

"I'm done here. It was her wish. I didn't want to come, but Mom will rest in peace now." And Francis turns away and walks out the door, down the hall where Adeen is washing the lobby floor.

"S'cuse me, ma'am, and thank you for telling me the whereabouts of my father."

"Anything to bring families together is my motto. Hope you had a nice visit."

But he doesn't reply. He is gone.

Payton wonders what just happened here. He lets the radiant mahogany box, heavy with Johanna's ashes, rest on the kitchen table and crosses the room to pull out a drawer containing files and papers that he has always meant to organize. He removes a couple of photographs hidden under a pile of folders — one from the day of their wedding posing as newlyweds and the other of baby Francis on his first birthday. He hasn't looked at them since she abandoned him for the fisherman so many years ago. He positions Johanna's photo against the receptacle and lays the smaller one of Francis before him on the table. He searches for his bell and then shuts all the lights and draws the drapes until the room is dark.

He meditates on his life in the pitch-blackness and relives his years as an altar boy, when the priest transformed the Holy Eucharist into the body and blood of the Lord. The bell would tinkle to alert the parishioners that a miracle was about to occur.

Payton lights an assortment of beeswax candles in various lengths and thicknesses, transforming the kitchen table into a radiant altar. The bell trembles and then peals faster and faster until it escalates into an alarm. Out of control. He opens his Bible and begins to read in a shrill voice: "Romans 6:23. For the wages of sin is death; but the gift of God is eternal life through Jesus Christ our Lord." And he begins to weep.

ADEEN

I told Payton he could live at the Complex Arms on the condition that he didn't bother any of my tenants with his preaching. "Respect other religions," I said. "I've got atheists living here along with your Muslims, Russian and Greek Orthodox, Roman Catholics, Protestants, Baptists, pagans, and your everyday generic Christian."

Me, I'm an agnostic. Don't talk religion to me. Just causes a lot of arguments and bad feelings all around. That, and money and politics. How can something so good like religion start so many wars and cause such hate? Don't answer. It's a rhetorical question. Oh, I am a spiritual person, don't get me wrong. If there is one God, why are there so many religions? Answer that for me. No. Never mind. Don't want to waste my day listening to pompous lies. Seems to me if you all honour one God, there should only be one religion, but then every church thinks theirs is the true one. Come on. It's really about increasing the size of a congregation so more money in the coffers on Sunday.

Maybe if the Vatican sold off all that gold and distributed the money to all the poor, maybe if they paid taxes, maybe if they punished all those priests and nuns who abused altar boys and Native children in those residential schools, maybe if they weren't such plaster saints, maybe, maybe, I might become a believer again. So I went against my rule and talked religion. What are you going to do? Burn me at the stake?

Since Irene was born, I stopped believing. Payton told me once that here, this life, this earth, is hell. We are all living in hell. He tried to get me to join the JWs and I almost fell for his prepared speeches, I mean propaganda. He can be quite persuasive, I tell you, but I'm educated enough and can think for myself. Don't need anyone telling me how I should live my life. I'm a good person. Better than some of those Christian hypocrites. Am I disturbing you? Yeah, go get a hankie.

Anyhow, I never met Johanna. He was already divorced when he moved into the building. Said he wouldn't bother anyone. One of the rules of his religion is to keep away from non-JWs as much as possible. So he isolated himself from the tenants as best he could, except for that bell ringing. Told him to give it a rest. Some of our tenants worked at night, so they slept during the day. I had complaints about Payton, but he was such a sad sack. He kept talking about the next Armageddon. The end was supposed to happen in 1975 and still there is no end in sight. Still waiting. Not much has changed. People are still miserable and wicked. Don't look at me like that. Told you, get a hankie if you're going to cry for me, Argentina. The date, as I understand it, has changed again. I let him clang his bell outside in the courtyard. Melded with the ice cream truck's ring-a-ding-ding. No harm done. Just alerted people that the nutcase was out or maybe the ice cream man.

Francis seemed like a nice young man, well-mannered. He bumped into me on his way out as I was mopping the floor and excused himself. His mother brought him up well, considering.

Anyhow, Payton's door was half-open so I just walked in as I also needed to get his rent for the month, and there he was sitting at the kitchen table, his eyes beaming on this shining box in the dark and all these candles lit like it was midnight Mass and the choir was waiting in the wings. He was sniffling, or maybe it was a cold coming on. "What you got there, Payton," I said, and he didn't even look up. Not an eyeball. He just seemed mesmerized by that polished box. Told him I came for the rent, and he nodded and pointed to an envelope on his desk across the room as though he were expecting me to find it in the dark. I turned on the light switch and he seemed to have been crying. "You okay, Payton? Right lovely son you got there," I said.

"Shut the light, Adeen," he said. "It's Johanna," he finally confessed.

"Oh," I said, "she coming back?" He shook his head.

"That's her in there," he said, and pointed to the little box that looked like it might contain a jewel instead of her ashes.

After that day, he would park himself on his balcony and carry Johanna with him for company, set her on the patio table beside him near the jug of iced tea. He'd sit there and talk to the box for hours, like they were just having a friendly conversation. "I knew you'd come back," I heard him say once.

Okay, so I'm nosy. After what happened to Wayne, I was more concerned about my tenants than ever. He kept repeating, "We could have been a family, Johanna. Francis is a handsome fellow ... you did a good job on raising the boy, even Adeen said so. Johanna ... you understand I had no choice but to let you go ... funny that you brought me to this religion and then left me hanging. You should have told me how you felt before breaking my heart. We could have been a family. We could have been a family," he kept repeating like he was trying to convince himself. I felt I was intruding but I was really concerned about him.

His voice sounded forced and strident, like he was drunk. I know that alcohol is a no-no in their religion, but I guess he had nothing to lose, no Witnesses around, so what the heck. A jug of iced tea could camouflage rum very smartly, which I know he loved because he told me so, but because of his being a Witness and all, he only drank moderately for certain occasions like a wedding ... or a death, I guess. Felt sad for him. Felt sad for me. Felt sad for the entire galaxy of stars and planets. I let him talk to the beautiful shining box — what did I care? If it made him feel better ... Everyone has had the sharp corners of their lives blunted by bad things that happen. So many broken spirits walking around here like zombies. People's lives. As long as he didn't bother anyone or hurt himself, I didn't see the harm. Maybe Payton was right. We are living in hell. Here, right now. Irene and Frosty ... I don't know anymore.

S'cuse me. I need a moment.

Anyhow, that's the story there.

SHYLENE

hy Shylene is in one of her throw-away-everything moods. Adeen, who has parked herself on the edge of the queen-size mattress, watches her rummage through the closet and dresser drawers tossing various garments onto the bed. Shylene wears only expensive designer clothes purchased at Holt Renfrew downtown or in specialty boutiques, so when she posted a notice on the building's bulletin board that she would be holding a wardrobe sale, Adeen insisted on first dibs.

"Only winter clothes? How come?"

Shylene pauses for a moment and caresses the silky burgundy blouse against her cheek.

"Bought this one in a boutique in Montreal when I was there as an exchange student. Long time ago. Hardly worn. I mean, it's for special occasions. Here, yours free just because you're my friend." And the blouse takes flight, landing in Adeen's arms.

"Oh, Shylene, you should keep this. Montreal. My hometown. Did you know that?"

"Yes, you've mentioned several times."

Adeen, deaf to the comment, continues, "Aw, yes. Used to window shop on rue Elle in Place Ville Marie on my lunch hour and drool over all the clothes I couldn't afford."

"Ever want to go back?"

"No, nothing for me there."

"Nothing here either." Shylene raises her arms above her head and snaps her fingers as though she is a flamenco dancer who has lost her castanets.

"Oh, Shylene, you sure you don't want to keep this."

"Nah, bored stiff with it. Going to get myself a whole new winter wardrobe."

"How can you think of winter when it's a hundred degrees out there in the shade?"

"Keeps me busy, plus I like to be prepared." Snap snap. "Doc said to keep those neurons in my brain busy."

"Oh, thank you. I love it." Adeen throws her arms around Shylene's neck, concealing her worry about Shylene's looming change in behaviour. She knows the drill. The finger snapping was the first sign.

Shylene exists. She was an only child who spent days in her room relishing the solitude; then, without warning, she transformed into an anti-social, rebellious delinquent. At fifteen, she had a break-down, and her mother took her for a psychological evaluation. The therapist reported nothing positive. Only that signs of mental disturbance were likely present at an early age, which made her parents miserable. She was diagnosed as suffering from clinical depression.

"My mind's not right," she once confessed to Adeen. "Hope that doesn't change things."

"Why should it?" Adeen said. "We're all just people trying to do our best with what we've been given."

"It's a genetic inheritance."

"No explanations needed. Come here. You need a hug." Adeen reached over, taking hold of Shylene in her arms, and with that gesture alone, their friendship took root.

Later, as Shylene's trust in Adeen developed to a closeness bordering on obsession, she shared more of her former life. Her mother had been committed several times to the Centennial Centre for Mental Health in Ponoka, where she was described as having a paralysis of the mind. After three years at Ponoka, her mother returned home, permanently depressed and inaccessible to all until her death. The manic behaviour in the household had sent Shylene's father to an early death from a heart attack.

She had no other relatives, except for an estranged distant cousin in Millet whom Shylene presumed dead. She had gone against her parents' wishes and sold the ancestral farm near Ponoka, and with the proceeds and a sufficient small inheritance, she settled in the Complex Arms and lived a charmed life. She carried herself with some dignity in public on the rare occasions when she went out.

Nights were often spent playing solitaire in her kitchen. Adeen would sometimes join her in a game of bridge or hearts or Scrabble. Those were the cheerless hours when both craved companionship.

In her manic phases, when Shylene yearns for male attention, she searches the downtown bars. She is a creature of contrasts: a lonely child one minute and a promiscuous spirit entertaining men in her apartment the next. In the morning she comes to her senses and, in a rage of contempt, throws out the bewildered "dates" like so much garbage. Adeen ignores the comings and goings. It is none of her business, as Frosty always reminds her, unless Shylene's behaviour crosses a line, and infringes on the rights of her other tenants. A complicated woman, whom Adeen accepted without judgment.

One day Shylene rescued an abandoned ginger-coloured kitten in the field across the road from the Complex Arms. She couldn't believe how cruel people could be. She hid the poor thing inside her shirt and carried the animal home. No pets were allowed, and when Adeen heard the meowing from somewhere in the building, she confronted Derrick, who denied harbouring any pets except for the store-bought white mice. Shylene admitted ownership, insisting he was family, a harmless addition, a companion in need of mutual affection, so Adeen, being the understanding compassionate human being that she was, yielded and allowed Shylene to keep Cumin. Perhaps it would help her depression.

"Oh, thank you. Thank you. He won't be any trouble."

"Okay, just watch that she doesn't go wandering into the hallways peeing. Don't want to hear from the Swanks. Between Derrick's mice and your kitten, something will give eventually."

The window air conditioner, which Frosty had installed earlier, had chilled the apartment to a comfortable temperature. Adeen notices that Shylene has purged most of her furnishings and is keeping the decor to a minimum.

"You leaving and not telling me or something?" Adeen says. "We would really miss you."

"Leaving?" Shylene possesses the startled look of a frightened winter hare about to be attacked by a wild dog. "Oh, heaven's no. This is my home."

Adeen fondles a well-worn tan leather jacket, just lying there begging to be bought. She waits for Shylene to speak, to take a break from sorting through the pile of shirts, skirts, and Gucci bags and shoes. "I love this belt. Leather. Haven't worn it in ages. Too fat."

"But you've lost so much weight. You're looking really good — even too thin."

The last month or so, Adeen has also become aware of how Shylene is always on the brink of tears, complaining about the eternal exhaustion that never seems to leave, no matter how long or how often she sleeps. Adeen knows the signs.

"You coming for the big barbecue?" Adeen is picking over more clothes.

"Wouldn't miss that for the world. When is it again?"

"Friday, July twenty-seventh. Two p.m. Just bring yourself, okay."

"I'll make a potato salad."

"How much for the leather jacket?"

"Keep it, Adeen. I owe you more than any jacket." The finger snapping, a comforting obsession, accompanies the words.

"Really? I love it. You sure?" Adeen sniffs the scent of sheep-skin and says, "I always wanted one."

After the final giveaway of her worldly possessions, Shylene says, "Well, that's so liberating. Don't know why we need to cram our lives with such useless things."

Oh, what Shylene wouldn't give to have someone put their arms around her now and not some crummy jacket. Someone to tell her she is loved. Where is Cumin? Nothing can compensate, not even a lost cat. Before leaving, Adeen gives her the long-needed hug. Shylene prolongs the moment with a minute's worth of heartbeats, as though this act alone will ward off her loneliness.

Later, Shylene polishes her apartment until it sparkles like a diamond and circles the living room, examining the floors and windows. Then she goes out to her patio, lies there on the lounge chair studying the vacant sky. She instantly falls asleep, slumbering in the oppressive heat until the squabbling of birds wakes her up.

Shylene steps back inside; the apartment's coolness contrasts to the heat wave outside, and this seems to invigorate her mood momentarily, or perhaps it was the nap? In any case, she pulls her will out from a drawer in her desk and places the envelope on the kitchen counter beside the sink. Her pep leaves her as suddenly as it appeared and now she feels engulfed in a lethargy, as though all her brain cells have been destroyed. Nothing left. Running on empty.

She reclines on top of the duvet covers and dozes off again. Is too much sleep a sign that death is near? Some days she sleeps for twenty-two hours at a time, and other times she is a night owl with insomnia, dusting her collection of vinyl records from the sixties, fondling her favourite books lining the numerous shelves, and snacking on fresh strawberries from the market. She wakes up intermittently to use the washroom, checks the medicine cabinet, and in her fogginess from waking up, she swallows her pills until the container drops empty into the sink. She slumps over and spills to the floor.

ADEEN

I hadn't seen or heard from Shylene in over a week after I left her apartment. Worried sick, I knocked on her door several times and when there was no answer ... I mean she rarely went out, except with me, withdrawn as she was, and I understood that part of her. But she always allowed me to enter her world, and we'd have a cuppa tea or glass of wine and talk about what was happening in the world and how we could change it for the better. Zita would sometimes join us.

That day, I unlocked the door with my spare key, and notwithstanding the chase of cool air from her unit in the window, there was a faint musky odour that hit my nostrils as I peered inside.

"Shylene," I called out, "are you here?"

I shut off the noisy air conditioner, which seemed to have been in a spin since I left her that day. The apartment felt like an iceberg. I slid open the patio door to release the cold and let in some fresh air and then checked the bedroom. The bed was a holy mess, as though she had to rush out while changing the sheets. The bathroom door was slightly ajar, and when I peeked in, there she was sprawled on the tile floor, her scrawny back to me.

"Shylene!"

I ran to her but I could see it was too late. I screamed when I turned her over: she was the portrait of death — her face and body, bones protruding like a child from some Third World country. I can't describe the scene without tearing up.

S'cuse me. Give me a moment.

Okay, so I called emergency and they came and took her away. I found the envelope addressed to me on the kitchen counter. There was her rent money for the rest of her lease and her will. Her only possessions were her car and Cumin. Couldn't find the cat anywhere. She left the car to Frosty and me "for our generosity." She remembered how I was getting tired of riding around on that two-wheeler or having to take the bus everywhere. So thoughtful of her, I thought. So Shylene.

After the coroner removed her corpse, I mean, they had to ascertain whether her death was natural or a killing apparently — but who would want to kill Shylene? — I sat on my patio, waiting for night, which takes forever here because we are so far north. I was catatonic, couldn't move. Guess it hadn't hit me yet. Death always makes me think of life. I thought of my mother and my father, Irene and what will become of her after Frosty and I are gone. Frosty, who always left the workload to me while he gallivanted around town like a horny dog.

I left Shylene's that day, with all these expensive clothes, feeling quite uneasy. Should have trusted my instincts, I never do. I should have gone back, stayed with her, played a couple of games of Scrabble. I knew the signs.

Not too many people at her memorial service: a couple from Ponoka who knew her parents; her psychiatrist; all the tenants from the Complex Arms; three unfamiliar faces, one of whom showed up as this distant cousin from Millet and who immediately accosted me and asked straight out at the reception later if she was in the will. What nerve!

Didn't know what was expected of me at the memorial service, but I read a short eulogy and stressed the positive nature that was Shylene — intelligent, generous, kind, creative, a lover of the arts, and protector of animals, a voracious reader, and good friend. That's all anyone had to know.

She was a private person. I guess because of her illness. Sometimes she sounded so happy, snapping her fingers like a fool and flirting with Frosty, and other times, so miserable, irritable, and yelling at Derrick and Irene. I put a halt to that nonsense and came right out to ask if she had forgotten to take her meds. And then she would guffaw, snap her fingers like a period at the end of a sentence, and say she had taken them. I knew she was lying and changed the subject. She was always joking when she was in a manic phase. A camouflage, a facade, I realize now. Comedians have the saddest lives, I read somewhere. How they can find humour in tragedy, I don't know. With all the weight loss, she'd been looking pretty good, except toward the end. All bone and cartilage. I would always remember the joy that was Shylene and the great times we had, which made up for the bad.

She willed me a small amount of money if I would be the executrix. Guess I was as close to a family as she got, notwithstanding that distant cousin whom she never knew. I cried. No one should be so lonely. She was a good friend. I gave her hugs like I did for all my tenants who needed to feel someone's arms around them. But Shy Shylene was so needy, could drain the life out of you sometimes. But so special nonetheless.

I still can't believe she's gone. People's lives. At one point yoga replenished her energy. I thought that was a positive sign, but she quit after a month's worth of headstands and meditation. She mentioned wanting to travel and asked me about Montreal. Told me how she wanted to live there one day and learn French and marry a Frenchman because of her ancestry. I told her to go to France if she wanted a real Frenchman. She rarely laughed, but when she did, it was one of those ballsy, earthy, rolling-in-the-dirt kind of laughs accompanied always by those jazzy snap-snap fingers. She wanted to experience the cosmos, she told me once. Everything. Didn't understand what she meant. But I guess she meant death. As you can see, she was a complex person, a broken spirit, like most of my tenants. And now she was stardust.

Anyhow, that's the story there.

BLUE VELVET

He had sent her the plane tickets, said he would meet her at the arrival gate from Toronto, 1700 hours. The flight was late getting into Edmonton and she couldn't find him. She wandered around the airport, stopped, leaned her slight body against the gigantic windows, surveying planes landing and taking off. She returned to the baggage carousel in case he had been delayed and had just arrived, but the area was almost empty except for a few suitcases meandering in circles. She had him paged and remained in waiting mode. Nothing. She went to the ladies' room, thought she would freshen up. For sure he would be there by the time she finished, but no. She was getting hungry and plucked up a turkey sandwich from the autovend. He would surely surface, all aflutter with apologies, and from the corner of her eye there he was. A tall, blond, sturdy hunk, dressed in khakis and a black T-shirt. Baseball cap turned front to back. She broke her stride. "Ryan, Ryan," she cried out, but when the fellow turned around, she saw it wasn't him. Always the anticipation.

As the day wore on, she realized something must have happened to him. He wouldn't stand her up in this godforsaken place. He'd said he would buy her the moon when she got here. So cliché and yet she believed him. A small-town girl, a dreamer, a romantic, a Saultite — that's what they called residents from Sault Ste. Marie, or the Soo. She didn't want the moon, just him. She remembered the slip of paper where he had scribbled an address and phone number. "Call me if I'm not there." She thrashed about her purse and pulled the note from her wallet and, at a pay phone, followed his instructions.

"May I speak with Ryan?" The girl on the other end giggled, her voice barely audible as though she had put a hand over the receiver and was having a conversation with someone else in the room.

A muffle of nervous laughter and then sharp and loud: "Sorry, but you have the wrong number."

"Is this —"

But the girl had already hung up. Dead, except for the beeping tone.

Velvet sat back on the unyielding plastic airport chair. Night now, and the stars seemed to blend with the lights from the aircrafts approaching the runway. Had she been here that long? Eventually, the hum of engines lulled her to sleep. Even the sudden screech of planes braking didn't wake her.

And then it was morning. The airport was abuzz with travellers, everyone in a rush of living, going somewhere. She could smell roasted coffee from the nearby eatery. Maybe she had the wrong day and so she decided to run back to the arrivals gate from Toronto. Passengers were awaiting their luggage and she circled the carousel again looking for that blond head of hair. He was a musician, tattoos climbing his arm, a button earring in his right ear, so against the grain of what was considered normal here in the West. How could she miss him? But he was nowhere. Vanished.

Velvet had withdrawn all the money she'd saved from her sales job at a record store in Sault Ste. Marie where she first met him. Said he was passing through, but he stayed. Played some of the bars around the Soo with a backup band, and hung around long enough for her to fall in love. Then with a sudden turn of events he announced he was heading for a gig in Calgary and another in Edmonton.

"Lots of money to be made in Alberta," he said. "I'll send for you when I get settled." She thought that was a new pickup line but he did call and he mailed her the airfare. He was working in a town called Red Deer.

"Red Deer. What kind of name is that?"

"A stopping point in the middle of Alberta. On my way to Calgary first and then back up to Edmonton next month if things work out. I'll meet you in Edmonton. I'll be staying with a buddy of mine in this new part of town called Mill Woods. There's a future for us there, babe," he said. "There's a future." And here she was, still waiting for her future.

She cleaned up in the ladies' room at the airport café then ordered a coffee. Black. She picked up the *Edmonton Journal* that someone had forgotten at her table and read the headlines. It occurred to her that perhaps something had happened to him. A small article caught her eye. An elderly couple had stumbled over a dead body in a Mill Woods ravine. Could it be? She shook that notion out of her head and took another sip of coffee, ignoring her anxiety. What would she do if that dead body was Ryan? How would she find him? She fingered his folded note and decided to present herself. She had been prudent and had stayed within her meagre budget, but considering the situation, she decided to forget her thriftiness and splurge on a taxi. She gave the Punjabi driver the Mill Woods address.

It was an apartment building across the street from the Moravian Church cemetery. How could he choose to live near the dead? With tentative fingers, she buzzed the apartment number and, after a few seconds, a female voice barked over the intercom, "Yeah?"

"Does Ryan live here?"

"Who?"

"Ryan. I called last night from the airport. He was to meet me there but never showed up. He gave me this address and —"

"Oh, sweetie, I would take the next plane back to wherever you came from. You don't want to know Ryan."

"But he's my boyfriend."

The girl began to chortle and then a male voice intruded, "Who's that?"

"Another one of Ryan's whores." The intercom went dead.

Velvet buzzed again and waited a moment in case the male voice would let her in, but there was only silence. Despondent, she turned around and headed out. The building was one of those four-storey walk-ups common to the neighbourhood. When she met the sidewalk, she decided to let logic guide her. She had some money but that could evaporate in a moment's temptation if she wasn't careful. The cab fare from the airport alone was more than expected. She needed a job and a place to live. She strolled around Mill Woods, in and out of farmers' fields and meadows, choice real estate yet to be developed. She came across a vacancy sign at the Complex Arms and walked in.

A waiter at the airport café mentioned rents were quite cheap now. The price of oil in a downward spiral. People on the Klondike Trail looking for black gold now returned to their origins: the Maritimes, Quebec, northern Ontario. The server also suggested that perhaps she, too, should follow their course and head on back to the Sault. "A young girl like you alone in the Wild West. Yep, if

I were you, I would go back and make your little life there." She ignored his suggestion, a stranger to her. What did he know of her life?

The Complex Arms was in an area designated as Burnwood. A woodsy scent in the surroundings seemed to energize her. Nature abounded. Birds cheeped and squeaked, which reminded her of the Sault. Small-town living felt comfortable. She could be on the verge of happiness, contentment, if only she could find Ryan. Her thinking was that, living in Mill Woods, she could easily bump into him in the street, the mall, the park nearby, maybe at a bus stop.

The following day, after she moved in with her sparse belongings and a new bed from a wholesaler, she checked out the various bars in the vicinity. She hoped that perhaps Ryan had played in one of the venues in or around Mill Woods since the address he had given was in that section of town.

Her first stop: Black Jack's on Calgary Trail. She was drawn by the small blinking neon light in the bar's window, advertising two dancing feet in stilettos. They were hiring dancers. She had some experience as a backup dancer for every band that came through her hometown. She could do that, she thought. No Ryan at Black Jack's but everything was not lost. She had landed a job as a waitress. Minimum wage to start, but the tips made the work worthwhile for a naive girl from the Soo. The owner told her that she could earn more money if she stripped and would receive an additional bonus if she persuaded customers to buy her drinks, watered-down shots masquerading as vodka. Her innocence would not let her commit to taking her clothes off. Not yet. She wasn't that desperate.

Black Jack, the proprietor, made fun of her, mocking her reluctance. "You know, if you're gonna work here, even if you're just a waitress, you're gonna have to show a lot of skin. Sheer bra and a tiny skirt. Fellows here just want to see tits. I can tell you have nice ones. So you might as well give the guys what they want. You'll make a lot more dough."

"I really don't —"

"Look, I've seen a lot of girls like you. Come in here and think, 'Oh no, I couldn't do that.' Well, let me tell you, they all change their minds once they see how much money they can make. So if you're smart, you should just follow my advice and dive right in."

Velvet couldn't believe what she was hearing. Did all the waitresses really end up as strippers? She had a nice body, she knew — guys were always ogling her — and she wasn't shy about showing it off a little. Her bikini was pretty revealing. But still, stripping was something else entirely. She could use the money, of course.

"Tell you what. Why don't you come to my office? We can talk some more, take a few photos."

She felt herself drifting behind him to his office upstairs above the bar.

"Sometimes, my clients are looking for dates. An escort. You okay with that?" he said as they reached the door.

"Just a date?" Her head low, eyes raised in the dusky hall before entering his office.

"If you want more money, arrangements can be made for other, shall we say, lucrative activities."

"I don't think so," Velvet said. "Thanks anyway. I'll just serve drinks, okay, and then maybe I'll see."

"Just putting it out there for you. Think about it," said Black Jack. "For now, bring that chair over here and pose so I can get some shots."

Black Jack sighed. "Now don't be a tease and get shy on me, doll. Your tits are practically falling out of that halter. Take off the top and don't waste my time. Thought you needed a job." And he started to walk away.

"Wait. Wait. I'll be working as a waitress, right? So why do you need naked photos of me?"

He returned to face her. "Policy, doll, you got nice tits. Do you understand? This is a strip joint. First you dance, and if the customers like you, you get to remove your clothes down to the G-string. No waste of time taking photos if we do that now. Time is money. What did you expect? You're just meat to my customers. You all look the same to them. Ready?"

She vowed that she would make sure the customers didn't like her dancing so she would never have to strip. Right now, though, she knew she had to take off her top. She swallowed and, shaking somewhat, pulled it over her head.

He manipulated her body in various positions, sitting demurely, hands between her thighs, ankles hooked behind the back of the chair legs, her head resting, hair a mess of knots and tangles as though Black Jack had seen the movie *Blow Up* too many times.

"Okay, time to take off your skirt."

"But —"

"Look, you're really startin' to piss me off. Do you want this job or not? Guys want to see topless and they want to see you in tiny little panties. You gotta show them what you got. So either you grow up and take off your skirt, or get out of here and stop wasting my time."

She knew there was nothing more to say. She took another deep breath, pulled off her skirt, kicked off her shoes, and stood there. She wanted to cover herself up but she knew that that would just make him angry. So she stood there, staring at the floor, knowing that his eyes were roving over her almost naked body.

"Nice," he said.

She felt in a daze, like she was someone else. He had her sprawled on the plank floor, writhing and sweeping the tresses back and forth like a mop, murmuring, her throat gulping for air at each titillating movement of her breasts. She fell in love with the camera; forgot Black Jack; forgot Ryan; and remembered all the models she had worshipped on the fashion covers of magazines like *Vogue, Glamour, Vanity Fair*. She was Christie Brinkley, Cheryl Tiegs, Cindy Crawford wrapped in one Blue Velvet Coburn. She wondered if maybe she should go to modelling school and become a model.

"Good, good, good. You're a natural. Good, good. Lovely. Do it again." David Hemmings photographing Veruschka.

He kept shooting nonstop from various angles, the flash blinding; he, moving closer and closer for the kill.

"Let me see your face, doll." Black Jack pulled back her hair with such abruptness, it frightened her. He hovered over her face and took aim, his pelvis close to her mouth, and then he caressed her breasts.

"Nice tits, doll. You're hired."

She feared the inevitable but he backed away with clumsy steps as though he had unsealed an envelope and realized it was the wrong one for the prize.

"Don't worry, doll, I love men. Put your clothes back on."

"Is that it then?"

"Start tomorrow. Night shift, six p.m. to two a.m. when we close. You start serving drinks. Watch the other girls for a couple of shifts. Nice girls. In a week we'll get you that dance audition. If my customers like you, well, we'll move you to stripper."

She signed the contract. No escorting. A deal.

Velvet dressed herself with a shield of mixed emotions, but she had a job that could pay well if she played it right. Temporary. An opportunity to ask around for Ryan. He was bound to show up all apologetic and forgetful as was his way. It's all the drugs he takes, she reasoned. And, hopefully, he would present himself before she had to strip.

It happens as she is leaving. Frosty is rushing up to the door just as she is on her way out. They collide and she goes flying onto the cement walk.

"Sorry, ma'am," he says, removing his cowboy hat.

"Asshole." She struggles to stand up, but keeps slipping backwards on her dress shoes until he catches her.

"Well, well, well. Lookit here."

"Frosty."

"What were you doin' in Black Jack's? Don't usually find too many women visiting a strip club."

"I just got a job here," Velvet says, feeling rather ashamed to admit it.

"Black Jack hired you?" He shakes his head. "Trust me, you don't wanna be stripping for Black Jack. Before you know it, he'll have you whoring for his customers. You don't want that, do you? No. Stick by me, girl, before you get yourself into some nasty trouble. I can get you a job groomin' horses at the racetrack. Pay's not bad. They's always on the lookout for a pretty girl. You don't want to work for Black Jack."

"I can take care of myself." She thrusts her body past him and is gone, hurrying toward Calgary Trail and a bus back to Mill Woods.

With the late light of summer beginning to wane, Velvet sits on the bench in front of the Complex Arms and reviews her day — work at Black Jack's tomorrow, the photography session, bumping into Frosty. Maybe by the end of the week Ryan would show up, or maybe she'd get lucky and find a better job. She has no expectations. Only hope.

The sun's dying rays flatter her. Basking in the light, her face looks radiant and wholesome. Velvet relaxes, absorbing the summer day's aromatic senses and the city's sounds.

Suddenly, cool fingers tap her bare shoulders. She looks over her shoulder and there he is. Again.

"You moved in all right? Need anythin', just holler."

"Frosty."

"It's okay. Adeen don't need to know we bumped into each other at Black Jack's. She don't like me goin' there."

"Well, I gotta go there."

"I told you I can get you something at the track."

"I don't think that's for me."

"You wanna strip?"

Velvet doesn't say anything.

"Okay, it's your life ... but you be careful of Black Jack. Like I said, he's going to want you to do a whole lot more."

"Like I said," Velvet replies, "I can take care of myself."

"What's your boyfriend going to say?"

"Ryan? Who knows."

Velvet goes on to share her concerns about Ryan, the boyfriend from hell, who has deserted her.

"I want an explanation, and he owes me some money."

Frosty's head drops almost to his knees. "Yeah, well, dudes can be that way. I can maybe help you find him if you want. I know practically everyone in town and I know the bar scene. I can ask around."

She gives him a perplexed scrutiny and says, "Why would you want to do that. You don't even know me."

"'Cause I'm a good person. May not go to church on Sundays but I like to help damsels in distress."

"I bet you do. What does Adeen think of that?"

"Who cares what she thinks."

But Frosty, for all his faults, is a man of his word, and the next morning before she heads for Black Jack's, they check several bars and restaurants in Mill Woods, showing a photo of Ryan that Velvet carries in her wallet. Their search widens that week to include the downtown core, Boyle Street, Chinatown, Little Italy, the library, Winston Churchill Square. She is also getting a tour of a city that she currently calls home.

Eventually, they land on Whyte Avenue, where they do a round of all the clubs. Finally, they call it a week at the seedy Commercial Hotel. They sit at a sidewalk table and inhale the smoke from exhaust pipes and weed, shielding their ears against the sputter of deranged motorcycles and old jalopies that should have died a long time ago.

"Don't want to go back to the Soo. Nothing there. I'm here now so have to keep moving."

"Looks to me like he don't want to be found."

"Maybe I'll go to Calgary. Said he was going there first. Lots of jobs there, someone told me. Maybe I'll go to school, get my degree in education ... or become a model ..."

"And change the world, Velvet? The world changes on its own terms."

"And you?" she asks.

"Gonna keep writin' my poetry. There're different ways to change the world."

"You write poetry?"

"Wanna hear?" And before she can reply he is reciting four stanzas about his land and how corporations are raping it to dig out its resources; about the corruption of man and the purity of nature.

"I don't know poetry, Frosty, but it rhymes, so must be good."

He smiles and orders another beer for each of them. He has a fan.

ADEEN

So hot, Edmonton was hidden in a haze from all the forest fires now burning up north in the mountains. Couldn't see two feet in front of me. The last couple of days Payton had pealed his bell in the corridors at all hours of the day and night like a small-craft warning.

"Armageddon chasing us. Beware, all you heathens. We will all burn in hell. The end is near." Payton was a bundle of joy, if you know what I mean.

"For God's sake, stop that, Payton!" And I ripped his bell from his hands. "You'll get it back tomorrow," I said.

That night even Payton remained alert. Come take me, Lord, he would count quotes from the Bible instead of sheep until he was dead to the world. That's how he fell asleep. Told me to give it a try. Reading the Bible would put anyone to sleep, I guess.

I was getting ready for bed when Mona called. Irene was asleep and doing well, she said. The new medicines were making her docile. I must be a bad mother if Mona could handle and love her like an angel. She wanted to know how I was doing. I have to admit that with Irene out of the picture, I felt a freedom and peace that had been lacking from my life for so long. Even Frosty's absences no longer bothered me. Not much.

By ten o'clock I had slipped into bed and fallen asleep; an hour later I awoke to feel Frosty's side of the bed. Nothing there but cool sheets. He had been missing since morning. I had come to terms with his impulsive, irresponsible, cheating behaviour, his characteristic histrionics and self-pity, playing the unsung Poet Laureate of the Complex Arms. Big shit! Nonetheless, I tossed and turned with worry until I eventually dozed off. I didn't hear the poetic hound, reeking of cigarettes, booze, and weed creep under the sheets beside me.

The back of my head felt damp against the pillow. I had earlier shut off the oscillating fan on the nightstand as the continuous whirling gave me a headache. I heard a dog barking somewhere nearby, perhaps in a neighbour's yard. Light filtered through the venetians. I was wide awake now and thirsty. I reached over to Frosty's side of the bed again and screamed, not expecting to find Zita's husband, Howard, lying there.

He apparently had lost his way to his apartment after an all-nighter. In his drunken state of confusion, all the floors and doors looked the same. I had left my door unlocked for Frosty so he would not disturb me when he came home. Howard just walked in and headed straight for the closet in the entrance. Saw his error and shifted toward the bedroom and fell into bed with me, think-ing I was Zita. So goes his story. It might have been funny if it had happened to someone else, not me.

"What are you doing here? This is not your apartment." I was hysterical. I mean, did he try anything while I was asleep? I wanted to know. He apologized and said no.

"You're in the wrong apartment," I kept screaming.

"Sorry, sorry Adeen." He was so contrite, looked pathetic as he shuffled off like a zombie into the living room, the entry closet, in and out, and finally out the door, me cursing behind him, and Frosty, buttoning up his shirt, racing down the stairs from Velvet's apartment. Who else? Not surprised. I know my man. It was full daylight now.

"And you ... you ... cowboy, what are you doing up there with that bitch?" I yelled at him, slapping his chest left and right, left and right. Embarrassed. Tenants watching. I didn't care.

"Nothin', hon," he said.

Such a liar.

"Takin' her on an early search for her boyfriend before she starts work today at Black Jack's at noon," he said. "Was comin' right down to get the car ready. That's all." His fine excuse.

And the bitch from the Soo was now at the top of the stairs in her nightie backing Frosty's version. "That's right, Mrs. Whitlaw," she said. "Frosty came to my rescue at Mr. Black Jack's the other day and said he'd help me find Ryan. We just talked all night about where to look, come up with ideas, and before we knew it, the sun came out and —"

Yada yada yada. The bitch. Only a couple of days here and already she was making a spectacle of herself.

I told her not to come near Frosty ever again and then turned to him with a punch and told him to stay away from me for a while, to just leave me alone, or I'd ditch him just like that. I was getting tired of all his excuses. I knew he was getting it on with Velvet. Did he think I'm stupid?

"Ouch, Adeen, that hurt."

"Good," I said.

Since Velvet moved into the Complex Arms, Frosty was never around. I knew where he went. I knew. I couldn't help noticing how no sooner did she leave, he was right behind. Said I'm not stupid. Then one day, I think it was her first week here, I heard that voice,

Bobby Vinton singing "Blue Velvet" somewhere in the building. I followed the music and sure enough it was coming from Velvet's apartment. I knew that if I went in I would find Frosty there. I didn't even knock on the door. It was unlocked and what a sight — Velvet, naked, prancing about with a photo clutched to her breast. She stopped dancing when she noticed me watching.

"Is this what girls do in the Soo? Have affairs with married men?"

"Adeen. You got it wrong."

And I jumped at the naked bitch, snatching the photo from her hands and ripping the thing to pieces.

"Hey, you can't do that. That's personal." Velvet was hysterical. "That's the only photo I have."

"Right, I want you out of here as soon as you can get your shit together. Stay away from Frosty," I spat at her. Felt good.

She simmered down and said, "But that was a photo of my boyfriend, Ryan. Frosty is helping me find him."

"I want you out of here end of the month," I said.

"You have to give me three months' notice."

Well, she was right about that. She did sign a lease, so nothing I could do.

Overkill? I don't think I was overreacting. Do you? There are no happy marriages. Mona told me back when I was considering marrying Frosty. "Couples," she would say, "who brag that they are happy with their partners, well, it means they haven't been married long enough or one of them is lying or has been silenced. It's usually the woman."

Who the hell invented marriage? I want to kill that guy because it certainly wasn't a woman. I forgave Frosty again for being a horny cowpoke. Okay, I'm stupid. And by the way, I never told Zita about Howard sleeping in my bed. I had enough problems already.

Anyhow, that's the story there.

THE MOUSE INCIDENT

They are both up now, the hostile sun penetrating across the horizon. Frosty is making coffee. Adeen waits like a teardrop about to descend, hands vanishing behind her.

"So how much money did you lose?"

"Came out even-steven."

"Who'd you stay with?" Adeen picks up the old newspaper section with the photo of the Complex Arms and the balcony with the child's tricycle.

No response.

"I asked who you stayed with. You were gone two days." She tosses the newspaper on the table.

"What's with the interrogation? I was at the casino. Mario let me sleep there, in his office. I was dead drunk."

"Good thing you weren't dead, or I'd be arranging a funeral right now."

"Should throw that thing out. Old news," Frosty said pointing at the tabloid.

"Yeah, well." And she rips the pages into smithereens except for the article about Jan and Nina, keeping it as a reminder of the vulnerability of women who marry the first thing that crosses their world, as though they were unworthy of more.

Velvet has settled into the Complex Arms; Frosty has been furnishing her apartment with second-hand furniture that he salvaged from runaway former tenants: a sofa, a coffee table, a chest of drawers, and a bookshelf. He continues to assist in her search for the elusive Ryan.

Adeen has a thirst for a cold Molson. Nothing in the fridge and no stash left behind Irene's bedroom door.

Frosty steps out under a blistering midday sun, excusing himself from the yardwork that Adeen assigned him. "But my wrist is sore today," he complains. Her eyes beam threats at him, but he splits before she can shove a mop in his arms.

Velvet, at the same time, decides to explore the neighbourhood, stop off at the Mac's store around the corner for an ice cream sandwich, and maybe inquire again about Ryan. She is in the lobby heading out when Frosty, sprinting down the hall, collides with her. Frosty signals with his finger to his lips to shush, to stay quiet, and gestures for Velvet to walk backwards. There in the lobby, under the threadbare welcome mat, a mouse is birthing a brood of scrawny, hairless, pink babies. Frosty counts four but more may be flushing out.

Velvet shrieks and Frosty hushes her up again, but the mother mouse, the doe, is deaf to any startling sound, so occupied is she in cleansing her brood. Two more pinkies emerge. Frosty again cautions Velvet to stay back then he removes his T-shirt and uses it as leverage to lift the two ends of the welcome mat. He flings the entire contents out the open doorway, like so much garbage, into a nearby shrub. The mice sift down through the interior branches, eventually finding soft landings. One puny pinky, the smallest, the weakest, slips out and hits the pavement, dead. The carpet lies motionless, one part folded over, like a discarded opened envelope. The doe seems oblivious to the fact that she has lost one of her pups.

"You've killed them! A mother and her babies. You've killed them all."

"Nah, I didn't. See." And he points to sudden movement under the mat.

"They are probably hurt for sure," Velvet said.

"Thought you didn't care. Want to go rescue them. Go ahead." And he bows from his waist and grandly gestures toward the floral shrub, a bleeding heart.

"At your disposal, ma'am," Frosty says.

"Leave them alone. Leave them. They are creatures. They breathe."

"All right. Want the critters? I'll get them for you."

"Murderer!" Velvet's voice is an anxious squall. "Murderer!"

And she is gone. She springs back blindly inside the building with the speed of a runaway horse, up the stairs to her apartment, sobbing for all the dead creatures in the world, leaving Frosty behind scratching his head.

Adeen pokes her head out of her apartment and can see Frosty through the glass lobby door bent over laying out his T-shirt on the ground like a picnic blanket.

"Always have to show off your chest, eh, Frosty. What's going on? Who screamed?" She is outside now nagging him.

Frosty hurries up the steps, ignoring the rants. He passes Adeen, and before she can utter another word, he says, "Mouse in the entryway gave birth and Velvet went crazy like I was some kind of monster 'cause I threw the mat with its package of vermin onto the front lawn. They landed under your blessed bleeding heart. One baby hit the pavement. Just gettin' somethin' to clean the mess before any of the kids get at 'em, especially Derrick. Spread germs, you know."

"I'll have a talk with Derrick. He promised me, only pet mice and in a cage. I thought we had evicted them all."

"Never get rid of mice here. We live too close to the fields and marshes. We're the ones intrudin' on their livin' quarters."

"Only the strong survive," Adeen said.

He passes in front of her and she says, "I have to see Rosemary upstairs. She's inconsolable. Still mourning her husband."

"Why don't you just let her be?"

"She's grieving, don't you understand. She knows no one here but me. Have to go."

"Go then. See your crazy tenants. Take care of them first. You could help me get rid of the dead mouse."

"You know I can't see anything die, Frosty. And mice. Not even cuddly."

Adeen heads for Rosemary's while Frosty stops at the broom closet to fetch a pail, mop, and trowel. The closet abuts their apartment and he can hear the phone ringing. He makes a hasty decision to ignore the dead mouse for the moment. He drops the cleaning equipment in the hallway, returns inside, and picks up the receiver.

"Hey, Burp. How's it going?" Frosty checks over his shoulder to ensure he is alone. "Not now," he whispers. One of his casino friends. "This place is a fuckin' zoo. There's a family of mice checkin' out the real estate on the front lawn."

A knock on the door.

"Hold on, Burp." Knock again and there stands Velvet, shimmering like a newly minted loonie.

He's already in the hallway, arms held out, reaching for her. "What's the matter, hon?"

"Mouse and her babies. They deserve a decent funeral."

"I was just gonna check and do that."

And then he remembers Burp. "Come in, Velvet. Just on the phone. Only take a minute."

Frosty is listening, nodding, then hangs up with a forlorn, disoriented expression, a grinding of teeth moving his jawline, a touch of red anger coating his cheeks.

Velvet follows Frosty and she begins to squeal as they near the front door.

"I can't bear to look."

"You better stay behind, Velvet, if you're gonna act that way. Have enough crazy here to last another lifetime."

"I won't, I won't. I promise." Her fingers latch on to the back of his leather belt until she and Frosty near the bleeding heart. Frosty bends over it with deliberation and teases the lower branches with his trowel for a better view.

"Nothin' here, Velvet. Come see. They musta taken off." And the earth seems to once again settle back into place until the next round of drama.

With a caution bordering on paranoia, she tiptoes toward the scene of the mouse massacre, only to come unglued when she feels a light scampering over her sandal. The mother mouse is beating its way across the lawn in search of her lost pups. Velvet is hopping up and down like the soles of her feet are on fire. "Mouse, mouse."

Frosty is grabbing her arm, drawing her toward him, and she is breathing into his heart, whimpering, and he likes it. He is squashing her with his long arms, chest to chest, his mouth sucking her neck and face.

She does the same, seeming to acknowledge this affection between them. She lets him kiss her full out on the lips, a lizard's flicking tongue, and then she pushes him away and says, "I have Ryan."

"Well, where's the highfalutin dude, huh?"

"And you have Adeen."

He lurches forward, grabs her waist, and spins her around again, his eyes on hers.

"I don't have Adeen."

"Don't hurt her, Frosty. Besides, I love Ryan. Don't confuse me. I still haven't uncovered all the places he could be hiding."

"But, Velvet."

"Fuck off," she shouts with a surprised finality and marches back inside the building.

"They is all crazy. All crazy."

After burying the dead baby mouse under the bleeding heart, he drags the mat behind him by a corner, stops to hurl it inside the Dumpster in back. The dry grass, the colour of steeped green tea, tickles his ankles as he returns to the lobby. He thinks it's a mouse and kicks it, but nothing there.

"Those critters still alive somewhere. Now I'll never hear the end of it. Maybe I can flush them out. Besides, the lawn needs waterin' and that tree is askin' for refreshments." He is talking to the birch now. "I know what we both can use. Whisky. At least for me. You get water and maybe some fertilizer."

"Talking to yourself again, Frosty?" says Payton.

"Haha. Funny."

"Heat got to you, too?"

"Lay off."

Payton retires inside with a smugness bordering on conceit. Frosty slaps his hands against his naked chest, trying to erase the dirt and sweat.

The drought singes the City of Edmonton and the surrounding area. For Sale signs pop up along roadways. Prescribed burns in forests up north wait to ignite into an accident.

"Bloody heat wave," Frosty says to no one and directs the garden hose on himself before drenching the birches.

ADEEN

People who need people always rely on the kindness of strangers. They say we all need someone, which is just a lot of bullshit as far as I'm concerned. Me, I don't need anyone. You need yourself first. You are whole without another person hanging on to your rib cage, whether it is a husband or a child. If I had to do it over again ... if I had to do it over again ... Irene and Frosty need me, so I guess they are lucky they have me.

Told you not to judge me.

Rosemary wasn't home, so I went back to wait for Frosty, see if he had cleaned up the mice mess. Interesting that the mother mouse, so oblivious to her brood she didn't expect all of them to live anyway, was grateful for nature to lighten the load for her. Christ! I wondered if we should tell the Swanks about the mice? I knew I'd have to have a talk with Derrick first. At least there were no cockroaches like in Montreal.

Don't I sound like a native Albertan? Hate this province. Never should have listened to Mona. I don't know anymore. I'm losing whatever goodness I had left. Only so much a body can take.

Anyhow, as I was saying before the mice interrupted, I saw Frosty out our bedroom window lunging for Velvet, arms all over her like she was freezing and needed someone to keep her warm. When he started kissing her, I backed off. I'm no fool. He'd done this before to me. I knew it. Those nights when he was gone ... Where do you think he went? Not midnight Mass, I can assure you.

Later that day, Frosty neglected his janitorial duties, took his notebook of poems to Black Jack's, and waited until Velvet's shift was over. How did I know? I followed him. He was still latched to his little dream of becoming one of those cowboy poets who read at fairs and rodeos. Bet Velvet liked that romantic side of him. Everyone did. His horsing days were over, and I guess he'd decided that he'd rather horse around with anyone who would listen to his stupid poems. He was convinced he would be famous one day, make money. "You'll get your house, Adeen," he would tell me.

Well, those days were gone. I'd stopped waiting for him to make good on his promises, stopped waiting for him to help me make my dreams come true. Stopped waiting for him, period. At night, I'd hear him come back to the Complex Arms, his voice raised in a drunken stupor after a night of drinking at Black Jack's and sharing a cab with Velvet after her shift ended. I could hear them both laughing in the hallway like a couple on a date and then not a word.

One night I couldn't stand it anymore. I stormed upstairs and I flung the door wide open, angry with hurt. The building seemed to vibrate. And there they were, eyes locked, Frosty deaf to anything but her sweet murmurs, and his hands under her elbows. Velvet spotted me over his shoulder and indicated my presence with raised eyebrows and further whisperings, speaking soft like I was interrupting something important.

Frosty looked over his shoulder, like he had just noticed me, and with a sheepish grin said, "Oh, hi, Adeen. Just deliverin' Velvet home from Black Jack's."

"Full of shit" is what I said. But it was always the alcohol talking. I knew that.

"What more do you want from me?" He'd always throw that bit of nonsense at me. "What more do you want from me?"

Lots more, I wanted to say.

I didn't want him cheating on me. I didn't want him gambling. I wanted him to actually do some work, help me run the Complex Arms. Once upon a time he would check out the classifieds in the back of musical periodicals like *Variety* and *Billboard*, and at first I supported his sorry efforts. I hooked on to his dream. This was early in our relationship. Frosty would send his paltry lyrics to unscrupulous American music producers who greedily praised his poetics, pocketed his money — money that was not his to spend — and then he'd never hear from them again.

After he fell off that horse at Northlands Raceway and broke his wrist bones, and after his workers' compensation ran out, he would complain that he could no longer carry a mop, that his back and neck would give out, that his wrist tired from the lifting. And so I took on a bigger load and left the watering to him until he complained about how heavy the garden hose was, so I finally relented and told him to take care of the banking and write his stupid poems. I didn't want the Swanks to fire us because we couldn't do the job.

I took comfort in my tenants. They were a distraction.

Mrs. Lapinberg, with the aid of her oldest son, was preparing to move out. I had mixed feelings. Such a dear soul. There are good people in the world.

Zita found a part-time job to keep busy and would leave Derrick with me when she worked the night shift at McDonald's. Not much money, of course, and she developed a bad back from all that stooping and lifting, all day on her feet. Seemed strange, she, a young woman in her midthirties. "Not right," I said.

Howard kept working up north at Fort Mac, and Zita's extra wage helped with the groceries. He would come home every two weeks but, according to Zita, there never seemed to be enough to pay all the bills. Sometimes I would give her an extension on the rent during a particularly bad month. Where did his money go? I could have told her but kept my mouth shut … I would have told her if she asked but she never asked. I did what I could to help.

And Rosemary no longer wept for her Walter. Guess she kept everything inside. Days after the funeral, a friend set her up with a blind date, an old geezer in search of someone to take care of him in his old age. The usual story. She would have none of that and broke up the relationship rather quickly, I thought.

Instead, she returned to finishing the memoir she'd started so many years before. I guess she had an ending now that Walter was gone. Her emotional condition improved somewhat. I did notice, however, she was becoming more reclusive, self-absorbed, withdrawing from everything. A way of protecting herself, I suspect. Can't blame her. I understood she wanted to tell her story. But memoirs bug me. They are all about me me me; I hated this narcissistic part of her. Everyone should listen to her whining as though everyone else lived a life of bedazzlement, but hers was one of martyrdom and sacrifice. I could tell her a thing or two. She asked me to help type the manuscript, but I declined this time. I didn't want to know any more details of her life.

There was one happy senior in the building. That nice man, Jack, on the second floor, who dressed in women's clothing, and went by the name of Jackie, after Jackie Onassis. Even dressed like her. Pillbox hats and spiffy pastel suits. A compulsive hoarder, he felt it was his mission to keep the world clean and beautiful, so he spent his days thrashing through Dumpsters in a bid to recycle every discarded can, bottle, and paper. He and Payton battled over the garbage until they eventually arranged a daily schedule of who went when to unearth his treasures. Civilized they were. Jack also painted in the manner of Modigliani, so I was drawn to him and our common love of art. We'd sit in the courtyard on the bench under the apple tree, Irene stretched out on one of the other benches, and we'd talk about paintings and books and music — all the things that nourished my spirit in the face of the absurdity that was the Complex Arms.

"Oh, Modigliani is my favourite painter right after Degas," I would say.

He would chirp, "You must come up and see my paintings, dear, one of these days."

And we would both laugh.

"That is so cliché, Jack," I'd say.

"Oh, you know what I mean." He would flop his wrist like a magician readying to perform a trick.

That was about as close as I got to being an artist. I only had a high-school education, and it is from Jack/Jackie (depending on the day), the retired principal, that I learned about art and literature. So he was no bother, an oddball who wore pink lipstick like his other namesake and a woman's wig in the fashion of the sixties. To me he was a precious friend. I can accept just about anything in a person except dishonesty or lack of integrity. He had bucketloads of honesty and integrity and more.

"He's harmless," I would tell Frosty if he complained, "and doesn't make trouble unlike some regular folks here."

"What's the world comin' to?" Frosty would say. "The city has changed a lot since I was a kid."

"You should talk," I would say, but he didn't understand. I mean, he was not the man I thought I had married.

Jack kept to himself most of the time, painting in isolation, forgetful of time. I understood. One day I dropped by to see if he needed anything and was taken aback by the filth of his apartment — worse than Payton's. The man was a contradiction — like Shylene in some ways, like most of us in many ways. I guess Jackie must have been the clean freak, and Jack, the hoarder. Wall-to-wall stacks of newspapers, magazines, CDs, empty jam jars, discarded chocolate bar wrappers, and God knows what else. No wonder mice now nested in the complex. A hot pot of canned beans with ketchup on the stove was his daily nourishment, along with his bologna sandwiches. He still thought it was the Age of Aquarius and kept humming songs from *Hair*.

One day I said, "Jack" — he wasn't wearing lipstick, so he was Jack — "I want you to clean up this mess immediately before I get in trouble with the Swanks and we all end up on the street."

"Yes, Adeen," he said. "After I finish this painting. I'm almost done." He smiled an odd smile and then spun around his easel, revealing the canvas. I saw it was a self-portrait in the manner of a crazed Van Gogh, gloomy and dark, amateurish, primitive, with ugly slashes of colour drowning his face, giving him the illusion of a werewolf.

"That's a nice hobby you have there, Jack," I said, "but this is an apartment, not an artist's studio, and if you don't clean up, out you go." I scolded him good.

"Yes, Adeen." Always yes, yes, yes, Adeen, and nothing ever got done.

I had come for the rent. He was a month late, which never happened. He pleaded that his pension cheque hadn't arrived yet and if I could wait another couple of weeks, he would be good for it. It's a shame how we treat our seniors. He was always on time. Swank Property had raised the tenants' rent because the city had increased property taxes. Nothing I could do about that. Jack/

Jackie asked me if I could write a letter, telling management about his career as a public servant educating their children, and could they take pity on him and keep his rent at the same level for at least another year. Defer his misery, as he put it.

I felt sorry for the man/woman. Amazingly, Ed Swank, being the humanitarian and philanthropist that he was, deferred his increase for another year. Still, every month, Jack/Jackie needed to budget expenses, choosing between food and makeup or rent. Very often he would go to the food bank to load up on necessities like milk and bread. He could live on that for a week. He was not entitled to welfare as the powers that be considered his pension cheque adequate, enough to keep him in the style he had become unaccustomed to. Often, I would bring him leftovers. Frosty would yell at me, "He's a Molly, a homophilic." And I would answer back, "He's a human being," adding, "and a very interesting one at that."

I understood Jack/Jackie. I've noticed outsiders are the most interesting people. But everyone needs someone. People do need other people just to live. We are social creatures. My tenants needed someone, needed me. So here I am.

Anyhow, that's the story there.

THE SUMMER FAIR

Edmonton's hot season is always filled with family activities: visiting water parks, camping, hiking, swimming, canoeing, biking, and celebrating at street festivals of every make and model. Tourists overrun the province, stop at historical sites, holler at the Drumheller hoodoos — or doodoos, as Adeen called these rock formations in the Badlands where dinosaurs once ruled the earth — and always there are the side trips to the wild, to escape the oppressive heat near a lake or hotel pool: Banff, Canmore, Jasper. City folks blend with the travellers on the highways and roadways where the Rockies reveal themselves in all their glory, and everyone sighs and says, "Oh, wow, look at the mountains!" And then there are Klondike Days for those with no recourse but to vacation close to home.

Adeen carries an unbearable guilt for ignoring Irene, but Mona insists the girl is thriving in her home. If truth be told, Adeen likes the freedom of not having to deal with her damaged daughter and experiences a liberating joy akin to winning the lotto. No parental responsibilities for a change, she can pretend that she is a solitary figure without a past, or present, pretend that she's been given a chance to redesign her life, obliterate all the errors and misjudgments, a second chance to get it right. If she could, she would run away with a new identity and push life's restart button.

Mona called instead. "I'm taking Irene to the fairground and thought you might like to come."

"Do you think that's a good idea? You know how she can get."

"Adeen, Irene is just fine. She likes the kids around here, and she hasn't had a tantrum since she got here. I make sure she takes her meds. I'm there until I see her swallow those yellow pills."

"Are you saying it's my fault, Mona, that my daughter hates me, that I can't control her, that I don't give her proper care? Want to adopt her?"

"Don't be silly. Irene doesn't know what hate is."

Silence on the other end. "Besides, I can't. Told Zita I would babysit Derrick."

"Hey, we can take him with us. Irene loves Derrick and it would be fun for both of them and us. Remember fun? Remember all those corndogs and rides and games when you and Irene first came out here? Adeen, you could use a change. Get out more."

So Mona collects them, Irene sitting in the back seat, clapping to an old Merle Haggard tune on the car radio. When Derrick spots Irene, he comes charging at her like a battering ram, flings open the back door and slides in, his arms almost a chokehold around her neck, knocking her over on the seat, tickling her sides while she shrieks and snorts, her giggles spilling out the open window with pure joy.

Adeen waits her turn to hug and kiss her daughter's cheek before joining Mona in the front. Irene stops laughing and applauding, joy now deflating like a punctured tire. This breathing space away from each other reaffirmed Adeen's affection for her daughter. She'd just needed a brief respite from the distress that was Irene.

They park the car on a residential side street specifically designated for those attending the midway. Northlands Coliseum is in a low-income neighbourhood, and this playground, every summer, provides extra income for the residents who open their streets for parking; after all, they have to contend with the cacophonic headache of a carnival and exposition in their midst. The four stroll toward the gate, Irene clutching Derrick's hand, both arms swinging in wide strides of anticipation. They burst into fits of nonsensical sniggering and deliberate fart sounds over the noise of the midway. "Do you have to go to the bathroom?" says Adeen to Derrick's head shaking while Irene continues skipping and cheering with her hands in a show of *I am happy*. Just being kids. Behind them, Mona and Adeen drag on cigarettes, blowing gusts of smoke into the density of another hot summer day.

The heat hits them like a heavyweight boxer, but as soon as they hear the roar within the gates, Irene and Derrick release their armholds and sprint in the direction of the music. Mona chases after them while Adeen lags behind, moving in a desultory fashion; her face is devoid of any obvious signs of enthusiasm. They purchase day passes and are in the swim of the moment when Adeen spots him. Payton. Heedful of possible converts, gatekeeper to Jehovah's kingdom, he has positioned himself in front of the fenced grounds, clutching a handful of pamphlets in one hand. In the other, he cradles a simple small shining box against his heart. The lid carries an engraving, a name, with calligraphic lettering which she can't decipher.

"Payton?" Adeen says.

"The end is near." His focus is levelled into the oblivion of some other world he has yet to experience.

"Oh, Payton, that's enough now. Are you allowed to be here?"

"They will come. Prepare." And he searches the pewter sky for a ticking watch forecasting the termination of everything that belongs to mankind.

Mona, impatient to jump-start the afternoon, repositions herself next to Adeen, nudges her and says, "Who's that?"

"One of my tenants. Strange fellow but harmless. Remember I told you about him when we took on the building. He thinks we're all going to die and go to hell unless we are Jehovah's Witnesses."

"Not before we have some fun first."

Though the sky has shifted and there is a sudden appearance of clouds, a spot of sun is determined to push through. A prediction of showers is in the forecast, but the day, nevertheless, remains hot and sluggish, overburdened by humidity.

The day's turnout compares with the largest in the history of Klondike Days, and there are long lineups for all of the rides and for the more popular amusements and games of chance and skill, like hitting a target with either a ball or a weapon. Irene and Derrick are enthralled by the duck pond because it produces a winner every time. The player selects one of the rubber ducks floating in the water. Writing on the bottom of the duck reveals the prize. Everyone is a winner. Mona and Adeen can't coax the children away until they are bribed with ice cream cones.

By the end of the afternoon fatigue has set in, but Mona wants to guzzle down a cool beer, so they place Irene and Derrick at the children's centre and make their way to the makeshift saloon after buying a couple of tickets for the home lottery. Adeen bumps into a woman of a plus size, wearing a swirl of pink-and-green chiffon and adorned with bright yellow hair, false eyelashes blackened with mascara, feathers in her pompadour, wrists encased in layers of rhinestones over long-sleeved white gloves reaching to the elbows, and at her throat a remarkable display of amber in a silver necklace. It's Diamond Lil, reincarnated from a daguerreotype photo, a woman from another era, before they fought for emancipation from the kitchen and bedroom. Adeen is spellbound.

"Excuse me," says Adeen. When she looks more closely, there is a familiarity in the woman's comportment. Jack in drag, makeup smudged from the smear and sweat of the day, Jackie extends her arm.

"Adeen!"

"Jackie? You look … you look … fantastic. Wow! Anybody else here from the Complex Arms?"

"Oh, sweetie, isn't it a lovely day for a parade of costumes. Got my photo taken. Look." And she whips out a shot of herself under a parasol, pouty and sexy. "I've entered the contest for best-looking male in drag. Isn't Edmonton wonderful?"

"Aren't you hot in that getup?"

"Oh, Adeen, you are too funny. What's a bit of sweat. Going in?" She harrumphs and opens the old-fashioned saloon door that swings back and forth.

Wall-to-wall patrons pack the room. Anthracitic lighting and a substantial odour choke the air conditioning vents with smoke and stink. The waitress leads them to a table for three that has just been vacated near an open window and returns with the cocktail menus as a starter. In the meantime, while both Jackie and Mona muse about how lucky they are to get window seats, Adeen studies the room. Over the hills of heads, she comes across something that she will archive in her memory folder for many years.

"Let's go," she whispers.

"Hey, I haven't gotten my order yet. I'm starving." Mona is grouchy. She attributes it to the heat. And Jackie just wants company. She doesn't want to eat alone.

"See over there?" Adeen points to the other end of the room, opposite to where they are sitting. There is Frosty, dressed as Roy Rogers, sitting at a table with Velvet costumed in red and black boas, corseted like a dance hall girl from the days of the original Klondike. On her other side is a masked stranger outfitted as the Lone Ranger. Frosty leans over to give Velvet a kiss on her cherry-coloured lips and then it is the stranger's turn. They are all obviously drunk. Joshing, laughing, and slapping the edge of the table like a conga drum, they seem oblivious to their surroundings.

"Oh, my, doesn't she have a waist!" says Jackie as she soaks in the scene. "I see what you mean, Adeen. It's getting hot as hell in here." And she fans herself with her hands, bracelets a jingle like everyone's nerves.

Adeen dashes out in a fury of anger, and the noise of the crowded room seems to thunder behind her like a distant engine revving up. Mona chases after her.

When they reach the children's centre, they finally plop down on a nearby bench, breathing heavily, and Adeen cries out, "Bastard! Did you see him kissing that bitch?"

"I was hoping you wouldn't notice. But, yeah, he's drunk, Adeen. Doesn't even know what he's doing. He won't remember a thing tomorrow."

"Well, I will. I don't think I can go on living like this. I do have some pride left."

They both sit still. What to do next? Each is in their own world of oblivion and then Adeen perks up and says, "I want to go home. Get the kids."

When they enter the children's centre, one of the workers is frantic and says Irene and Derrick have disappeared, that they slipped out and volunteers are scouring the grounds.

"We were hoping to find them before you got here."

"They weren't here long. How could you have been so negligent?" Adeen yells, her voice rising at each hit of rage.

"These things happen. The kids want to go on the rides, play the games, so sometimes they just wander off."

"Wander off? You guys are supposed to make sure they don't wander off."

Adeen rushes back to the saloon with Mona trailing her again. Frosty is bending over the table, both elbows up, hilariously laughing at someone's joke, choking on his beer. Velvet sees her first and her demeanour changes to outright fear.

Frosty says, "What's the matter?"

Velvet motions behind him. "Your wife."

With a sharp look over his shoulder, he notices Adeen, who is now screeching, "Irene's missing and you're sitting here having a grand old time. I hate you, Frosty Whitlaw."

"I can explain, Adeen. We was just havin' fun. I have a good explanation. Honest." He stumbles in a drunken whirl of words that mean nothing.

"Cliché excuse. Go write yourself a poem and shove it up your ass."

And she is gone, leaving the Lone Ranger and Velvet to muddle through the evening while Frosty stumbles after Adeen mumbling, " What you mean Irene is missin'? What you mean?"

One of the employees at the duck pond reports finding a young girl, Irene's description, who talks gibberish, accompanied by another child of ten or so. They had been loitering around the stall without adult supervision. The children's centre pages the fairground, announcing like a broken record: "Mrs. Adeen Whitlaw, report to the children's centre. Your children have been found. Mrs. Adeen Whitlaw, report to the children's centre. Your children have been found."

ADEEN

wasn't frantic at the possibility of losing Irene. Isn't that awful? I was just mad at Frosty and the situation. I've had this buildup of anger inside of me simmering for a while. Every time he did something moronic, he'd strip another chunk out of my heart. I'll be without a heart at this rate. But the weird thing is I didn't really blame Frosty for all he did to me. No, I blamed his behaviour on the alcohol and the weed. It must do something to the brain. The idiot. Don't say I was asking for it because I always took him back. No one asked me, not even Mona, but I was relieved that they were found, of course, but, honestly, I wanted Irene dead. Isn't that awful? Don't judge me.

I forgave Frosty again. Gave him another chance. I think the medical profession calls it *enabling*. Anyhow, he told me he just bumped into Velvet at the fair with her friend, the Lone Ranger, so they stopped off for drinks. That's all. He just tagged along for the ride. I so wanted to believe that, but what the hell was he doing at the fairgrounds alone except he knew she would be there, or they had gone together. The liar!

I wasn't ready to take Irene back after that. My blood pressure was up again, and the doc said I needed to relax, do some yoga maybe. Find a hobby. Find a hobby? When would I have had time? I get these anxiety attacks sometimes. I know I'm hard to get along with, but what can you expect when I was living with someone like Frosty, who was making all those promises to me about his poetry and how one day he'd be rich and famous and we'd live in a house of our own. Can you believe that I believed him? And now?

Thank God for Mona. She had a way with Irene. I don't know how she did it. I guess it's always easier when it's not your kid. I really needed more time to figure out what I wanted to do. I knew that Frosty was fooling around with Velvet. I'm not stupid. Maybe I am. Maybe I'm in denial. Despite my feelings about her, I felt sorry for the girl. She still couldn't find that boyfriend of hers, who'd left her stranded here.

Look, I get it. Women are such pushovers. Here was Velvet — God, I keep thinking of Bobby Vinton every time I say her name. Anyhow, okay, I get it. She was alone in this big town, Edmonton, and no boyfriend to meet her. If it was me, I would have gone right back to the Soo. I'm an independent kind of woman. I don't need anyone. Not anymore. I was keeping my eye on her and Frosty. I should've just left. Escaped to some foreign country, an exotic island, and no one would hear from me ever again. No one would miss me, I'm sure.

Anyhow, as I was saying, thank God for Mona, who had the patience of an angel. Irene was in good hands. Mona was just somehow a born mother. Knew just what to do, say, and well, she just loves kids. Loved Irene the best. And she couldn't have any of her own. She told me once that she had a hysterectomy. Isn't it always the way? Those who should be mothers can't, and those who shouldn't be are like bunny rabbits. Just one baby after the other.

And then there was Zita's mom. Marietta wanted to control her daughter, organize her life. Never severed that umbilical cord that tied them together. Zita told me she just wanted to hear her mother say *I love you*. When Marietta ignored her daughter's birthday, in effect she was saying *You were never born*. So Zita lost her mother, and then she lost her baby. The pain must have been horrendous for Zita. I can only imagine.

And my mother? Her daughter was the bottle. I know a little bit of what Zita feels. The mother-daughter thing can be special, but it is not without its problems. I'm sure somewhere in this world there are mothers who exemplify Mary, the mother of Jesus.

Nothing is ever easy. I so wanted to believe Frosty, but my trust in people was diminishing every day. People always disappoint me. I'm a good person, you know. I just wanted to live a decent life. Be happy. Whatever that is.

Anyhow, that's the story there.

AFTER THE FAIR

Mona drops off Adeen and Derrick at the Complex Arms and continues back to the Evergreen Mobile Home Park with Irene, who copies Derrick's hand movements with a baffled expression. "Bye, bye, Irene." He waves. She throws a hissy fit inside the car, kicking and screaming, repeatedly calling for Derrick: "De-d-d-d-d."

Mona brings the car to a halt. "Oh, Irene, you'll see Derrick again soon."

And Irene retorts with her own language of love for Derrick: "De-d-d-d-d." Confusion masks her face until Mona offers a chocolate mint. The distraction calms her, Derrick forgotten for the moment as she focuses on licking the coating from the candy. Then Mona accelerates the car and they are back on the highway.

It is almost suppertime when Adeen hands Derrick over to Zita, who seems out of sorts, tired. Her face is partially hidden by a cotton scarf. She is sitting on the front steps.

"Oh, there you are. Knocked on your door but there was no answer."

"Sorry, Adeen. Just got here. I wanted to sit a bit before going inside."

"Well, he was a good boy. Went to the fair, won himself a toy …"

Derrick pulls out a small stuffed monkey, his prize at the duck pond.

"Derrick had fun at the fair, didn't you?" Adeen says as he nods, yawns, *yes, yes.*

"Thank you, Adeen."

"Something wrong?"

"Does it show?"

"Well, you're usually more energetic."

"Just got fired today." Zita lowers her voice, as though it is a deep ugly secret, not for her son's ears. "Not a big deal. Wasn't cut out to sling hamburgers anyway. There are other joints I can find work. It's not like we really need the money, you know."

"Yes, I know." A happy marriage? Adeen didn't want to hazard a guess.

Indeed, she knows how men working up north, away from home for weeks at a time, are tempted to live dangerously, spend their money frivolously, and when the time comes to return to their families, there is little left for household expenses.

Adeen keeps her mouth shut, determined only to offer advice if asked. Next to Mona, Zita is her closest friend. As though through osmosis, they understand each other without explanation. They share a love of cooking and they both have issues with their mothers. Zita's husband, a sociable extrovert, prefers the company of others to an intimate dinner with his wife. Summer evenings when he is home, they sometimes invite the Whitlaws for a balcony barbecue or a spaghetti dinner. Zita makes the best marinara sauce, he would say and give her a slap on the rump as she scurried past him from the dining room to the kitchen.

"Well, Derrick will sleep well tonight," Adeen says. "He has a bit of a tummy ache from all those corndogs. And Irene loved seeing him again. She didn't want to leave him."

No mention of losing the kids at the fairgrounds.

"Must be a vacation for you to have Irene with Mona. When she coming back?"

"Another week. I do miss her." And then Adeen spits out the words she has been avoiding admitting to anyone. "I'm considering putting her in the Michener Centre. She's getting too much for me, and I think it's a burden on our marriage."

"Yes, children can do that."

And then Adeen stops in midair. She wants to share something, her fears about her treatment of Irene, about Frosty's infidelities, his lies. She is thinking of leaving him, but where would she go and how to keep living? She could never tell Mona because Mona would just rub it in, reminding her that she told her so. She'd offer no solutions. Adeen's life was never going to untangle itself unless she did something. Zita would listen. But what would she think?

Adeen decides to keep her secrets to herself for now. She reaches over and pats Zita's arm. "Not to worry. Everything will work out. You'll find an even better job, or maybe Howard will get a job in Edmonton. Stay positive."

So Adeen leaves Zita on a note of hope; stops to check her mailbox; and in the hallway bumps into Mrs. Lapinberg and her son who are just returning from their customary weekly dinner.

"Such a show at the Mayfield Dinner Theatre, Adeen. A bit schmaltzy but the food was *geshmak*."

"*Geshmak?*"

"She means it was delicious." Pause. "Mrs. Whitlaw. I need to have a talk with you. I'll just put mother to bed. Are you available?" says Barney.

THE COMPLEX ARMS   217

"Sure."

"I'll be right back."

A few minutes later, a knock on the door. "Come on in," shouts Adeen.

Barney stands in the doorway with a nervous tic in his right eye.

"Well, come in now. I won't bite you."

"Mrs. Whitlaw." Barney is catching his breath. "Did my mother by chance give you a Royal Copenhagen 1908 Christmas plate, 'Madonna and Child'? It's worth about four thousand dollars."

"Oh, my! Yes, yes. She did give me a pretty plate of some kind, but I don't know where I put it. Four thousand dollars?"

"I hate to say this, but that was an heirloom and should stay in the family. It belonged to my grandfather and is of some value as a collector's item. He died in a concentration camp, Dachau. So you can understand the significance of keeping it in the family. I know mother meant well, but sometimes she doesn't understand what she's doing. May we have it back?"

"Oh, goodness, I told her I didn't want it but she kept insisting. Of course, you can have it back." Adeen goes to the glass cabinet to retrieve it.

"No! Oh, Barney, it's not here. I'll return it to you as soon as I find out what happened to it."

"I'd hate for it to get lost. It belongs to the family, you know."

"Yes, you said. I'll ask Frosty when he gets home. Maybe he moved it somewhere else. It's been chaotic lately."

After Barney leaves, Adeen searches the apartment, every nook and cranny, and not a trace. When Frosty shows up, just before midnight, she is in no mood for any of his shenanigans.

"Finally," she confronts him. "Did you have fun with Velvet?"

"Adeen, it's not like that. Stop it."

"I bet."

"We had some drinks. That's all."

"She find the boyfriend?"

"No. That was her date from the club. A friend of Black Jack's."

"Oh," says Adeen. "What were you doing at the grounds anyway? You're too big for the merry-go-round. Or maybe that's your style?"

"Adeen. Look, Adeen. Stop with the questions." And he pulls out an envelope overflowing with lottery tickets. "You wanted a house and so I bought tickets for the home lottery. We have a good chance. A beauty of a house. Did you see it?"

"Yeah, I did. Where in the heck did you get the money? Certainly didn't sell any of your poems, I bet." And then it occurs to her. "Frosty, did you come across an antique plate in the back of my glass cabinet? The one Mrs. Lapinberg gave me as a gift."

He trips over his words and then spits them out with a slow stutter like a six-year-old sent to the principal's office. "Yes. Wasn't worth much. Got a hundred bucks for it, enough for a lot of chances."

And she is on him like a dog with rabies, arms repeatedly thrashing him. "You stupid idiot. Fool."

Frosty stops her arms in midair and her head falls back in defeat. "Barney came over to get it back." Tears now. "His mother never should have given it away. It's an heirloom, now what am I to tell him? It's worth more than you got for it. How are we going to pay them? It's worth four thousand dollars. Better try to get back your money."

"Are you kiddin' me? Man, oh, man, Adeen. Can't do that." He's walking in circles. "The draw is tonight and all sales final." His voice is penitent, confused.

"You stupid idiot. You idiot. You go and tell Barney what you did, you idiot. I'm not cleaning up this mess. Die. Just let me die. Can't take too much more of this shit anymore."

Frosty with a hangdog face says, "But hon, it's not my fault. I didn't know and neither did you when you took the plate."

"Oh, it's my fault now. It was a gift from an old lady. It was her way of thanking me for helping her over the years. My gift. MINE, not yours. You didn't even consult me." And she throws a cup at him that shatters at his feet.

"All right. I'll talk to Barney," he says.

Frosty winds his way out through a familiar tunnel of disoriented darkness where there are no signs of light anywhere. He really has done it this time. Years later, he would attribute the incident to an early attack of dementia, and Adeen would just file it away with all the other amnesiac to-do lists that never got done, forgiven but not forgotten.

ADEEN

I just didn't know what to do anymore.

A week later, Barney again inquired about the antique plate and I pretended ignorance. Don't think he believed me when I told him I was still looking for it and that it was probably stashed in a strong box with our important papers and to please leave me his number so I could call when I found it. You should have seen his face. Full of disgust. People aren't stupid and he's a lawyer so I was really scared he would sue or something, but he didn't. I guess a Copenhagen plate was not high on his money-making list of priorities, and he didn't seem hurt that he lost an heirloom belonging to his grandfather. And where was Frosty through all this? God knows. He liked to avoid problems, so I was always left mopping the shit out of his way. I was getting tired.

Temperatures soared from hell: thirty-seven degrees Celsius; higher if you included the humidex. Against all rules, I opened the sprinklers for the neighbourhood kids to cool down, and even Jack slipped into his bathing trunks and went cavorting in and out of the spray of water.

Anyhow, the week before the barbecue, which was to be held the last Friday of July, I put the Complex Arms *Bulletin* into everyone's mailbox as a reminder. I ignored Frosty, who had fallen into a cloudy day of writing poetry. He sat there, cigarette ashes dripping on the kitchen table like he was Leonard Cohen. A trio of Molsons by his side, a joint or two in the ashtray to summon his muse, and he was set for the evening. He still believed that one day his words would find their rightful place in Nashville's Grand Ole Opry, sung by the likes of Merle Haggard or Dolly Parton. "We'll live off the royalties easy," he said. Nothing was ever easy when it came to Frosty. He never saved a penny in his life. Ask his mom. I no longer believed in his dream and had abandoned mine when Irene was born. Life's roadblocks.

If I had known the consequences of raising Irene alone, how my life would twist and turn with disruptions like a wild thunderstorm, I might have taken another course, perhaps abandoned the baby girl on the Catholic Church's doorstep for the nuns to find. Cliché now, but common then. They, the nuns, always made me feel insignificant and bad. There, I said it. Actually, I can't blame them because I let them make me feel that way. Wish I had been more aggressive when I was a kid. I must have done something wrong in another life that this one was so difficult. The nuns could have had Irene. But that was not what I chose. I kept Irene because I am a kind person, a good person. Ask any of my tenants. I've always been there for them. It's in my blood. I took a test once, and the results showed that I was one of those "feeling" intuitive types who should look at becoming a nun or social worker as a calling. Too late now.

And, the thing is, I love Irene. With all her violent tantrums and pain, she is still a part of me. She is my responsibility. I know I keep contradicting myself. Some days I love her and some days I hate her. I'm trying to work things out. I think it unfair that she has the mental faculties of a two-year-old, but I brought her into this world … I had no options. Yeah, yeah, yeah, I know, I made my bed …

Some days, I'd sit on the front steps of the Complex Arms, pretend I was lying on a bed of clouds in a hammock looking down at the universe, trying to figure things out. I wonder why all kids aren't born healthy and perfect. Don't answer. It's a rhetorical question.

Irene was a beautiful girl and I worried about her every day. I feared she'd come to harm by some insensitive bully, and she wouldn't know what was happening or what to do. Even scream-ing against pain was not in her. Irene thought everything was a game; just laughed and clapped and shook her hands as though she were drying nail polish. She didn't have a clue. Happy, always happy. Well, most of the time. How did she find joy amid all her dark, violent moments? It was the drugs. Yes, the drugs settled her. Maybe I should've taken some of what she was taking.

But I couldn't let my personal problems interfere with the lives of my tenants; although, I was always there to listen and lend a hand if they asked. I'm not a monster. Are we not all part of the human race? Do we all not shit, bleed, and then die? We are all dying every day. We are born to die. Yes. I believe that.

I am a caring person, but some days I'd wonder what would happen to Irene, who would take care of her when Frosty and I were gone? It still weighed heavy on me the day I hit her, but Irene's memory is short. Give her a rattle and all is forgiven, and always that clap clap clap. That applause for being pleased with herself or others. Her way of saying *I love you*. I was sure of that. Maybe I should take a lesson from my daughter. After all, Irene hugged me when we parted at Klondike Days when Mona dropped off me and Derrick. I should really call, I told myself, and see how they are doing. Mona was such a good friend. The best.

Irene was going to be home Friday to enjoy the long weekend and Heritage Days at Hawrelak Park with all its pavilions from various countries — Poland, Ghana, Germany, Japan — serving up their dishes, their cultural dances in their ethnic costumes. It was always hot and spicy that weekend. Something the city looked forward to. Me, I prefer a cold day. Should move to Iceland. Just saying.

I'd usually go with Zita. Girls' day out. Our time to sit and yadder. And I'd always do the barbecue on the Friday before the long weekend. I was hoping Mrs. Lapinberg could join us and bring her knishes, and Rosemary usually had a dip of some kind. Irene always enjoyed these yearly community meals. It'd become tradition now at the Complex Arms. She loved the buckets of ice cream and watermelon that the Ukrainian lady next door would bring from her family's farm in Barrhead. I hoped it was going to be a good day.

Anyhow, that's the story there.

BLACK FRIDAY

T he heat wave persisted all week into Friday. The night before, the hottest, most humid on record, multiple layers of haze — yellow and light tan — brushed the sky. *Going to be a perfect day for an outdoor get-together*, Adeen thought. Even so, the population was advised to stay indoors, close their drapes, keep cool, and be vigilant for folks who could easily succumb to heatstroke. Newspapers reported seniors dying from dehydration. Steam smoked through sewers; hydrants were opened to dampen the streets. For a moment, water conservation was not an issue.

Environment Canada forecasted cooler temperatures moving in, with a heavy thunderstorm heading toward Edmonton. Relief was in sight. But there were warning signs, too. Hints of the consequences sometimes faced by those living in a place where the heat of a burning sun that produced cracked, dry soil where nothing grew could suddenly converge with a cold front, a dangerous combination. The farmers, bless them, ignored the forecasts from the government and still raised their weary heads, scrutinized the formation of storm clouds and lamented the loss of their harvest one way or another.

That Friday morning, the last day of an emotionally turbulent month, the sky, a teal green, no breeze in sight, Frosty is on his way out when words get in the way.

"I need your help here, Frosty," she says.

"Promised to help Velvet for another round of findin' Ryan."

"And what about me? Perhaps he just doesn't want to be found. Ever think of that? It's been almost a month now."

"Adeen, today is the last day, okay. I promise. I just feel sorry for the kid."

She lets him go.

Because of the precarious weather, Adeen announces the barbecue, or block party as she now calls it, will move indoors to the spacious lobby of the Complex Arms. Folks can use the stairs as seating, and she suggests everyone bring their own cushions for added comfort. Adeen opens her apartment for any spillovers of people or food. The tenants busy themselves setting up a beverage table in her kitchen for the beer, soda, water, and various platters of cold cuts, cheeses, baguettes, crackers, and crudités. Mrs. Antoniuk arranges slices of watermelon on a plate and sets it on the coffee table; the freezer is stocked with homemade ice cream. Adeen has extended an invitation to the neighbourhood kids and their parents. There is enough food to outlive Armageddon.

By noon that corner of Mill Woods rocks to the hot tropical sounds from *Billboard*, including Adeen's favourites: Whitney Houston's "I Wanna Dance with Somebody" and "Livin' on a Prayer" by Bon Jovi. Someone has had the foresight to bring a boom box and taped enough music to last the long summer day into night. The music echoes throughout the building, escaping through the open double doors of the entrance and into the countryside, scaring the gophers and magpies.

The storm rolls in around 2:00 p.m., one raindrop at a time, then thicker and thicker, faster and faster, falling in slants; lightning explodes on the horizon over the dilapidated farmhouse. Adeen usually thrills to a light show. This time the flash of light and clap of thunder are so fierce and near that she backs away. The power and phones are already down, so there is no communication to the outside. The block party guests either sit pat or depart to their upstairs apartments and wait. No one is hungry.

Zita, head bent down, tumbles into the lobby and joins the delayed party to report how she had picked up Derrick at the summer day camp, the Green Shack, and driven into the teeth of the wind. Adeen changes the tuner on the battery-powered radio from music to a news station.

"I saw thousands of birds in the sky," Derrick reports.

Adeen wrinkles her brow and Zita leans over and whispers, "The birds were all the cars, trees, and people flying in the air."

Adeen reaches over and suffocates the child with hugs.

At 2:30 p.m. the radio interrupts its usual broadcast with a piercing emergency signal, warning citizens of a tornado watch in effect.

There is a dangerous beauty in how the multiple layers of the fast-moving winds shift the sky from an eerie green with a yellow pulse to, later, a vibrant tangerine — the northern lights unplugged. The tornado touches down south of them, off 23rd Avenue, picking up a large oil container and tossing it into the middle of the avenue. Cars and trucks are upended, pitched like Hot Wheels vehicles in the hands of a child with a temper tantrum. The Complex Arms stands its ground on 34th Street and on the other side closer to the Whitemud Drive. It is safe for now.

Witnesses and the media will later describe the thunderstorm as a wall of black cloud that shape-shifted into a funnel and finally morphed into the green bulk of the tornado, fat with power, a demented furious twist to its face, rising and falling like an out-of-control spinning top, veering toward the outskirts of Mill Woods, past the Complex Arms. All of a sudden, it pivots on its heels, makes a sharp ninety-degree angle, bounces along the railway tracks, and heads north, wiping out several businesses on its route of destruction. It trips across the Sherwood Park Freeway, carries itself through the industrial section, the refineries in Sherwood Park around 3:00 to 3:30 p.m. Buildings are flattened, entire warehouses collapse, and vehicles are ditched helter-skelter. And then the hail begins. Dear God! The twister jumps in the direction of the Evergreen Mobile Home Park and cuts a devastating swath through the community of Clareview on its way to the north side, moving with a raging defiance bordering on insanity.

Disobedient children with umbrellas venture outside in the heavy downpour, gathering hailstones and storing them in their freezers. Chunks collide and grow as they descend and smash through windshields and rooftops. The boom box with its battery-operated radio keeps everyone in tune to the wild storm seething outside the Complex Arms.

Adeen shushes everyone. "Listen, listen," she says.

> *Tossed around like toys ... signs of devastation ... people trapped in collapsed buildings. The tornado claimed most of its victims northeast of Edmonton in the Evergreen Mobile Home Park, with fifteen people killed and almost two hundred homes destroyed or damaged. Flooding on major freeways making it impossible for emergency crews to get through.*

At the mention of the Evergreen Mobile Home Park, Adeen remembers Mona and Irene. Where are they? She tries to phone Mona but the line is dead. The lines are still down. Tenants and neighbours whine and moan, appeal to a higher power to keep them safe. Even the atheists plead for salvation.

"Where's Payton?" a female voice calls out over the crush, now gathered into a crowded corner of fear.

"He went up to his place," Adeen says.

The heavy rain continues its rampage, rattling windows and doors like a ghost determined to enter. If they were going to die, they would all go down together. Adeen suddenly bolts toward the building's entrance. The violent storm is so fierce that a tug of war ensues between her and the wind as she attempts to shut the door. Tenants come to her aid. No sooner have they returned to the lobby when the raging wind retaliates, uprooting a young dogwood and hurling the tree through the just-latched glass door with a thunderous crash.

"That was a close call," someone mumbles. There is another crash, followed by a chorus of wails and Oh Gods.

"Everyone, downstairs into the basement. Quick," Adeen commands like a colonel in the throes of battle against an insane enemy.

The room, dim and dingy, with its wall-to-wall insulation of people, feels like a tomb, smells like a barrel of herring in urine. Some begin to pray; others remain stoic, silent. One mother, a neighbour, shrieks that she panicked when she saw the tornado and threw her five-year-old son into a closet. She heard windows breaking and fled outside into the hailstones. Jack discovered her wandering near the Complex Arms and accompanied her into the basement.

"Reminds me of Holland," a voice stabs into the gloomy room. Only a line of light from the one narrow window filters through.

"I left my son. How could I forget?" The woman heads to the exit calling out the boy's name until Adeen catches up and guides her back into the familiarity of her private hellish hideout.

"If he's in a closet, he's in a safe place," Adeen says.

"But he is only five years old. He'll be traumatized." A mother's guilt. Thinking of herself again, leaving a small child behind.

Adeen notices Mrs. Lapinberg hiding in the room's shadows, grabs her arm and leads her to assemble with the other tenants. "You'll be fine until Barney gets here," she says.

"But how will he find me?" Mrs. Lapinberg is on the verge of tears. "Are we being rounded up for the train?"

"Oh, no, Mrs. Lapinberg, no train. Just want to keep everyone together until the storm passes."

Jack is now comforting Mrs. Lapinberg, and Rosemary is crying out: "We're all going to die."

Adeen can't take it anymore and tells her to shut up. "Here," she says, "take a humour pill and see me in the morning." She hands Rosemary a Smartie.

Nobody laughs. Zita, protective arms around her son, still crushed against his mother's heart. Howard, his father, is unreachable. Everyone accounted for except Velvet and Frosty. The group stays huddled in the basement; the hail seems to smack throughout the four floors of the Complex Arms like a series of grenades exploding.

Payton considers the spectacle before him from his balcony as though he is viewing a movie on IMAX. The rotating column of air suddenly takes an unexpected sharp turn, changes direction, swerves to the northeast, and disappears. The rain and hail seem to have abated, fooling him into a false sense of safety. Then, within seconds, the spinning top reappears carrying the storm. Payton, at this point, is unaware of a pending tornado. He thinks it is a mere thunderstorm, unaware this tempest is likely the closest thing to Armageddon he will ever see.

Johanna, his wife, sits by his side in the sleek wooden box on the patio table. He warned her to be prepared for the imminent gusts, the vulgar green vomit surfacing like an exorcism of evil.

"You should see this, Johanna. But you probably can already. Unbelievable!"

The storm transforms the sky; the noise of thunder almost disappears in the screaming winds of the vortex; hailstones like a thousand projectiles rip shingles from rooftops and ding the hoods of parked cars.

Payton remains rooted on the balcony, enthralled by the drama unfurling before him. He continues to tinkle his little bell, but its tiny note of warning is overwhelmed by the deafening symphony of the elements. He increases the speed of his ringing only to find the storm has snapped off the clapper, leaving the bell silent.

At last Payton understands that the heavens are about to wreak havoc on the land. "Prepare thyselves for salvation. Sinners you are doomed. Armageddon is upon us," he shouts, his voice lost in the turbulence. A capricious gust of wind whips around the balcony. Payton, disoriented, knocks the box from its perch and sends it airborne over the railing. It plunges, smashing to the cement walk below. Johanna melds into a frenzy of sooty dust and debris floating toward the tornado, and he is now wailing, "Johanna! Wait for me." Her ashes blow back at him, sifting through his clothes, into his face, but he keeps sputtering, "Johanna, Johanna!" He reaches out with both arms to catch the flying particles, ignoring the danger of leaning out into the overpowering force swirling around him. He stands on the balcony, arms outstretched into the storm, looking like a prophet in holy ecstasy.

"Johanna! I'm coming." He repeats his mantra like an inconsolable widow whose family has gone missing. As Payton leans over, he loses his footing and, like Johanna's ashes, becomes airborne. There follows the heavy thud to the sidewalk, like a horse tripping in a gopher hole.

Adeen follows the storm through the narrow basement window, held spellbound by its crazy actions. Suddenly, she hears a thump. Pressing her nose against the windowpane for a closer investigation, she recognizes Payton's body; an installment of bones and skin and blood spilling onto the lawn not three feet away from her observation post, his silenced bell by his side. Taken by surprise, Adeen, a human android, detaches herself from the sight of another death. The sole basement fixture flickers; the radio, tuned down to a messy garble of gibberish racked by more static, pierces the air in a duet with the wind outside.

Across Mill Woods on Calgary Trail, Frosty and Velvet are oblivious of the tragedy developing outside. They have abandoned efforts to search for Ryan. A month was enough time to find the man who didn't want to be found, so they have spent the afternoon at Black Jack's, sitting at the bar, sharing warmth along with the whisky. The power goes out momentarily then returns.

Black Jack's is deserted except for the two. Scottie, the barman, compulsively wipes the counter to a polish as there is nothing else to do. The TV screen is tuned to the game show *The Price is Right*. Frosty asks Scottie to lower the volume and change the TV to a sports channel.

The bartender turns the dial to find something more interesting than a game show, but it is daytime, so other than the soaps and talk shows, there aren't many choices.

"Wait, wait, wait," Velvet says. "Stop there."

"Looks like there's a tornado somewhere," Frosty says, "Must be Nebraska. They have lots there. Turn up the sound."

But Scottie continues to rotate the channels with the speed of impatience as the TV screen flickers, showing the occasional image of a funnel cloud, now growing into an all-out tornado. Suddenly, everything goes black again. The freezer and ceiling fan stop humming. A death of silence.

It isn't until Frosty and Velvet leave the premises that they notice the sky is a ceiling of various shades of green and turquoise. They switch on the car radio but no music plays; there are only the frantic reports from across the city of the tornado and its devastation.

"Wow!" Velvet says. "We missed it."

And Frosty laughs. "Must be a joke. Someone doin' a movie here." And then he thinks of Adeen and Irene and Mona and the Evergreen Mobile Home Park and races the car toward Mill Woods like an Indy driver. Just in case it wasn't a movie.

ADEEN

The lights flickered briefly and the power returned an hour later. We all hugged each other as though a touch would confirm we were alive. I went outside to assess the damage to the Complex Arms. The building was mostly okay, but the rest of the neighbourhood was a disaster. Missing shingles and rooftops unhinged, cars on their sides, an upheaval of pavement, trash cans and garbage strewn in the parking stalls in back, trees ripped from their roots, a collage of damage created by an angry tornado, which missed us by a hair; and Payton lying there mangled in rubble like a toppled mannequin in a store window display. I couldn't look death in the eye anymore. I removed my jacket and covered him as best I could, hustled back inside to call emergency, and then tried Mona again. Nothing. A dead line. I called the number for inquiries about family and friends but it was busy.

Everyone returned to their respective apartments carrying their food. Nobody felt like celebrating and nobody had much of an appetite. We watched the news for updates.

One journalist interviewed a woman who lived in the Evergreen Mobile Home Park. I hoped to see Mona and Irene standing amid the group behind her, but there was only a background of noise and destruction: homes flattened like an unstable house of cards. She said her husband looked out the window and said, "Have you ever been in a tornado?" and she replied, "No," and he said, "Well, now you are." And they ran to the bedroom and pulled the mattress on top of them and their two kids and she said she felt the trailer lift as though she were on a flying carpet and then drop back down hard, their home off its foundation. They looked around and everything was levelled; their trailer was the only one in the compound escaping any damage. They were lucky, but years later on one of those Black Friday anniversary dates, reporters would provide an update on the family. The children had nightmares for years after and didn't want to sleep alone, only with their parents' assuring arms around them.

Anyhow, I still couldn't reach Mona or anyone at the number provided for inquiries. I tried not to worry. Mona was smart and resourceful, so I knew she would find a place of safety for both her and Irene. And where was Frosty? If I knew where Velvet was, I would surely find Frosty. But at that point, I had no idea and didn't care.

As it happened, Frosty and Velvet reached the Complex Arms when everything had calmed down. There they stood with Frosty stuttering and muttering, "I'm sorry, sorry, Adeen, I wasn't here for you."

"Hell with you a hundred times over!"

I ignored them, locked the apartment behind me, and just bawled my eyes out. I couldn't help myself. He kept kicking at the door until I got tired of the racket and let him in, fearing some of the tenants might complain to the Swanks. Everyone was on edge, stressed out. I let him in, but I slammed the door in Velvet's face. Who invited you?

I withdrew to the balcony and felt my spirit levitate outside my body as though I were dying. I was on the patio looking down at the damage across the road from the Complex Arms, and Frosty kept saying, "I'm sorry, sorry."

"Sorry doesn't count." I whacked him hard in the face.

The barn and rusted truck in the distance had disappeared, landing in another field or county perhaps; the vegetation hunched over as though in pain from the punch of the hail. The sky in its film of blue seemed to mock me, seemed to say, *What do you mean a tornado passed by?*

I called the inquiry number again and finally got through. They were still conducting their search and rescue.

"I'll be right there," I said, but they ordered me to stay back. There was no point going out there. To see the destruction would be unbearable, they warned me; it looked like a war zone, as though someone had dropped an atomic bomb. Besides, I would only get in their way. They said they would let me know when they found Irene and Mona.

"I'm sorry, Adeen. I'm sorry," Frosty, the asshole, kept mumbling. "Maybe they went for a drive and weren't anywhere near the park when it happened. They'll show up. You'll see."

I kept hitting the idiot; I was getting good at beating him up. Such fury unleashed! *Get the heck out of my way, my life*, each blow seemed to say, and all he could muster was "Adeen, Adeen, I'm sorry." I was tired of sorry. Sorry excuse for a man. He was out there with that bitch and not a thought about me or Irene or Mona.

Frosty had tossed the car keys onto the kitchen table when he returned from his outing with Velvet. I grabbed them and made a dash for the door.

"Where you goin'?" Frosty bleated like a goat.

I silently thanked Shylene for bequeathing me her car, and I flew out of there with Frosty's words tagging behind: "You haven't driven in years."

I was overwhelmed with grief at the thought that I — me, Adeen — was responsible for the loss of my best friend and my daughter. I jumped into the car with Frosty scampering behind. He kept shouting, "I'll come with you," but I just sped away, propelled by the idea that perhaps I'd lost two important people in my life.

Shylene's car was a gem, a Toyota Tercel, only a year old. I drove it with an initial clumsiness until I got the hang of it and was finally buzzing along on the open highway. The summer sun hogged the day; the night snatched its light sometime around 10 p.m. I accelerated and thought about the size of that tornado: almost one mile wide at times, the newspapers would later report. Who could survive its wrath? I had never seen anything like it. The idea that it would take my baby and best friend was unthinkable.

I followed its path toward Sherwood Park and Baseline Road. I saw more of the same destruction: overturned oil tankers, the landscape thick with levelled industrial buildings, silos lying face down. The wind had swept the debris into scattered piles in and around the industrial park; power poles were pitched in midair; there were trees snapped in half, derailed train cars.

I was going ninety miles per hour now.

Evergreen Mobile Home Park, nestled in a beautiful, naturally wooded ravine, was normally a twenty-six-minute ride from the Complex Arms. I made it in ten minutes flat — irrational driving all the way. I ignored the radio announcements' warning of flooding in low-lying areas and underpasses caused by the excessive rainwater. I took the main new multi-lane highway, and as I neared Evergreen, I could see the old scenic road beside it, now overflowing with sludge, water spreading like thick lava. Downed trees and power lines created a barrier to traffic; vehicles partially submerged under the tide floated like recreational boats. I kept to the high ground and wept all the way.

I cry easy, one of my weaknesses, I know, I have to let it all out. Can you imagine how I felt? Yet somewhere in the back of my murmuring heart where my spirit slept, there was a skip in its beat, that maybe it was a good thing. Everything happens for a reason, or as Payton told me after Cody's death, *It is God the Jehovah's will.* I dismissed that notion immediately. What kind of God causes such damage? And how could a mother even consider such evil thoughts, especially for a daughter who needed more love and attention than the average child?

I veered the car past the Market Gardens at 167th Avenue. The sweet breeze from the open window whipped my face as I sped down the road tailgating all the cars in the space between me and the Evergreen Mobile Home Park. I was almost there.

I stopped for water and gas, delaying my entry into the park. I don't know if I did it on purpose because of a fear of what I'd discover. I shielded my eyes using my hands like a visor, the sun a brilliant gold, blinding my view. There was a garden centre behind a small grocery store, but nothing was flourishing there. A dog barked behind the gas station, and a van pulled up to refuel. The air was charged with a hushed reverence, the end of the world as we knew it. Perhaps Payton was right: Armageddon or some semblance of it was closing in.

Irene. I thought maybe she'd be sitting there on Mona's deck licking a soft ice cream cone when I got there; or maybe the emergency crew had discovered them both relaxing on a mound near the marsh having a picnic. Maybe I'd find Mona waving at me and yelling, "Time you got here, Adeen."And Irene. Oh, poor Irene. I was trying to remember the good things.

That day, en route to the Evergreen, I gave the skies a once-over and inhaled deeply as though I was fixing to die. We always remember pain because it leaves scars, and scars can open up at any time. Joy, on the other hand, is a fleeting three-letter word and leaves no scars, so it is easily forgotten. Right there I felt such sadness. The scars exposed themselves. I psyched myself to enter the "war zone."

After I filled the gas tank, I closed my eyes briefly and drove like a car chase into the trailer park, a flat slice of landscape, only to halt at the entry. Stuck in muck, a barrier of felled trees prevented me from moving farther.

I rallied around to the back, got out of the car, and headed toward Mona's trailer. The living dead staggered toward me through great clouds of asbestos and insulation, bleeding, moaning, and screaming in agony. Some just sat there in a catatonic state amid the devastation.

Maybe Mona was there cleaning up the mess like some of the survivors I saw. I reached for anything resembling the life that had been there: a dented saucepan, a blanket, toys, or a teddy bear. Irene had one of those. I dug with my hands alongside the rescuers for signs of life: a family pet, a father, mother, grandparents, and children. Nothing. I skipped over heaps of destroyed mobile homes shredded like matchsticks for kindling, and then I swung in the direction of Mona's trailer, smashed to smithereens. I began to run like I was approaching the finishing line in a marathon, a last-minute push of energy behind my back, and then I stopped, dropped to my knees, kneeled down amid a pile of ripped insulation. "NO!" I cried so loud, but no one took notice. Everyone who survived was now familiar with the noise of grief and ignored me, busy searching for their own.

My voice seemed to carry across the rubble of what was once a thriving community for young families and retired seniors. Only one trailer and a wall of mobile homes bordering the park remained upright. Those lucky residents had escaped. I stood up and began a systematic hunt for anything I might recognize. "Irene! Mona!" I kept calling out. I pulled up a blow-dryer, hairbrush, and Irene's teddy bear blanket from under a pile of siding. In the adjacent yard I came across a ripped chair with stuffing poking out of the faux leather; it was from Mona's salon. She and Irene had to be nearby.

The rescuers dragged out the injured from under the rubble of mattresses and broken furniture. None of the mobile homes had basements. The only place with one was the rental office, which was connected to the residence of the park manager and to the community hall. When we boarded with Mona on our arrival to Edmonton, we often took Irene to the hall for various child-centred activities. We would leave her there while Mona and I went shopping, knowing she was safe. She adored Mr. Pumpkinhead, the kids' nickname for the park manager, and his wife, Mrs. Pumpkinhead, who was the children's supervisor. Irene was in good hands. A childless couple, the Pumpkinheads had a knack for handling youngsters of all ages and temperaments. I never knew their real names.

I sprinted toward the community hall, still standing, having survived the effects of the tornado. I tumbled inside and Irene was sitting on a bench, Mr. and Mrs. Pumpkinhead on either side of her like bookends. All the other children had been picked up. My arms reached over with hugs and kisses, but she remained stone-faced with a queer look of puzzlement until I showed her the teddy bear blanket. Her eyes grew wide and brightened as she snatched it from me and smothered it against her face.

I beamed, tears streaming down my face. That look of recognition returned, her arms aflutter. "EEEeeeeeee. Momma!"

"Yes, Irene," I said, "Moma."

Did she mean Mona? I asked Mr. Pumpkinhead about Mona. Evergreen, with a population a little over a thousand, was a friendly community where just about everyone knew just about everyone else. However, he didn't know her whereabouts; only that she was to pick up Irene at the end of the day. "I suspect she went home," said Mrs. Pumpkinhead. But her home had disappeared off the face of the world as though by magic. They convinced me to leave as there was not much I could do but get in everyone's way. I left with Irene and hope.

The emergency crews were still sifting through the ruins for signs of the living as we headed for the car. Irene played with her blanket, distracted from the chaotic mess around her. I had forgotten to eat and felt a sudden light-headedness, so I rested for a minute and talked to a couple of volunteers who were taking a breather. I inquired again about Mona but they suggested that, one way or another, someone would call me if she was found and that I best just go on home and wait for that call. I obeyed.

With their reassurance, Irene and I traipsed back to the car keeping our heads down. Water surged up to our knees in places; the landscape was overrun with photos, paper money, garbage, sewage, furniture, and torn clothing. I prayed we wouldn't step on a submerged body. All around me, people, digging, crawling from under flattened roofs or missing siding. A young woman, cuts to her face, was stationed at the park's back entrance, her long arms stretched around her four babies. She was in shock — I could see that because I asked her if she needed any assistance and she just stared past me like she was in another galaxy. An Edmonton Transit bus pulled up in front of us. They were taking the injured to Alberta Hospital and the driver asked if we needed a lift. I told them we were okay but to take the young woman with her children. Perhaps Mona was at the hospital. Returning from Evergreen, out of habit, I ended up taking the old scenic road, forgetting that most of the low roads were now flooded, and I had to turn around to get back onto the main highway and home.

As we drove back from that scene of destruction and suffering, I thought back to how it used to be. When Irene and I moved out here, Mona and I would sometimes go sit and picnic at this special place in the ravine near a creek. Being a city girl, I always felt anything with a small amount of water was either a puddle or a spill needing a mopping. Irene tagged along, and we would relax on a log while Irene pulled up dandelions and other prairie weeds and presented a bouquet to me and one for Mona, her "auntie." Mona, with the patience of a saint, showed her how to make a crown of dandelions. She'd place it on Irene's head and, well, we'd be entertained by Irene's usual happy dance, all that clapping and bouncing up and down, pirouetting like a circus dog. Somehow it conveyed a simple contagious joy that was unfortunately lost in a world of too much suffering.

The Evergreen community was built in 1982; Irene was five then, and Mona was one of their first occupants. Everything was on the verge of polish, a newness you could feel in the shine of new windows and neat rows of planted gardens, shrubs and flowers framing yards and patios. Now, everything gone.

Three days later, a police officer called to say they unearthed a body with a description "similar to your friend, Mona."

"Irene," I said, "they found Mona. They found Mona." I had to repeat the news as though saying the words out loud would make her appear right there. Irene just applauded as she always did whenever she heard Mona's name. "Momma, Momma," she said.

"Where is she? Where is she? I'll come and get her," I told the guy. And then he soberly gave me the address to the medical examiner's office and told me to go and identify her. I dropped the receiver, letting the cord dangle like a noose. Wailed like a banshee and Irene still doing her happy dance. Clap clap clap. I wanted to hit her. Told you not to judge me!

Not a happy moment. Frosty picked up the receiver and said, "Hey, you, who's this? Who am I talkin' to?" And when the voice on the other end finished, Frosty hung up and turned to me and just said, "I'm sorry, Adeen."

They recovered Mona's body under the wreckage of her neighbour's trailer, which landed atop her own damaged home.

I couldn't stop crying. I became a fountain of tears. I wept until there was nothing left inside me, a hollow shell. Life didn't seem worth living anymore. Oh, you can't see my tears anymore because they are hidden inside my heart, scar tissue. She was my only family. Always there for me and now I felt so alone. And what's left is still the anger. I don't know why. S'cuse me while I get a tissue.

Anyhow, that's the story there.

JULY 2007

HOME IS LIVING IN A TRAILER PARK

At a time when most women her age were settled in adult condos somewhere in Canmore with the Three Sisters Mountains as backdrop, Adeen never thought that she would instead be living in a glove compartment, as she called the six-hundred-square-foot mobile home, set in the Arboreau Trailer Park on the outskirts of Hinton. Her life, at fifty, had come full circle. This circumstance brought to mind Mona and the tragedy at the Evergreen Mobile Home Park. She hesitated to live in a flimsy fabricated building without a basement.

"It won't happen again. That was a fluke of nature," Frosty convinced her. "What are the chances?"

Frosty and Adeen settled in and continued their emotional roller-coaster ride as one year sprung into the next. "I won't be around much longer," he'd say after another explosion of words. Such outbursts were typically followed by days of noncommunication until one or the other eventually decided to break the intolerable chill. Over the last twenty years the relationship had vacillated between volatile words and stony silence. It was not unusual for them to renew the armistice until the next altercation. They became indifferent to lapses in conversation that bordered on rebellious inertia. A couple in a room, yet separate; two strangers passing through.

The cowboy poet had traded writing poetry for driving a truck, transporting horses, food, furniture, and electronics to various parts of northern Alberta. "It's a job," Frosty would say, "so don't complain." She didn't. He was now contributing to the household expenses, and those distant delivery days when he was on the road were a respite for Adeen from their stormy marriage.

Their mobile home, an older model with a carport, was far removed from prying eyes, sheltered in a woodsy area so Adeen could sporadically neglect its upkeep; however, what little self-pride remained ensured that at least the front yard and deck, with its floral containers and window boxes on view, were kept tidy. Appearances were essential.

"If you're going to smoke, you can at least pick up the butts. This isn't the city dump, you know," she would scold Frosty.

He feigned deafness, or a purposeful absent-mindedness that he'd acquired over the years as a coping mechanism for Adeen's constant nagging.

The previous summer she counted two hundred cigarette stubs scattered in various planters, window boxes, the in-between spaces of the deck floor, and the front yard. When they first moved into the Arboreau Park, she put down her foot and forbade smoking inside their home, so Frosty spent winters and spring by a portable heater, ensconced in blankets on a patio chair, puffing away, contemplating, his chest a pillow for his chin.

Adeen had quit smoking after witnessing the devastation at the Evergreen Mobile Home Park. The fetor of decay had saturated her lungs, and nicotine now made her ill. She increased her consumption of beer and hid the tower of empties in a crate behind the compost bin concealed by the dogwood. Petty cash, she called it. Payton would have praised her resourcefulness. She thought of him whenever she piled the empty beer bottles. The isolation of life in a rural community and Frosty's chilly behaviour reduced her to introversion and self-conversation. All traces of the city girl were erased now except for her name.

Adeen was free from the usual physical ailments afflicting premenopausal women who've spent a lifetime working with their hands in fast food joints, packing boxes in clothing warehouses, watering plants in gardening centres, cleaning other people's houses or apartments, including the Complex Arms. Her doctor pronounced her a healthy specimen for a woman her age and disposition. No arthritis to speak of, except for a recent tricky injury; a slide down a slippery embankment on wet grass after a rainfall — she tumbled to the bottom and shattered a shinbone, which never healed properly. She now walked with a slight, albeit noticeable, limp, especially when tired. Otherwise, Adeen was still quite fit — a bit more full-bodied, perhaps — but she definitely didn't have the kind of body to appear on the cover of magazines such as *Zoomer*, which celebrated "women of a certain age."

Over the years, Adeen had gradually become slovenly in her grooming. She now sometimes forgot to shower, or perhaps just didn't care, forgot to brush her teeth, and wore the same T-shirt and shorts for days at a time until permanent stains marked her meagre wardrobe. It saved on laundry work, she would say, should Frosty comment. Her only exception was when appearing in public.

Alberta summers with their intense heat and dry patches mirrored each other from one year to the next. She squandered her days napping or chewing miniature ice cubes, an acquired nervous habit, until her teeth cracked from the cold tension.

Adeen never expected to reach fifty, a milestone in her eyes. Too many of her friends and former tenants had already succumbed to the pale reaper from drugs, heart attacks, suicide, and cancer. She was almost certain Alberta's ecosystem, with all its airborne fossil fuels, bred cancerous cells in the body and mind.

For a time, after the tornado, she kept in touch with some of the ones who had vacated the Complex Arms — Zita and Derrick, Rosemary, and Mrs. Lapinberg — and several Evergreen residents who were Mona's neighbours and clients. Very often it was just a phone call to say hello. But once she herself moved away, they were eliminated from her memory bank. Payton, Wayne and Cody, Shylene — gone. The endurance of continuously living in the face of a magnitude of life's challenges was too difficult for some of them. For others, like Rosemary and Mrs. Lapinberg, old age dealt the final knockout punch. And always, Mona was on her mind.

On those sleepless nights, and there were many, she would softly hum John Lennon's lyrics from "In My Life," and remember all the places and people who had touched her, both dead and the few still living; how they impacted her, reduced her to what she had become. She would hum until she fell asleep or Frosty, in one of his moods, would yell at her to shut up. He was trying to sleep and just needed quiet.

Velvet returned to the Soo hoping to hear from her absent boyfriend, only to find her whimsical life had become a futile chase after something that never existed in the first place except in her imagination. Frosty was transparent about their relationship. Or so I thought.

"Nothin' happened," he kept insisting once they set up house at the Arboreau Park. "She had a schoolgirl crush on me is all. Forget it, Adeen. Let's just move on."

And to prove his loyalty, he shared Velvet's postcards from the Soo, along with the photos, in compromising positions. The girl now made her living pole dancing around the "hot spots" of northern Ontario — Thunder Bay, Sudbury, North Bay, Timmins, Elliot

Lake — numbing her life against the fierce light of day with what-ever drug was available to get her through the night. Adeen wit-nessed Frosty tossing everything into the shredder after sharing it and he never mentioned Velvet again. He pitched everything except for one black-and-white photo. This one he held hidden in an enve-lope taped behind the bottom, rarely-used dresser drawer. There was Velvet, naked as a newborn, on her back, legs splayed, enticing arms reaching out, inviting the onlooker to come and consume her.

Mrs. Lapinberg's son, Barney, rescued his mother from the Complex Arms the morning after the tornado had done its dam-age. He set her up in a plush Jewish seniors residence somewhere in Sherwood Park.

And Zita, poor Zita, she relocated with her husband, Howard, to Houston, Texas, to follow his engineering career with a large oil company. They lost touch and Adeen wondered if she ever roared against the shackles of a loveless marriage. Zita told her once that she was getting tired of her nomadic existence and longed for a solid, secure commitment. If anyone asked her if she was happy, Zita would lie and say, "Yes, of course." Derrick cried when he bid Irene a final farewell, and Irene, poised like a statue, fixed her attention somewhere in space, an existential moment watching Zita's car disappear around the corner from the Complex Arms. Years later Adeen heard from Jack that Zita had borne a daughter.

As for Jan, in 1988 her husband stood trial for manslaugh-ter in a case of domestic violence. Jan's best friend, Norma, was a character witness for the defence. Norma's husband threatened to toss her over the balcony in the same manner if she took sides against his best friend. So Norma lied and painted Jan's husband as a perfect specimen of manhood who loved his family and would never harm his wife or baby daughter in any way. It was an unfor-tunate accident, his lawyer pleaded. Because of Norma's testimony, her lie, the jury declared Jan's husband innocent and he was set free. Norma fell into a deep depression of guilt that stayed with her until one day she went missing and a motorist discovered her body in a ditch near Beaumont, a community south of Edmonton. The consensus was that she had left home, probably hitchhiking, and had accepted a ride, only to find herself in the clutches of a rapist and killer. The suspect was never apprehended and Norma's husband remarried after a reasonable period of mourning. People's lives, Adeen would shake her head in disbelief.

Jack remained at the Complex Arms.

"Where would I go?" he said. "This is home."

He felt a familiar comfort in his compact one-bedroom apartment, convenient to everything, and continued to depict his world on the blank Masonite boards sprawled around the living room floor. He no longer painted dead flowers. Eventually, he connected with a dealer at the Wild Rose Art House, a cozy gallery off Whyte Avenue, where Jack surprisingly sold all his paintings that captured Black Friday in all its force and fury, as well as the anger he felt living a lie, a woman in a man's body, and the turbulent lives of the tenants in the Complex Arms. He and Adeen kept in touch by phone for a number of years, Jack supplying the latest gossip about the new building manager and residents of the Complex Arms. She often attended his exhibitions and purchased paintings of Irene and Mona to support his talent. And then she never heard from him again.

Those days when Frosty brought her down, she would go hiking in the foothills of the Rockies, outside Hinton, and scream at the range of mountains, "He's destroying me."

This persistent pattern eventually rendered Adeen a semi-recluse. She hid herself in the vale of trailer parks, surrounded by snow-capped ridges far off in the distance, and trees that camouflaged her misery. She would ask Miss Pauline, her neighbour and Arboreau's resident manager, to babysit Irene while she drove to Hinton, parked the car, and hiked alone into the nearby woods, toting a couple of beers. She would sit on her familiar boulder in a clearing not far from the road and meditate on the flawless sky, the valley below with its vegetation and streams.

In these reflective moods, Adeen often wondered how many more years remained before she expired. She was prone to self-analysis. Why should she be the one to take care of everyone? She always prided herself on never being sick. Her only hospital stay, the birth of Irene, had drained her of all vitality, both physically and mentally.

"The baby takes everything it needs from its mother before birth," her obstetrician had warned. She understood now.

Irene's birth was as vivid as though it were yesterday; she wondered what her life would have been if she could delete that one night of reckless abandon in her boyfriend's bedroom while his parents were away for the weekend.

"Man, you're hot," he teased his lips against hers, pushing his body toward her warmth until she yielded. She was seventeen and still untouched. He would be leaving shortly for Carleton University in Ottawa and then a career in journalism.

"It's not like I don't love you, Adeen," he said. "Do you love me?"

"Yes," she demurred as he pulled up her skirt.

"You made your bed, now you can lie in it," her mother's words always a haunting beam away from reality.

"Shut up, shut up."

This weekly hike always invigorated her and sparked a temporary rejuvenation of energy and creativity until the darkness would once again overtake her.

ADEEN

wenty years later, I still live here because I have no other home. And there are the memories of Irene and Mona and Frosty. I sometimes feel like an unwanted orphan; I still don't know where I belong. Other times I feel like a tourist. I'm really trying. Here's the thing: I just don't think like a prairie girl. Never have. And yet, I no longer feel like a Montreal girl. I've lost a lot of my French. *Je me souviens? Non.* Miss Pauline told me once cities, like people, can grow on you. After living through that horror, I don't want this city to grow on me.

End of this month Edmonton will memorialize the twentieth anniversary of when the tornado hit. The days leading to the event are always the most difficult, so why do we need to capture that loss every year and endure more torture? How can anyone forget? The media named it Black Friday. Final count according to Environment Canada: 27 dead, 600 injured, 1,700 evacuees, and 750 families left homeless. "One of the worst natural disasters in Canadian history," said the commentator.

The mayor at that time, Laurence Decore, coined the phrase *City of Champions* for Edmonton's response to the tornado on

July 31, 1987. It also became the city's official slogan on its Welcome to Edmonton signs at the entry points, but then, as time elapsed — and I suppose that is why we need to recognize that day — the motto evolved to include sporting events, winning Oilers games. The *City of Champions* was now about Wayne Gretzky and the Edmonton hockey team, the Edmonton Eskimos football team, and the famous Edmonton Grads — the champion women's basketball team. It's pathetic how everything eventually gets sanitized, commercialized. I suppose it is a marketing ploy to attract tourists: a sports event versus a tornado. Which one would bring you here?

Twenty years later and, for me, it's as fresh as the day it happened. *Global News*, as they do every year, will broadcast a half-hour special report paying tribute to the victims. Don't know if I'll be watching. Will I be allowed to watch the ceremony on TV, sir, if I can't attend? I have to water the trees, you know.

Anyhow, I don't need a reminder on my calendar; it's here in my heart and it's enough to wear the scars. Not a day goes by that I don't think about Black Friday, about Mona. Those images never leave me. On those hot summer days, like today, I was always out there looking up for the next one. Have you looked up lately? Sky okay? Never mind. Don't answer. And every year I visited the Evergreen Mobile Home Park where twenty-seven trees were planted in a memorial garden for the people who died. I'd take special trips out there and make sure all the trees were watered, stayed fresh and healthy so they didn't die.

And on every anniversary, newspapers insisted on interviewing survivors, publishing their stories and photos on the front page. Now, with the internet and social media, the news feeds have become agony, almost on par with a root canal.

I recently heard on the radio one Evergreen resident telling a reporter how she watched the funnel cloud approach her trailer, not realizing the threat to her family. It blew the roof off a house down the street from her, and suddenly she understood the gravity of the danger and ducked outside, gathering her children's toys and carrying them to a back shed just in time. What was she thinking of? I mean, come on, lady!

Anyhow, as she was closing the shed, the wind peeled off its roof and sent it skittering across the ground. She fought to get back inside when an addition to the building collapsed as someone's airborne mobile home landed on top of it. With the house bouncing up and down, she and her four kids hid under a doorway off the master bedroom. I can't imagine. Four years later the woman was diagnosed with post-traumatic stress disorder and began treatment. Stories like that are repeated to this day. I wish they would just stop it. You never forget. Let it go.

I sometimes wondered if I carry the same disorder. PTSD. Perhaps I should have immediately seen a therapist to unload all my emotional baggage, you know, going all the way back to my crazy mother, and Irene's birth, and Frosty's indiscretions and addictions, and then the tornado. But I've always been strong, stubborn; could take care of myself, thank you. The idea of talking to a stranger about my feelings didn't appeal to me. I always had Mona but now ... maybe ... I should have talked to a professional. Instead, I would go to the library and read these self-help books about depression and PTSD, and once I understood what happened to me — perhaps I was going crazy. Well, at least I was aware and could pull back on my bad days. I just kept fighting back, trying to get rid of the anger. I read somewhere that the anger always remains and is the last to leave, like grieving a death. Why Mona and not me? Why not Irene, even? Those questions continue to haunt me. Told you not to judge me or I'll stop right here. Again, it was only a fleeting rhetorical question, anyhow.

For a time I dug into various philosophies, religions, trying to understand the storm inside my head. I folded more and more into myself and became a shut-in for a spell. Doc gave me some antidepressants to take for three months; see how that worked for me. It did help, but I was concerned about side effects and stopped taking them after a month. I was sleeping my life into oblivion. The irony is that I kept pumping Irene with meds for her unpredictable behaviour, justifying her need as being a real health issue. Mine was fleeting.

We all have ways of dealing with traumatic events. Some will take the approach, here's a tragedy and there's a reason why some families survived the tornado, so we need to go on and be united and look at the bright side. The opposing thought is that this tragedy hit our community and so many people lost their lives, so how can we possibly recover? Everyone takes opposing views, especially when it affects their relationships or their own situation. It's difficult to move forward when you focus on what could have happened, rather than on what actually did happen. Heard a lot of couples filed for divorce a year later. Each in their world of denial and blame, I guess. Others remained united, steadfast. Must be something in their genetic makeup. Or they really loved one another and took their vows seriously. Until death do us part, as they say.

Frosty and I remained together. He was good to me for a while, sympathetic, bending over backwards to console me after I found out about Mona. Whenever I went off the deep end, he would submerge himself in his cowboy poetry and let me be. Patient guy. One of his qualities, I guess. Nonetheless, our marriage was still rocky. I couldn't trust him, but what choice did I have?

To this day, I still examine the skies and wait for the next tornado. I often thought about going back to Montreal alone, escaping. My mother was dead and there was nothing there for me anymore, as I told Zita. Keep moving forward, I kept telling myself.

I forgot to eat, sleep, and shower; just stayed in bed for months at a time after Mona's funeral. I didn't care about anything or anyone. Life seemed such a chore. Frosty took care of Irene and the Complex Arms. He just kept feeding her the drugs the doc prescribed. They would relax her, make her sleepy, and she wasn't a problem. Slept with that teddy bear blanket I found amid the wreckage of mobile homes. How can a sleeping beauty be a problem? She seemed to have forgotten about Mona, Mr. Pumpkinhead, and the Evergreen, but she wouldn't part with that blanket.

A year after the tornado I reconsidered placing Irene in the Michener. There have been changes at the facility, and Frosty suggested we give it another try for a month, at least. Irene would be with other kids like her and she would not be our burden anymore. I almost gave in to the idea this time because I just didn't care anymore. But we moved on, and things changed. Irene and I had come so far. Frosty and I got older and she grew up. Turned thirty! Hard to believe. When she had her birthday, I thought that perhaps I should give more thought to her future when Frosty and I die. I kept mulling over the idea. But there was still time. No?

I don't remember when I last felt joy. I've become one of those menopausal women going through a midlife crisis, carrying a lifetime of anger in my pocket, ready to explode. No, I guess I couldn't do that. I've lost my fighting spirit. Some days the fatigue and isolation overwhelm me. Some days I just want to run and keep running until I stop breathing. When sleepless nights exhaust me, I count the cracks in the ceiling above my bed and rewrite my life. Something to do. A comfort. Do you understand?

People's lives are so sad, and they make the lives of others around them even sadder. I am still filled with rage. I am depressed. I know it's not healthy. Frosty and Irene are still a burden. It's gotten worse, not better. They have stripped happy out of me. Again, don't judge me. It's the way I feel. I just want everyone to find some empathy for me. That's it. Empathy would solve some of the world's problems. We can't change people. Take care of yourselves, I say, then the world will take care of itself. People's lives. They come and go. Touch us, good or bad. Take what they need and leave. I've become cynical in my senior years. I know I'm jabbering but I need to hear my words out loud.

For the longest time I had no inclination to go back to Mill Woods, see if the Complex Arms was still there. I had blotted out that part of my life as though it had never existed. And then three years ago, must have been the summer of 2004 because I was at Evergreen for the memorial, watering the trees, I made a visit. I couldn't tell you what compelled me, but as I was leaving Evergreen, my car took a sharp turn toward Edmonton and then Mill Woods. I guess it was curiosity urging me to confront my past, or maybe I just wanted to see if Jack still lived there. Find out what happened to him.

I couldn't find the Complex Arms. Circled the area several times and then I realized I passed by it twice. Didn't recognize it. Two new add-on apartment buildings attached to the original. New aluminum siding replaced the wooden, and the sign in front now read "Birchwood Estates. No Vacancy." I walked around to the parking stalls in back. Trees framed the perimeter. The original birch, now the height of the four-storey walk-up, showed wear and tear, stooped over in old age, like me. Pests had stripped the top branches, which pointed to heaven like arrows. The tree was dying.

I checked out the front of the building, flattened my face against the familiar glassed door, shading my eyes against the reflection of light. Then I walked in and buzzed Jack's bell and waited. A loud woman's voice on the intercom barked, "YEAH?"

"Is. Does Jack live here?" My timidity barely escaped my mouth.

"No Jack here." And the intercom went dead.

I felt a tap on my shoulder. "May I help you, ma'am?"

Turns out he was the resident manager. Told him I used to be in his shoes twenty years before and that I was looking for a tenant who used to live there when it was the Complex Arms.

"That's a long time ago," he said. He was hired by the new property management group who bought the building in the mid-nineties, made renovations, added the adjacent buildings to the compound and upgraded the landscaping.

"Rents went up, so Jack might have moved out," he said.

Disheartened, I left with an invitation to return any time and maybe we could have coffee or something. I kept walking; didn't want to complicate my life further. He reminded me of an aging circus clown or carnival barker who had spent too many years working and sleeping in the sun. Perhaps we passed each other at the fairgrounds during Klondike Days at some point. Now he seemed just another lonely persona, another broken spirit, someone to avoid.

"You know where to find me," I heard him shout as he waved. "What's your name again?"

I turned the ignition, rounded the corner, and said goodbye to my past. I got lost trying to find my way out of Mill Woods. The farmers' fields and wildlife were all gone now. Just a spread of new housing called the Meadows and more neighbourhoods along the way. The Pits had been levelled to make room for an extension to the circle road, called the Anthony Henday, to ease the traffic as Edmonton's population continued to increase. I realize the danger of attachment to things, people, and places because everything changes eventually. I knew I would never return.

Anyhow, that's the story there.

THE MONARCH

On hot breathless days like today, when Adeen needs to escape everything that is Frosty and Irene, she drives to the mountains and hikes alone to restore her sanity. So many trails to explore near Hinton: Athabasca Ranch Trails, Beaver Boardwalk, Bighorn Trail, Emerson Lakes. Today she treks the Bighorn Trail, which runs through to the foothills of the Rockies. Didn't need to walk too far; just enough to experience some space and communicate with nature, and then she could go home and face her world. Lost in the stillness of the woods, the distant mountains for a backdrop, she spreads an old blanket on the earth's flooring to create a bed among the cluster of tall reed grasses, a semi-private nest of her own. She meditates.

Adeen can hear echoes of Mona's voice and wicked laugh from whenever her friend cut a client's hair. "I decided to grow mine long and let the premature grey show through. What do you think?" Mona was ballsy and dared anyone to criticize her sense of style.

Adeen tries to remember instead those childhood years of happy, warm days growing up in Montreal; how she and Mona bonded against a life of poverty, played in cat-stained sandboxes until the park closed down for the day. Mona would challenge her to hang upside down on the monkey bars and view the world from the perspective of a trapeze artist, but she would experience vertigo and fall into the sand below. They would end up in hysterics, on the verge of peeing, but Adeen would pull back, trying to resume some sense of decorum in her seven-year-old self.

"Stop it, Mona, I have to piss," she would giggle, but Mona loved to take risks, jump off roofs from low-lying sheds in the laneway, run past the wicked witch's house, old Mrs. Mombi, with her stringy carrot-coloured hair, toothless grin, and black clothing that she wore as though every day were Halloween. The girls dubbed her after the Wicked Witch of the West from *The Wizard of Oz*, their favourite story. Mona would toss bits of grit at Mrs. Mombi's bedroom window, which overlooked the alley, and dart to the main street as fast as her cheap shoes would allow. Adeen always lagged behind and Mrs. Mombi would howl at her like a wolf, threatening to call the police or tell her mother. "I know where you live," she would intimidate. They were like sisters, Mona and Adeen, and twenty years after her death, Adeen still senses Mona's presence every day.

Adeen would always tie herself into a knot whenever it came to men, food, or career opportunities. She realized now that her penchant for self-destruction was her way to seek attention, as though she didn't deserve anything good. Mona, on the other hand, was smart and full of steam: confident, precocious. After her first failed marriage, she vowed never to marry again, adding that if she did, it would be for money so she could purchase beauty salons across Canada and create a franchise, be the next Vidal Sassoon and get Adeen a house because she never lived in one and she should have that experience. Neither had a desire to move back to Montreal. There was nothing left for them there but referendums on whether to separate Quebec from the rest of Canada, and that was a political tension neither wanted to submit herself to. Their lives, especially Adeen's with Irene, were stressful enough. No turning back.

ADEEN

Most grateful to the childless Miss Pauline, my neighbour from Vulcan, who at seventy, still spry and ballsy, had a real affection for Irene. I thought that the feeling was mutual. Irene seemed to relish her moments with Miss Pauline. She seemed to have no memory of the Complex Arms or the day of her rescue at the Evergreen Mobile Home Park. Perhaps that's the solution to a happy life. Rewire the brain to that of an amnesiac; live only in the moment, obliterate the past. There must be a pill for that.

It was lovely to see Irene happy, skipping after butterflies and moths in the playground across the road from our mobile home. She only showed her dark, violent side when she was alone with me or off her meds. Who could believe that Irene was anything but an affectionate daughter? I would fuss over her long blond hair, still braiding it even though she was now thirty, and then unravelling the weave so the strands fell in tight waves down her back. From afar, she was a lovely young woman, and several men flirted with her until they came within hugging distance and realized there was something wrong with her.

I will always remember the first week we moved to the Arboreau. This incident really left me reeling. Irene and I were sitting out front on the seat swing enjoying the summer breeze when a stranger stopped to say hello and Irene smiled back at him. I thought, *What a friendly place.*

"Pretty thing you got there," he said pointing at Irene. "Can she talk or does she just make noise?"

Irene's smile shifted into a frown as though she understood what the old guy was saying. I guess it was his voice that annoyed her.

"How much to take her off your hands?" he said. "I'm a widower and could use some help, take care of me, clean house."

"S'cuse me," I said. "You an idiot or something? Get out of here." And I came at him, reached down for some gravel, and threw a handful into his ugly face. You should have seen him skedaddle down the road and Irene doing her happy dance. Miss Pauline had just come to sit on her deck to see what the fuss was.

"What's old Braggs up to?"

"He's a lecherous old man," I said. "He wanted to buy Irene. What's the matter with people! This is the twenty-first century last time I looked."

"Oh, don't mind him," Miss Pauline said. "Harmless codger. Dumber than a doorknob. I think you scared him, though." She laughed.

When Irene showed her dark side, I would shove her medication down her throat as usual and she would gag, try to spit out the pills — they *were* big, almost like they were meant for thoroughbreds. The struggle would continue until I threw her into the closet screaming, whimpering, and Frosty would stand there and I would shout, "Do something, Frosty. Help me!" Frosty would make some effort but then always gave up, huffed out of there to the pub, his answer to everything. Then after a spell, I would feel remorse, open the closet door, hug my daughter, and sing "Goodnight, Irene," and Irene would just grin back at me with puzzled eyes like she didn't remember who I was. Nothing had changed. Told you not to judge me. I'm not a monster.

That's how it was the last twenty years after the tornado hit, after the loss of so many of my friends. And now another commemoration at the end of the month will open up all those scars, release the pain again. I've tried to move on, but they, the people in my head, won't let me.

And there are the butterflies.

Mona always had a fondness for butterflies and moths and wouldn't kill an ant or fly even if you paid her a million dollars, so every butterfly that landed in my flowers I thought it was Mona reincarnate. That must be why Irene liked to chase them. Bet she knew it was Mona flitting around like that.

We had formed a pact as children that whoever died first would have to send down a sign from above to verify that heaven existed. I know you won't believe this, but it rained the day of the memorial service for Mona. As I was leaving the church, for a brief moment, the sun showed itself. I closed my eyes for a second, felt the radiant warmth on my face, and when I opened my eyes, it was raining again. Just like that. So sudden. I took it as a sign from Mona that there indeed was a heaven so I best behave. A monarch butterfly had attached itself to the screen of the low-lying basement window. I walked toward it, extended my arm, and the butterfly perched on my index finger as though it were the most natural thing to do. It sat there for a bit before fluttering away. The odd thing is that it stopped raining, just like that, and the sun beamed down on us all day. Mona.

"That's crazy," Frosty said when I told him about the *miracle*. He didn't believe me and suggested I see a therapist.

I still couldn't delete Mona's name from my old-fashioned address book, and while everyone was embracing new things called the internet and BlackBerry, I remained fossilized in the world of July 1987. Mona. Lying on a slab of marble in the morgue. I could barely identify the remains; wasn't sure if it was even her. Every bone shattered beyond recognition, but she wore this distinguishing mark around her ankle — a lovely tattoo of a monarch butterfly. Still intact. She was a great fan of the monarch, with its two pairs of brilliant orange-red wings, black veins, and white spots along the edges. Unique, just like her. I later found out the adult butterfly lives for a maximum of four or six weeks. Why do beautiful things have a short life span?

Anyhow, I told her she was nuts to go put needles into her skin, but she thought the tattoo was an art form, the skin its canvas, a thing of beauty. At that time, not too many women were into decorating their bodies with symbols unless they were in motorcycle gangs, and now it's the hot trend. I persisted in blaming myself. If I had not left Irene with her; if they had been with me at the Complex Arms for the barbecue ... If. If. If.

Mona, bless her, left me a small inheritance, enough for a down payment on a house with the stipulation it be in my name. We couldn't afford a mortgage, but there was enough to purchase a mobile home and live rent-free until death do us part. The trailer fit into Frosty's *lafstyle*, as he kept reminding me again and again. But it still wasn't mine. He was ecstatic and I just went along because what choice did I have? We had to live somewhere.

It was my money, and I understood now why his grandmother listed me in her will instead of Frosty. She knew he would fritter away our lives with his gambling addiction. He would go into our joint account and make small withdrawals until, over the years, it was all gone. Whatever Shylene had left us, gone, lost at the casinos, trips to Vegas, Northlands Raceway, lotto tickets, smokes, weed, alcohol, and whatever schemes his friend Burp had up his sleeve playing the stock market. Frosty was such a sucker for any get-rich scheme, and I was the Bank of Adeen. Should have seen that when I first met him at the food court and he said he had forgotten his wallet. Never paid me back and all was forgotten when we married. To keep the peace, I always stayed quiet, said nothing. I was too tired to fight except when it came to the women, and oh yeah, the final blow when he took Mrs. Lapinberg's heirloom plate to buy the home lottery tickets. As I reached my midlife crisis, I ignored even his flirtations. Take him, I wanted to tell those oversexed broads. Plus the bills were getting paid, not knowing he was borrowing money to cover our monthly bills from the Bank of Burp. The wife is always the last to know, so they say. I wondered if he ever took the time from writing his pathetic poems to calculate the money we could have saved. We would be millionaires by now. This time would be different. I couldn't let Mona down. She brought me here for a better life, a house as we had planned, and here she was giving me the chance to make things right.

"You're my wife," Frosty said. "What's yours is mine."

I didn't like his raising his voice at me; it always put me in mind of my mother and her confrontational nature. This time I opened my mouth. "Heck with you," I said.

His calloused hand grazed my cheek in a slap. Irene was watching and began to lash out at her own face.

"Now see what you've done."

I attacked Frosty with my arms, scratching his face, and rushed over to Irene to stop the self-slapping. Frosty in his usual petulant, pathetic manner sulked out of the apartment only to return with an apology. Same routine. Some things just never change. I was done.

The next day when I received the inheritance cheque, we drove by the *dream house* around the corner from the Complex Arms. It was still standing there, waiting for me. We investigated its merits, the financing, but we didn't qualify for a mortgage.

Both Frosty and the bank convinced me we couldn't financially afford a house, but a mobile home was within our reach
and could be purchased outright with Mona's inheritance, and we
would at least have a roof over our heads. It would be a means
to leave the Complex Arms and all the complications that new
incoming tenants were going to bring. A move would also allow
us to be closer to nature, which I knew would make Irene happy.
Frosty said he would find a job, and with his sworn promise I gave
in to his *lafstyle* once again on the condition that he build a root
cellar with an ironclad lid that would accommodate the three of
us should a tornado strike again. Maybe I would grow to love mice
and wolves. At least wolves take care of their elderly.

One Sunday we drove into the country and came across the
Arboreau Trailer Park not far from Jasper. The mountains always
choked me — a claustrophobic malaise would set in if I got too
close to them — but they were far enough into the horizon from
the trailer park that I could manage. I would have preferred to
be near water, move to English Bay in Vancouver, but who could
afford a million-dollar outhouse by the ocean?

"Think about it, Adeen. We can get a dog for Irene. She'll have
fun playing with the other kids. Just like at Evergreen," Frosty
tried to convince me.

I didn't want anything like Evergreen. Irene, if she were like
normal kids her age, would have been dating by then. She no
longer played with anything, including pets, but instead spent
days sleeping under the influence of her medications, sometimes
reclining on a wooden park bench that we rescued from the garbage dump, restored, painted fire engine red, and set in back; other
times, she would doze off in front of the TV, even on the hottest
summer day when it was much more pleasant to be outside.

The Arboreau Trailer Park wasn't so bad once I became accustomed to that way of living. Miss Pauline, my neighbour, became

a good friend. Other residents of the park seemed fine; although, there was the occasional drunken party or fireworks thrown in on a hot Saturday night. I had a lovely deck with annuals cascading from planters and window boxes, tomatoes growing in jumbo containers. Best of all, the community was enclosed by forest and a density of foliage that hid the outside world. I liked the privacy. I had come to terms with Mother Nature and she had come to terms with me, leading my broken spirit to an oasis of tranquility in my hikes around Hinton. I had to look on the bright side.

This one day, on a walk along the Athabasca River Front Park near Hinton, I was asleep in a puddle of sunlight when something annoying twittered around my face. I suspected a fly or mosquito and swatted air several times, but it was still there. I remember rolling over to my right side, curled up like a fiddlehead, then stretching out on my back. I squinted through the angle of slender tall greenery, my hands a visor against the sun's reflection. I saw it: a monarch butterfly flickering in and out of the ornamental grasses. I lay still and followed its course until it hovered over me, landing on my stomach, and there it sat for a second. "Mona," I whispered, "Mona." Then the monarch flew away as though it had just wanted to drop by to ease my grief, to assure me that everything would be okay. Won't tell Frosty this time because, once again, he'll spoil everything, saying I dreamed it. I didn't. My hike was over.

I drove back to the rhythm of Carrie Underwood singing "Before He Cheats." I used to hate western music and now I listened only to the country station; all that heartbreak and divorce and cheating hearts and cowboys who subjugate their mates. I was an Albertan by osmosis now without realizing it. I no longer felt like the girl who left Montreal. I no longer slipped my hard-earned cash into expensive Gucci shoes when I was flush with money; instead, I wore comfortable, practical cowboy boots and faded baby blue jeans torn at the knees that said, "This girl has character."

That evening after Frosty and Irene settled down in front of the TV, I sat on the red bench and revisited my day. Miss Pauline was already out there contemplating the flat, leaden sky, awaiting night, which at this time of year was always late on arrival.

"We come full circle eventually," I told Miss Pauline, not looking at her. "Here I am living in a trailer park again."

"There are worse things, sweetie," she said.

Anyhow, that's the story there.

PRESCRIPTION: BURNS

With the defiance of a dying old man, Frosty spits the half-smoked cigarette in an arc onto the nearby grave of wilting petunias in the front yard. Bull's eye! Adeen lumbers to retrieve the stub, hobbling like a three-legged dog fetching a stick.

"You're going to start a fire. And then where will we be? Answer me that. Where will we be, huh, Frosty? Where will we be? You only think of yourself all the time."

He guns a lighter to another cigarette, relaxes his head back against the patio chair, and launches a line of fumes toward the unblemished blue sky. Frosty follows the smoke with his eyes as it diffuses into the heat of the day, inhales another drag of tobacco, then convulses into a fit of coughing, gasping for air. He reaches for a Kleenex in the pocket of his baggy shorts and wipes the spittle from his chin.

"I'm not the maid here, you know," Adeen bellows and slams the collection of butts into the compost bin behind their mobile home.

Frosty's hands dangle over the deck rail until his limp wrists go numb and the burning cigarette drops from his fingers onto the parched lawn below. He jerks his head, vaults from his thoughts, and hurries inside, the screen door halting for a split second before springing shut.

It is another weekend of silence, another weekend when words fail between them. Once again his increasing moodiness puts a damper on their relationship. There was a time, earlier in their twenty-five-year marriage, when his poetic disposition and attentiveness were endearing; after all, her chattiness and outgoing personality offset his more introverted nature. Later, she would find herself in survival mode, dissociating herself from his occasional emotional attacks, which increasingly decimated her self-esteem. Now, she falls into her own pattern of melancholy and out-silences him. Two can play the same game. When Frosty requests a truce, usually after the third day, he'll say, "Do you want me to leave?"

She always shakes her head and feels her eyes well up. He has gouged her spirit over time until now she feels nothing. She blames her escalating melancholy on the tornado and Mona's death.

Adeen now looks to the skies to reassure a safe day and busies herself killing dandelion weeds with a steak knife. She wipes the drip of perspiration from her forehead with the back of her hand, picks her nose in the absent-minded way children do when distracted, and slides her hand down the side of her shorts to wipe away the offending mucus.

"I should have left him a long time ago. A long time ago. Yessiree, a long time ago."

Over the years, it grew into another mantra. If Adeen said it often enough, she could be convinced that the best solution for everyone was for her to leave Frosty and Irene; revise her life on some tropical island where no one knew her name. The thought seriously crossed her mind when she received Mona's inheritance cheque. But she was a chicken shit, just as Mona rightfully nicknamed her as a kid. Chicken shit Adeen. *Dare you to steal that lipstick. Take a risk sometimes. No skin off my back. Go ahead.*

Adeen sniffs the air and searches the skies again. She follows the acidic odour to the patch of dry grass smouldering where Frosty discarded his cigarette.

"Damnit! That man is going to kill us all with his carelessness. I swear." She pulverizes the stub with the heel of her sandal, burying it into the cracked soil.

"EEEE-eeeeeeeee."

Adeen ignores the familiar cry. The screen door screeches open.

"It's the kid. She needs diaper changin'," Frosty says, his hand signalling the interior. A familiar complaint.

"I'll be there. Can't you see I'm busy here? You almost started a fire."

"Don't think she can make it. Stinks."

The screen door sways back and forth, back and forth, before finally stopping shut. He brushes by her in a rush of rebellion and is already on the gravel road, striking the fragments of stone with his boot, racking up a dust storm with each kick.

"Where you going?"

"Gettin' smokes."

The weekend silence broken.

"You promised to quit after the last pack. You promised. You have cancer, remember! Cancer," she repeats. "Cancer," she repeats and repeats like an echo.

But he delivers a backhanded wave as if to say "drop dead" and continues on his merry mission until he disappears around the corner. His treatments have ended, and now there is just the wait. He is dying, no doubt. How many months, days, minutes remain? Lung cancer shows no tender mercies. Adeen thrusts the knife into the ground and attends to an adult daughter who still wears diapers.

Red-faced and sweating from the flaming sun, breathless from the repetitive motion of pulling weeds, Adeen relaxes in a patio chair, scrapes dry elbows on the table. She juts out her neck and stretches it, as though she is in the midst of chin exercises. She shuts her eyes against the unforgiving heat and quiet of the afternoon; not even a birdsong, only the faint annoyance of flies buzzing around the compost and garbage in back. Summer days in Alberta, before branches of dogwood leaves turn amber and the first frost creeps across the land.

Miss Pauline now on her patio lobs a Popsicle over the fence.

"Got the internet going. Wanna come see?"

Adeen opens her eyes, feels the cold compress of the Popsicle on her lap.

"Miss Pauline. Hey, okay. I'll just make sure Irene is okay and I'll be right over."

Irene is asleep, snoring away. Adeen locks the doorknob and deadbolt so Irene will remain indoors until she or Frosty returns. It is the only way she can ensure her daughter's safety. An adult playpen.

Miss Pauline was one of the first in the trailer park to purchase a computer and just subscribed to Telus for internet service.

"Come here. Have a look-see. You won't believe this." Miss Pauline shows her over to the corner desk in the dining room area. She clicks away at various icons and googles a dating service.

"Now, when Frosty goes, you come here and we'll find you a man of wealth to take care of you."

"What are you talking about?"

"Or look, we can pretend we are widowed and we can chat on the web with a handsome engineer from Arizona."

"Oh, give me a break, Miss Pauline. Shut that thing down and let's play Scrabble."

"Or, lookie here." And on screen, Adeen views a couple, completely naked, having sex. She can't take her eyes of the erotic image.

"Rosemary would have loved this."

"Rosemary?"

"One of my tenants from the Complex Arms. I used to babysit her dying husband when she went out for errands or appointments. One day I happened to look inside a drawer of her nightstand and I found these sex tapes. Slipped one in, and that"— she points to the screen — "is what I saw. I never would have thought Rosemary was into pornography."

"You snooped? That's private. Can't believe you would do that, Adeen."

"You didn't know me then."

"And look, you can google Ask dot-com any question and get an answer," Miss Pauline says with excitement. "For example, let's ask what causes tornadoes."

"All right, I get it. I've seen enough. Come on. Let's play Scrabble, okay? Brought over a couple of beers."

"You're no fun, Adeen." And with a sigh leaning toward boredom, Miss Pauline shuts down the computer.

"Let's go sit outside then and cool off. I'm not liking this hot spell. Feels like déjà vu. Could happen again, and look where we are, Miss Pauline. In the middle of a trailer park."

She hates Frosty more than ever. She peers at the skies every ten minutes.

"I wouldn't worry if I were you, Adeen."

"See that smoke over there? I wondered why it smelled so bad, like something burning. That doesn't look right to me," she says, pointing out a dark patch in the sky. Adeen runs to her root cellar urging Miss Pauline to follow.

"What are you doing?"

"Hurry," Adeen says as she frantically lowers the lid, leaving Miss Pauline outside to fend for herself. She stomps on the iron clad top to get Adeen's attention.

Still in a panic, Adeen shouts, "Get off. I can't get the top up and you'll be left behind."

"It's over. Just a small dust storm flew by. You're safe."

The lid gently rises and Miss Pauline helps Adeen out of the root cellar.

"I guess that was a close call," Adeen says, "Looks like it skipped us. Everything is dry."

"It's okay. That smell is just from someone's barbecue, probably. Come on. Let's have another look at that internet."

"No, you go ahead. I just want to sit out here a bit. Maybe later." Adeen, on the wing of an anxiety attack.

Forests continue to burn near the foothills of the Rockies. Park wardens forbid campers to enter recreational areas and woodlands. Banff and Jasper take a financial nosedive as tourists begin to retreat to their cities and towns; thirsty canola fields forget to bloom; and farmers pray for rain again. *We need rain.* It is a yearly lament; anthem for a province that relies on agriculture and the oil patch as their main resources.

"EEEE-eeeeeeeee."

"Shit! Now what."

Adeen stands in the doorway of their mobile home and ignores the slovenly interior, with its air of fermenting garbage, a treasure trove of wall-to-wall piles of newspapers, magazines, corrugated boxes, empty paint cans, dirty laundry, and dishes spilling over the counter. Half-eaten ice cream melts in bowls arranged like a still life atop the broken-down seventeen-inch black-and-white

TV rescued from the rubble at Evergreen. A length of fabric from Fabricland transforms it into another side table. Adeen long ago abandoned the idea of having an immaculate home and has followed Jack's example, a panacea for her problems, one less thing to care for. Everything now seems overwhelming and unimportant. Nothing matters. Mona would have taken her to see a doctor for her continuous depression and regular anxiety attacks. Frosty always came first with his own health issues and concerns, and always her daughter front and centre.

Irene lies on the threadbare sofa, a soiled adult diaper discarded on the floor.

"Eeee-eeeee."

"I just cleaned you. Bad girl!"

Irene, agitated and perplexed, wobbles her head left to right, left to right, faster and faster until Adeen stammers, "It's okay, it's okay. Irene is a good girl." She cradles Irene's head against her chest and begins to sing "Goodnight, Irene," the song that is always a magic bullet.

Irene has a sturdy resistance to medication, so the lyrics, a distraction, always cool her down, allow Adeen enough time to force a tranquilizer down her throat and go about the business of cleaning her thirty-year-old baby.

Adeen can feel a borderline migraine about to spring. *You can't do this anymore*, the voices buzz around her like bees let loose from a hive.

She dashes to the kitchen sink with a compulsion to cleanse her hands of all excrement and germs. Adeen scrubs with a scouring pad, counting 1-2-3, 1-2-3, letting the cold water dribble in a spray over both her arms like a surgeon preparing to open a heart and insert a pacer. Then, full speed ahead, she rotates the faucet until a waterfall of scalding water gushes over her arms like Niagara Falls. She screams from the burn, so painful that she can't touch her skin.

Adeen swivels to face Irene, now scrubbed and decent, sitting on the sofa. Her interest has been piqued by her mother's activity, her brow is a wrinkled question mark.

"Ne? NEEEE?"

"Come, Irene." Adeen grabs Irene's scaly elbows and leads her to the kitchen table, opens a colouring book, and slides the box of crayons toward her.

"Excuse me, ma'am. Ma'am? Excuse me."

Adeen spins around to face the male voice. A man wearing a ball cap and T-shirt stands outside the screen door, arms clutching what appears to be a pile of posters. His legs stomp back and forth as if he is extinguishing a fire under his feet or has a need to empty his bladder.

"Yes?" Adeen walks over to greet him.

"Excuse me, ma'am, but everything okay here?"

"Why do you ask?"

"I heard screaming."

"Oh, that. Yes, hot-water burn. I was distracted and didn't notice until it was too late."

She steps outside and extends the man her scalded arms.

He removes his baseball cap.

"No one in the office, ma'am. Know where I can find the property manager?"

"You want Miss Pauline here. She's probably out shopping. I'm her assistant when she's not around. Can I help?"

He scratches his head as though that action alone would produce a solution to his dilemma. "Can I leave her a message or perhaps you can take care of it?"

Adeen is impatient to press on with her day, not that she has anything urgent to attend to, but she no longer cares to interact with strangers and forces herself to be sociable only on an as-needed basis.

"Sorry, ma'am, to trouble you but —"

"Who are you anyhow? I don't favour strangers," she says, clearly agitated.

The man seems rattled by her attitude. "I'm a park warden, work for Parks Canada." And he flips open his ID card with a photo.

"You don't look like one. Where's your uniform?"

"Oh, I see. We swapped the stetson and uniform for something less official looking so we don't scare off folks. It took a bit of getting used to for us, too, a ball cap and T-shirt. Just started the new look this year. Okay with you?"

"Makes no diff to me as long as you are who you say you are. Well, get on with it."

"We're just making the rounds to let people know about a prescribed burn in the forest near the Boule Range north of here. If anyone has asthma, they may want to evacuate in case the fire takes off."

"A prescribed burn, you say?"

"Sometimes it's called a control burn, ma'am. Yes. We occasionally set small fires to help Mother Nature with her housekeeping. Here, this will explain it." He hands her one of the posters.

Adeen glances at it, not reading the content, and says, "I don't understand."

"See, ma'am, it has to be done because when trees get sick, they die, and the branches and needles drop and pile on the forest floor. Insects love that dead stuff and end up infesting the other healthy trees, and then they get sick and die, too. Fire is just nature's way to clean up a forest so it renews itself, gets healthy again. Sometimes Mother Nature forgets, so we give her a helping hand."

"Well, isn't Mother Nature just clever? With all this dryness, you'd think she'd remember. Okay then, will have to google prescribed burns on the internet. Give Miss Pauline something to do. She'll love that."

"Yes, you can learn more if you're interested. We just want to make sure everyone here is aware what we're doing when they see the smoke, and not to panic."

"So that's what the smell was. What if it takes off, huh? Then what? Why don't you just leave Mother Nature alone and when she's ready, she'll clean up after herself? Let her take care of her own needles and branches."

"Can't, ma'am. Everyone needs a hand sometimes, including Mother Nature, so she doesn't get carried away and destroy the healthy trees along with the sick ones."

"Really? You sound just like the Discovery Channel, like someone told you to say that. Sure you're not selling smoke alarms?"

But the park warden stands his ground. "Give these to Miss Pauline to have on hand for any of her residents if they ask. I would appreciate her posting the flyers around the property in case I miss anyone. It explains everything."

"I'll make sure we also post them around the 'hot spots' in town."

"Got that covered, ma'am. But thank you."

He secures his baseball cap, tips goodbye with its brim, and is gone. "Hey," Adeen shouts. "When is this tree killing supposed to start?"

The park warden doesn't hear and continues his route around the Arboreau Trailer Park.

She shields her eyes and examines the skyline.

"Hell. That's what it is. Hell." She can already see and smell a ration of smoke in the forest skirting the range. Adeen goes inside to find her binoculars for a closer look at hell.

ADEEN

That Miss Pauline. Isn't she something else? Looking at all that porn at her age. She's very private in some respects, though. Never married, no kids, no relatives. Reminds me of Shylene.

People's lives. Who am I to judge?

Mona — I mean Miss Pauline — I must have scared her when I went flying out of her trailer into the root cellar. But when I looked up and the sky was overcast, it didn't feel right to me. I wasn't going to take any chances. I know, I know. I forgot about Irene asleep, but it was a spur-of-the-moment intuitive decision that just made me run. Like someone was pushing me. Don't make me feel guilty. I realize now that the haze in the distance was the smog from the prescribed burns. Every summer there seems to be a forest burning somewhere. Now I get it. They burn sick trees to save the healthy. Not unusual to have a rapid dust storm when things get dry.

Later that evening, I told Miss Pauline about the park warden and we googled "prescribed burns." We sure have come a long way since television, haven't we? Anyhow, we had no idea. Imagine Mother Nature destroying the sick trees so the healthy ones could live. What a thing! But come to think of it, I remember that mouse at the Complex Arms, cleaning all her baby pups except for a very weak one who was crushed to death by the mother doe. Only the strong survive, as they say. Mother Nature knows best, right? But that fire over there, it could have gotten out of hand and knocked everything down. I still say, don't tinker with Mother Nature. Leave her alone.

After the park warden left, I changed Irene again and gave her a sedative and let her fall into la-la land, asleep on the couch watching *Sesame Street*. I admit it was easier for me to just pop a pill into my daughter's mouth and go about my day. What did she know, anyhow? She lived in the comfort of her own body: sleeping, eating, drinking soda — lots of soda — and back to sleeping, eating, drinking soda, sleeping. Oh, and watching *Sesame Street*. It kept me sane. So don't judge me.

Once Irene had been taken care of, I bolted the door and went around putting up some of the flyers on trees in the entrance to the trailer park, one at the grocery store, and one at the community centre, which the warden had missed. Was going to tape one on the door of Bo's Bar, but I could see Miss Pauline and Frosty drinking and wasn't in the mood for a confrontation. She had a lot of spunk for an old lady, that Miss Pauline. She swore all that beer and smoking kept her healthy. I suppose it depends on your DNA because there was Frosty, dying of cancer and still smoking and drinking like there was no tomorrow. Perhaps there was no tomorrow. We die a bit every day, so maybe we should make the most of whatever time we have left. I don't know anymore. I just listen to the voices buzzing in my head. Like Payton's religion, they tell me what to do.

Anyhow, that's the story there.

BO'S BAR

L ocated in the heart of the Arboreau, Bo's Bar is the nerve centre of the trailer park. Bo lives in an apartment above the bar and has expanded the building to include a general store with a gasoline station next door. An active poker game always going in back, it is Frosty's playground, a refuge whenever he needs to run away from everything that is Adeen.

Miss Pauline favours a daily pint of beer after purchasing her cigarettes. She says it is the only beverage, apart from coffee, that could be said to give her good health and longevity, so it is not unusual to spot her sitting at a window table, absorbed in the world outside Bo's Bar.

She watches Frosty stumble a step or two as he heads for the back door, the familiar cigarette dangling from his lips, shoulders hunched as though it were a cold snappy day in February.

"Frosty, over here."

He scours the room searching for the voice, Miss Pauline in a frantic wave of *over here, over here*; she rises from her seat and beckons him to join her. A quick nod of his head toward the table, he pops by with a friendly howdy.

"Sit," Miss Pauline says. "Since you're here, I need to talk to you."

"Only have a minute. Don't want to keep Bo and the boys waitin' for our poker. Feel lucky tonight."

"As my daddy used to say, 'The quickest way to double your money is to fold it over and put it back into your pocket.'"

"Those are wise words your daddy told you. But not much fun."

"Okay, Frosty, I'll get right down to it. You and I have known each other for a while now."

"Yep, as memory has it, since we moved out here. What's on your mind?"

"I'm worried about Adeen."

"Well, that's Adeen for you. She likes the attention."

"She keeps talking about seeing these monarch butterflies. Says they are Mona reincarnate."

"I know. She's all beer and skittles. Crazy. I let her just talk. Keep tellin' her to get some counsellin' but she says I'm the one that needs it. Like hell. Just let her be, Miss Pauline. Don't worry. She's my problem. I married her. We all have pieces of crazy in us, some bigger pieces than others, so just let her be."

"All right, Frosty. None of my business. By the way, you're looking good these days. A bit of weight loss but suits you fine. How you feeling?"

"Feelin'? Feelin' right finer than frog hair. Look, Miss Pauline, I really have to go play that game. They're waitin'." He's keeping his eyes on the back of the room.

"Have to?"

"Somethin' to do. I have plans, you know."

"What kind of plans?"

"Can't say just yet."

They are staring at each other. Frosty reaches inside his shirt pocket and retrieves a pack of cigarettes.

"Should you be smoking? I mean in your condition."

"What condition?"

"The cancer. I guess it really doesn't matter at this point. But why rush the afterlife."

"I'm not a goner yet, Miss Pauline."

"Oh, but we all are dying in some way every day, as they say."

He lights his cigarette. "I'm in remission."

"Are you now? Does Adeen know?"

"I shouldna told you, but I trust you not to tell Adeen. I want to surprise her. Hey, Adeen, I'll be around a lot longer than you thought. Not dyin' just yet."

"Oh, she'll be surprised, all right. Did you just get the news?"

"Naw. Right after I finished my treatments, doc said there weren't any signs. No tumours. Didn't want to tell anyone, especially Adeen. Better if she thought I was terminal. Maybe she'd stop with her naggin'. Like I said, I have plans."

"My grandpa used to say, 'Treat a woman like a racehorse and she'll never be a nag.'"

"What you sayin', Miss Pauline? That I mistreat Adeen?"

"Not saying anything, Frosty. Think what you want. She did tell me once you are a chronic liar."

"Then don't mess with somethin' that ain't botherin' you. And you better keep our secret." He wags his finger at her. "I'll let you know when it's okay to spill the beans. S'cuse me."

"You plan on leaving Adeen?"

No answer. Bo pokes his head out the back door and motions Frosty to join the game immediately. No dawdling. Miss Pauline watches as he lumbers past her in that cowboy stride indicative of wranglers who've spent too many years in the saddle. She gulps down the beer, shakes her head from the warm bitter taste, smacks her lips with a loud *ahhhhhh*, anticipating the pending drama that always unfolds outside Bo's Bar and into the parking lot if you wait long enough. Showtime — a fight, a blooming romance, an argument, an exchange of illegal drugs — and that is in the light of a sunny day. Nighttime has its own playbill. Today brings an uneventful scene, though, a sluggish summer afternoon when chickadees nestle in comfortable perches to chirp, chatter, and cheep. Miss Pauline usually takes solace in the jargon of birds, but all she can think about now is Adeen and Frosty. A delicate situation. She orders another beer.

ADEEN

Been thinking about dying lately. Don't mean to sound maudlin. I guess because of Frosty's terminal cancer. I figure death is a sleep but we just never wake up. Or maybe we wake up in another galaxy. Stardust, someone once told me. I think it was Jack after Mona died. He was a comfort. And those dreams about people and places we used to know or read about, I believe they join us wherever we land. I'm not going religious on everyone here. It's always on my mind and I have no answers. Maybe because of my age. Fifty isn't old, but so many celebrities are dying now. Not that I measure the length of my years by the death of a pop star.

"Why the hell are we here?" I once asked Payton. "We're here to love," he told me. Sure, sure. How is that possible when people are so hateful? And when I asked Shylene the same question, she said that we're here to die. Then what's the point of living? Everyone has a different opinion, everyone a needful burden. I just don't know anymore. I guess faith is needed here and I lost mine a long time ago.

I didn't see how Frosty could be so strong and brave. Never complained about the pain and the nausea. Didn't know how much time he had left. He didn't say anything. Didn't tell me until it was time for the surgery to remove the tumour on his lung and then the chemotherapy and radiation treatments. He wasn't one to show emotion, except when he was angry. He didn't even want anyone to hear him vomit. I guess it's the cowboy way. Sometimes he couldn't help himself. Made me feel pukey just to listen. Still smoked his brains out, and I guess no harm done when you consider the inevitable. He seemed to be doing okay. His face was filling out some, as though he'd put on some weight. Must be all that beer he was drinking. Don't know how he did it.

Mona returned, a monarch butterfly, to show me that there is an afterlife. *Keep the faith*, she was telling me. My days were spent chasing butterflies, searching for her. She stayed a while and then disappeared, like she just wanted to land nearby to check if I was all right. I don't know anymore. Do you understand?

Anyhow, that's the story there.

DISCOVERY

In the evenings, before daylight trades places with the night, Adeen often joins Miss Pauline on her deck and shares the latest gossip. The long summer light still dapples through the trees framing the trailer park. This northern climate brings eighteen hours of daylight. Adeen now lives on four hours of sleep. She thinks of taking one of Irene's sedatives but decides against it.

"You don't think we should leave?" Adeen says. "Just in case this fire takes off?"

"Naw, well under control. These guys know what they're doing."

Miss Pauline is one of those well-worn cowgirls, skin like scuffed leather boots, always a cowboy hat perched on top of her bleached, damaged, Tammy Wynette–platinum hair. In her heyday she worked the rodeos, rode wild horses, roped cows. She can still balance herself standing up on a moving cow or doing a handstand after a couple of drinks, if asked. Miss Pauline would have been a perfect mate for Frosty had she been younger, or he older. Both wear the odour of horse manure and quiver for a wrangler's life that Adeen still struggles to grasp.

Adeen and Miss Pauline like talking to each other. Sometimes their conversation is chatty, casual; sometimes it's serious, reviewing the news of the day, arguing about politics.

"Did you see that editorial, Adeen, in the paper today about the Latimer case? He was released from Victoria jail for a four-day unescorted leave to visit his sick mother. Remember how he made headlines when he killed his twelve-year-old daughter because he couldn't stand to see her suffer anymore? The girl was a quadriplegic. He ran a hose from the exhaust to the cab of his truck and put the girl inside to die. Terrible. Terrible. Said he loved her. Compassionate homicide, they called it."

"Yes, I saw the article, too. Mercy killing. Mercy for whom?"

"You know," Miss Pauline changes the subject; it's her nature to flitter from one thought to another. "I just noticed the other day that when I get up from a night's sleep, an hour later I seem to have this new wrinkle, I mean, crease on my right cheek that won't go away, as though I don't have enough already. My skin doesn't snap back like it used to."

"Miss Pauline, you're seventy years old, for God's sake. We should all look so good."

And so they would google what to order in the way of creams and rubs, or marinades as Miss Pauline would call them, to revitalize their skin to its former lustre and elasticity. Adeen herself is beginning to resemble an overripe apricot. All that sun sucking up the moisture from her complexion.

"That warden sure was cute," Adeen digresses.

"Sure sorry I missed him."

"By the way, I left some posters in your office in case you needed more. He was going around telling everyone about these prescribed burns they do to save the healthy trees from the sick ones. Euthanasia with assistance from Mother Nature, I guess you'd call it. Makes me nervous. What if the fire takes off?"

Both women peer intently through the negative spaces of trees, with their dead branches and twigs.

Then Miss Pauline says, "Won't happen. By the way, saw Frosty at Bo's last night. He looked just fine. Didn't want to talk about the cancer. How's he managing?"

"I don't know. Blames me. Blames that I brought him to drink. Never mind all his smoking all these years. Like I'm the one who put the cigarettes in his mouth."

Adeen is despondent. Miss Pauline jumps out of her patio chair and hurries over to give an assuring hug.

"I can see you still love him. But, Adeen, we're all responsible for our own lives. We're adults. You're not his mother, so just stop it now. Not your fault." Miss Pauline is Adeen's new Mona. "Look at me and repeat. Not my fault. He's going to be okay. Miracles do happen."

She takes a moment, considering whether she should reveal Frosty's secret, but decides to keep her promise, at least for the time being. Let Frosty be the bearer of good news.

Always difficult to find true friendship in the later years. Adeen relishes Miss Pauline's company and wisdom. After their usual morning coffee on deck, they can hear Irene thumping on the trailer door.

"Better go. She's awake. Plus I have laundry to do." Adeen unbolts the door and Irene falls into her reluctant arms.

She follows the usual schedule for Irene: washing up, feeding, distributing the medication, and then setting her down in front of the TV as Adeen goes about the daily business of living. Frosty rarely hangs around, preferring the company of his cardplaying, gambling, drinking buddies at Bo's. He usually escapes from the trailer early, staying out all day until he tires and needs his rest. Adeen is stunned by his physicality and will to live, even in the face of a death sentence.

"It's the western air." He will pump out his chest. "Hard to keep a good man down." The ex–cowboy poet is determined to live forever.

Adeen is putting away clean laundry in the tallboy when she notices one of the bottom drawers is jammed, as though something has fallen behind. She jerks it open, causing the drawer to slip off its runner. Frosty's underwear spills to the floor. She spots something wedged in between. That's when she discovers the envelope with Velvet's photo — she's lying there naked, her arms reaching out to someone or something.

Adeen straightens up, transfixed by the image, unable to believe what she is seeing.

"You bastard," she says. "You damn asshole. You lied. I should have listened to Mona. You bastard. I gave you so many chances, you bastard."

She whips the envelope with the photo into her jeans pocket and holds it there until she decides her next move. Right now, she needs a moment to assimilate what she's just unearthed.

ADEEN

The following morning I could see a billowing mass of smoke beyond the distant mountains. Frosty, wearing only cut-offs, was already in the backyard, reclining on the hammock in the shade with his beer and cigarettes. He had found my spare six-pack of Molsons behind Irene's bedroom door. No surprise there.

"Reckon you thought me stupid," he said with such finesse. He told me that if I wanted to drink to just go ahead and don't be secretive about it. He didn't give a fuck, his word. That's what he said. Didn't give a fuck about me.

And I argued that it wasn't about me. I had enough things to deal with. I was just trying to help him by hiding the beers. I know, I know. It was stupid of me because I knew he went to Bo's and he was going to do what he was going to do.

He gave me this disgusted look, like he was ridiculing me, and with the defiance of a rebellious juvenile, he lit another cigarette, finished his beer, and opened another can right there in front of me.

I shivered against the memory of this past New Year's Eve when the roads were choked with the first winter snowstorm.

Freezing cold. Packed hills of powdered snow obstructed roads and highways as we bulldozed our way home from a party. It was Frosty's wish. One last boozy hurrah with friends in case this was his last year on the planet. Frosty lit the wood stove for more heat and stayed up to listen to the blustery wind that never let up. I went to bed and slept.

He was diagnosed just in time for Christmas 2006. "Merry Christmas," I said to him with a fatal sarcasm. Frosty broke the news to me after we opened our presents at midnight. In a drunken stupor, he bellowed, "If I'm dying, then I might as well enjoy myself for whatever time I have left!"

I retaliated in anger: "Bastard, you don't care about anyone, not even yourself. You stupid bastard! Bastard!"

Later the depression set in and that was the last straw for me. Those damn voices just never stopped. I guess Frosty's cancer was just one more thing to deal with, and I was so, so tired. *We are responsible for our own lives*, I remembered Miss Pauline's motto. But we are responsible for those who can't take care of themselves, no?

Frosty survived surgery early spring this year. They removed the growth in the right lung, followed the operation with some heavy artillery — various cocktails of chemo and radiation treatments to beat this sarcoma, as they called it. Two months ago the cancer returned, like scattered cigarette butts, on the surface of his lungs. He told me the doc said these fibroids were inoperable. They would leave the tumours there and see what happened. See what happened? See what happened? "You're dying," I said to him, that's what's happening. There wasn't much else they could do but wait. I wanted to talk to the doc but Frosty forbade me. Like I didn't trust him. Just a matter of time. I didn't know what to do.

But there he was, Frosty, in all his glory, maybe tired some days but still alive and kicking, drinking and smoking and carrying on like he was Superman. The man was made of steel. Even put on some weight.

So I kept my mouth shut and ignored Frosty's condition. I suppose I made it easier, hiding all that beer, but deep inside I suspected he would find them anyhow. *Enabler* is what you would call me. Perhaps he had a death wish, so who was I to interfere. His life. Not mine. I had enough problems. I just kept losing more and more respect for the man until that photo … well, that photo ripped out the last piece of whatever was left of my heart. I felt numb. I couldn't take any more. I'd reached my limit.

Anyhow, that's the story there.

SMOKE SUMMER

Adeen carries a large salad bowl of chipped ice and joins Frosty on the patio in back. She can feel the electrical currents of heat rippling around her like some magnetic field. "Oh, my, would you look at that smoke!"

Frosty, with an apathetic grimace, takes no notice of her and continues smoking — wheezing, hacking, rasping, coughing — spitting the thick mucus with purpose into the air. A half-inch cigarette sticks to the centre of his lower lip, seemingly in a mid-chew, as he rolls the thing side to side with his tongue. She cringes at the flying phlegm and averts her eyes, choosing instead to look at the flat colourless sky. She has grown accustomed to the loss of his body hair, his bald head, and lashless eyes. This poet cowboy now inhabits a putrescent body — the pasty skin, watery eyes, and burn marks branded on his chest from the radiation treatments.

One morning, in the early stages of his disease, she caught him spitting blood into the toilet, and he angrily motioned her to let him be. How many more months of endurance, Adeen wondered? His execution of his role as a dying ex-wrangler would have garnered him an Academy Award for best performance by a cowboy in a western drama.

"You feeling okay?" She tosses some of the chipped ice particles into her mouth like so many handfuls of salted peanuts and chomps down in a grind of torture. Crunch. Crunch. Crunch.

"Weatherman says it's going to be a blistering thirty-eight degrees Celsius," she says. "That would be somewhere about ninety-six Fahrenheit." She still converts everything from the Canadian metric measurement to the American imperial system just to understand the idea of how hot it *really* is.

She slurps the last shards of the pulverized ice cubes, the shrunken pieces sitting in her cheeks before they melt.

She grabs another mouthful and slathers more of the frozen crystals on her face, neck, and chest. "Want some?" Crunch. Crunch. Crunch. "It'll cool you down."

He winces at the sound of ice cracking, keeps his eyes focused on the fire looming over the skyline.

Day dwindles into an evening sky coated with lacerations of pink and pearl oyster. The patch of smoke has thickened and bears resemblance to a fireball. Adeen and Frosty observe the weighty sun spill its palette over the mountain peaks, which reflect in a nearby shallow lake, painting the trees and rocks along the shoreline.

"It's eerie, isn't it? Like someone just dropped the Hiroshima bomb over there." Adeen elongates the word: *Heerosheema.* "That cloud looks just like that, Frosty, doesn't it? So nuclear. Maybe we should get ready to hide in the root cellar."

He ignores her suggestion; she increases the nervous rhythm of mincing ice chips with a steady compulsion. He finally rouses from his seat, but Adeen halts him, forming a barrier with her arms.

"Where you going?"

"Can't take your crackin' them ice chips no more. Goin' inside."
And then she hurls the envelope at him.

"You might like to check what's inside, Frosty Whitlaw."

He picks it up from the ground and says, "What you doin'
goin' through my things?"

"Our things, Frosty, our things, remember. I was putting away
the clean laundry and when I couldn't pull out the bottom drawer,
I checked behind the drawer, and lo and behold that piece of shit
was blocking it. The Scotch tape came undone and screwed up
your secret."

His sallow face carries the expression of a schoolboy caught
reading *Playboy* in class and preparing himself for punishment. "I
liked the photo. Is all." He sheepishly lowers his head, avoiding
her angry gaze.

"Right," and she grabs the envelope from his hands and tears
it to smithereens, hurling the evidence into his face until the fragments trickle down to his feet like confetti.

"There was nothin' between me and Velvet. I just tried to
help her."

"I saw you guys kissing at Klondike Days and you hugging her
when you were evicting the mice at the Complex Arms."

"Thought you woulda forgotten all that by now. I just felt sorry
for her. Tried to help her find her boyfriend. Is all."

"Is all. Is all. You are such a lying hypocrite, Frosty Whitlaw.
Don't know what I ever saw in you. Die." And then she catches
herself. "I didn't mean that."

Adeen can hear his voice following her footsteps as she speeds
down the road in a confusion of emotions.

"Adeen, Adeen."

He angrily pitches his still-lit cigarette butt into the compost
bin and slumps to his knees to retrieve the ripped pieces, wills
his still-weak body to move inside, and begins to reassemble the

photo with Scotch tape, putting the pieces together like a jigsaw puzzle.

Adeen bolts for the nearby park and sits on a bench to evaluate the situation. She always thinks best in the dark, so she dawdles until the last blur of light in the west disappears. There is no moon. The street lamps startle her when they switch on. Adeen hurries home only to hear Frosty gagging, spitting phlegm in the bathroom, and Irene snuffling on the couch.

Midnight. Too hot to sleep in that sardine can of a trailer with its stifling smells and sounds. The small portable fan oscillates in its unsuccessful high-speed efforts to chill the interior.

Adeen rises, unlocks the door, and tiptoes outside to escape the somnolent noises of snoring and snorting. She parks herself at the picnic table, a pitcher of crushed ice by her side. It will cool her down, if nothing else.

Miss Pauline appears on her patio as though on cue. Their properties abut one another, separated only by a chain-link fence.

"Can't sleep either, sweetie?" She lights a cigarette. "I find smoking helps me."

"Oh, Miss Pauline. Hope I didn't wake you up."

"Yes, I could hear you chewing on those ice cubes." She laughs and blows smoke toward the ebony sky.

Adeen smiles. "Yep, can't sleep in that trailer. It's a furnace."

"Something happen?"

"Does it show?'

"According to Google I am an intuitive person. So spit it out."

Adeen tells her about the discovery of Velvet's nude photo behind the dresser drawer and how Frosty denied ever having an affair.

"I just don't know what to do. Why would he keep her photo if there was nothing going on?"

"You want to google to find out why?"

"Not in the mood for humour, Miss Pauline. I'm serious."

"Okay, so how about checking that dating service I showed you. Maybe it's time for you to have an affair yourself."

"Don't want to get involved with another man ever. They just want someone to take care of them, and I'm done with that, too."

"Can't blame you. Sorry to leave you, sweetie, but can't keep my eyes open anymore so off to beddy-bye I go." And she disappears inside.

"Be going in myself shortly," says Adeen.

A pungent smell, like a concoction of discarded simmering garbage, fills the air. At first Adeen thinks the stench is coming from Miss Pauline's firepit. She wonders if the nearby forest fire has escalated. Then she sees it! The compost is smouldering.

She is rooted there, paralyzed, terrified, in a panic; her mind escaping from her body. She dashes toward the bin as though approaching the finish line in a marathon but then suddenly stops in her tracks. The hot embers burrowed deep inside the compost heap burst into sudden, spontaneous flames. The fire, with a breakneck speed, licks up the sides of her trailer home and leaps over the roof. She stumbles toward the door, which is lava hot.

Miss Pauline, awakened again by the uncontrollable flames reflected through her bedroom window, rushes in a frantic fit of fear to find water.

It is one of those moments: Adeen makes a split-second decision to act on something that has been simmering in her subconscious for many years. She bows her head as though in prayer and locks the deadbolt.

"What are you doing, Adeen? Unlock the door."

A feeble knock comes from the interior, a mewling for help, and then nothing. Not a sound.

"What's the matter with you?" Miss Pauline strikes Adeen's hands away as she attempts to unbolt the door.

The heat from the blaze pushes Adeen back, back, back across to the other side of the road. She watches the fire consume her home, her family, her life. She babbles like a maniac, tearless. Without warning, a firefighter appears by her side, his rescuing arms pressing her back.

"You okay, lady? You okay?" he says.

Miss Pauline has positioned herself next to Adeen.

"What's your name, lady? What's your name?"

"Irene. Irene," Adeen whispers.

"It's all right. We'll take care of you, Irene." Then he turns to Miss Pauline. "Know her?"

"Her name's Adeen. Adeen Whitlaw."

ADEEN

I don't recall locking the door. Honest. When I saw the flames, I kept moving backwards, back across to the other side of the road. I didn't know what to do. I didn't know flames could scorch with that kind of speed and fury. I ran back to the door and tried to unlock it, truly I did, but the deadbolt burned my fingers. It was hot like a live volcano. I swear, I didn't mean it. I went back, didn't I? Ask Miss Pauline. She couldn't get it open herself, either. Too hot. See, we really did try.

Where were the firemen? They took forever. I guess they were out there trying to control those burning sick trees. I screamed. I know I screamed because Miss Pauline was by my side with her cellphone. She called for help and they were right there, but it was too late. I saw everything go to hell. I kept backing away from the trailer. Too hot, too hot to save anyone. It was hell, unstoppable. I couldn't hear a peep from the inside. Had to save myself. I was sure I was in a deep sleep, a nightmare, but as I got closer to the trailer, and Miss Pauline behind trying to stop me, I knew it was real and that I was alive and free. It's an awful thing to say. Put yourself in my place. Don't look at me like that.

I could hear the sirens blaring in that earsplitting way as the fire trucks moved onto the Arboreau grounds. I felt Miss Pauline by my side telling someone I was Adeen Whitlaw. This nice fireman was so kind to me. He hugged me and said everything would be fine. I believed him. Neighbours gathered 'round and we all watched like it was Monday Night Football as the men doused the mobile home with garden hoses and helped the firemen set up their equipment. A geyser of water, it seemed, but it was a fast fire. The flames jumped into Miss Pauline's yard and she lost her home, too. I feel bad about that. I apologized to her later, but she never said anything to me ever again. Not a word. In the end, nothing left but the stone foundation on both our homes.

Even mice take care of their own, you know. Derrick once told me that the mother mouse could love her newborn to death just by licking them with such intensity that they died. Only the strong survive a mother's love, and I did love Irene ... and Frosty. One time I did, yes, I did love them both. For everything that happened, I never wanted to hurt them.

Oh, s'cuse me, I am so, so tired. So sorry.

It's too hard to care, to get involved in other people's lives, get too close. I don't want to touch anything or anyone anymore. So tired. I don't care. I just don't care. I don't suppose you'll let me go to the commemoration ceremonies? No? I'll just have to remember what happened alone in my own way. Mona would understand. I wonder who will water the trees now at Evergreen. Do you know?

"Is that your story, Mrs. Whitlaw?" The officer from the Royal Canadian Mounted Police raises his head with distaste.

When she doesn't respond, he shuts off the tape recorder and gestures to the guard with a nod that the interview is over. The

THE COMPLEX ARMS   303

guard approaches Adeen and asks that she hold out her arms. He snaps the silver handcuffs back on her wrists.

"There's just one thing I don't understand. Why did you do it?" the officer says.

"They burn forests, don't they?"

ACKNOWLEDGEMENTS

First, a big thank you to my family for their continuous support of my creative life: my son, Tyler Dennis, and new family members Kerry-Ann Mueller and my grandson Calvin Mueller Dennis, who makes me laugh and entered the world the week I signed with Dundurn. I am most grateful to my husband, James Dennis, who supplied the coffee and snacks so I would meet my deadlines.

I would also like to thank everyone at Dundurn for taking a chance on me and the tremendous effort that went into the creation of *The Complex Arms*, especially Dominic Farrell for his patience, support and advice; Rachel Spence, who initially recognized the book's potential; Sara D'Agostino; marketing assistant Stephanie Ellis; art director Laura Boyle; the sales and marketing teams; project editor Jenny McWha and copy editor Kate Unrau; and managing editor Elena Radic. I am grateful to the talented Courtney Horner for her unique cover design.

Thanks also to my first readers for their valuable time, friendship, considerable knowledge and love of books: Jane Hikel, my best friend forever since the first grade; Christina Hardie and the Mill Woods Mythologies Project for telling me about the Pits; and Kathleen Betteridge for her significant contribution.

Grateful to all the folks in Edmonton who shared their stories with me; too many to personally name here but you know who you are. I do want to acknowledge Jerry Bellikka who was a radio reporter at that time and provided me with his on-the-scene remembrances of Black Friday.

My gratitude to the Edmonton Arts Council for giving me a grant to write this book.